P9-CSW-057

2/13/08 Ingram $16.99

THE
KEY TO RONDO

Library of Congress Cataloging-in-Publication Data
Rodda, Emily.
The key to Rondo / by Emily Rodda.
p. cm.
Summary: Through an heirloom music box, Leo, a serious, responsible boy, and his badly
behaved cousin Mimi enter the magical world of Rondo to rescue Mimi's dog from a
sorceress, who wishes to exchange him for the key that allows free travel between worlds.
ISBN 0-545-03535-X [1. Space and time—Fiction.   2. Adventure and
adventurers—Fiction.   3. Magic—Fiction.   4. Witches—Fiction.
5. Music box—Fiction.   6. Cousins—Fiction.]   I. Title.

PZ7.R5996Key 2008
[Fic]—dc22
2007016873

ISBN-13: 978-0-545-03535-4
ISBN-10: 0-545-03535-X

10 9 8 7 6 5 4 3 2 1   08 09 10 11 12

First edition, February 2008
Printed in the U.S.A.   23

FOR KATE, HAL, ALEX, AND CLEM

THE
KEY TO

RONDO

EMILY RODDA

Scholastic Press   New York

CONTENTS

1	FAMILY TREASURE	1
2	MIMI COMES TO STAY	13
3	UGLY DUCKLING	22
4	EXPERIMENT	33
5	THE KEY	44
6	THE NOTE	53
7	ON THE STREET	62
8	TOM	71
9	THE HIDEY-HOLE	80
10	CONKER	90
11	THE RED HOOKS	99
12	THE TROUBLE WITH MICE	109
13	FLITTER WOOD	118
14	THE NESTING TREE	129
15	FLIGHT	138
16	BERTHA	147
17	THE COTTAGE IN THE WOOD	159

18	"THE POM-POM POLKA"	169
19	GOOD ADVICE	179
20	TALES OF THE DARK TIME	189
21	THE FOREST WAY	198
22	DEEP WOOD	207
23	TROLL'S BRIDGE	215
24	TRIPLE TREAT	225
25	THE HOUSE BY THE RIVER	235
26	MIMI'S BARGAIN	245
27	ESCAPE	257
28	THE CASTLE	267
29	THE PLAN	277
30	THE MIRROR	288
31	WITCH'S TRICKS	298
32	DECISION	310
33	WONDERS	319
34	EXPLANATIONS	329

The day that Leo Zifkak became the owner of the music box, his life changed forever.

Leo didn't know this at the time. His heart didn't miss a beat as he took the box from his mother and put it on his desk. He had no idea what he was holding in his hands.

He was pleased, of course. Who wouldn't be pleased to be the new owner of something that had been a family treasure for hundreds of years? His father said that the music box should be in a museum. But Aunt Bethany Langlander had left it to Leo in her will and so here it was, making everything else in his room look plain and cheap and sort of . . . childish.

The music box had been in Leo's mother's family ever since a long-ago ancestor called Rollo had brought it home from one of his world trips. ("Rollo Langlander was a *great* traveler," Aunt Bethany always said, opening her blue eyes wide as if being a great traveler was as remarkable as being a fire-eater in a circus.)

The box was about as big as a shoe box, and had four short legs. Its lid was smooth, shining black, quite plain except for a narrow, oval-shaped ring of real silver in the center. Its sides, however, were painted with amazingly detailed scenes, and this was what made it so special, and so interesting.

The long side at the front was a town filled with houses, shops, and people. The long side at the back was green and peaceful, with a castle on a hill, a queen in a long blue gown, a dragon flying high in the sky, and a river winding down from misty mountains. One of the short sides was a coast of sea and golden sand. The other was mainly forest, where tall trees rose from a sea of lacy ferns and shadows seemed to flicker with the stripes of tigers.

Leo lifted the box and turned the winder in its base three times, counting under his breath. *One, two, three . . .*

He put the box down again and opened the lid. The familiar, chiming music began to play. His mother patted his shoulder and wandered out of the room.

And Leo was left alone with the treasure that might as well have been a bomb just waiting to explode.

The music slowed, and stopped. Leo wound the box again. *One, two, three.* As the music began, he heard his mother moving around in the spare room next door, and sighed. He wanted to forget that Mimi Langlander, his least-favorite second cousin, was coming to stay.

His mother wasn't looking forward to Mimi's visit, either. She hadn't said so, but he could tell. And Leo's father had, as usual, made his feelings very clear.

"Why can't Robert and Carol take the girl to Greece with them?" he'd demanded, when the news of Mimi's visit had been broken to him.

"She won't go," Leo's mother had said calmly. "She doesn't want to miss her violin lessons. And —"

Leo's father gave an explosive snort. "Then surely there's someone else who can take her?" he demanded.

"No, Tony, there isn't," said Suzanne. "Her brothers are both working, and can't possibly look after her. The twins are still in India. Chris and Kwon live too far away. Martin and Monique can't take Mutt because of Martin's allergy —"

"Mutt?" roared Leo's father. "Who's —?"

"Mimi's dog," said Suzanne, lifting her chin. "Mimi won't go anywhere without him."

Tony stared, speechless. Then he turned to look at Einstein, the dignified black cat dozing in a puddle of sunlight under the window.

"Oh, Mutt won't bother Einstein," Suzanne said confidently. "Mutt's a tiny little thing. And he'll sleep upstairs with Mimi."

Tony had groaned, and Leo had gloomily faced the fact that the matter was settled.

Tony Zifkak was a scientist. He was a big, untidy, funny, impatient man, who had no living relatives except his wife and son. He liked his home to be a comfortable refuge, and he loathed any kind of intrusion. But he loved his wife very much, and he knew that for her, blood was thicker than water. She had been born a Langlander, and Langlanders stuck together.

And if Mom hadn't been so determined, Leo thought later, wondering at the mysteries of fate, if Mom had caved and told Dad, okay, if it upsets you so much we won't have Mimi after all. . . .

Then maybe Aunt Bethany's music box would have kept its secret for another eighty years.

Aunt Bethany, Leo's *Great*-Aunt Bethany, had been a plump, fussy old lady with faded blue eyes, soft, powdery cheeks, and crinkly white hair. She had looked the same for as long as Leo had known her — which was all his life.

Aunt Bethany was the oldest surviving Langlander, and lived in the old family home. Every year she gave an afternoon tea to which all her nieces and nephews and their families (except children under five years old) were invited.

Leo's mother went every year, but his father never did. Tony flatly said that his marriage vows didn't include agreeing to be bored out of his mind.

The afternoon teas were held in Aunt Bethany's front room, where a table covered with a white lace cloth was always waiting. On the table were asparagus rolls, tiny sandwiches sprinkled with shredded lettuce, a sponge cake with jam and cream in the middle, small pink and white meringues, and gingerbread men from Aunt Bethany's local bakery, one for every child.

For the adults there was tea, in cups as delicate as eggshells. For the children there was sparkling lemonade. The lemonade was always warm and a little bit flat, as if it had been poured into the thick green glasses quite some time before everyone arrived.

The routine never changed, just as nothing ever changed in

Aunt Bethany's dim house, with its smell of curtains and furniture polish, its dried-flower arrangement on the table by the front windows, and the slow, loud ticking of the grandfather clock in the hall.

Aunt Bethany had lived in the house all her life, and liked everything to stay just as it had always been. Mr. Higgs, her regular gardener and handyman, had even had trouble persuading her to let him replace the ancient garden shed, which was so rotten that it leaned sideways. She'd agreed in the end, but she'd mourned "the dear old shed" for years afterward.

"I hated to see it go," she would say tearfully, "but I couldn't disappoint Mr. Higgs. He's *very* loyal, and *scrupulously* honest. And he's so good with the camellias."

Every year, while the children furtively cleaned up the last of the meringues and the adults restlessly sipped their lukewarm second cups of tea, Aunt Bethany meandered through a few favorite tales from her huge repertoire of old family stories. Then, without fail, she lifted the music box down from its usual place on the mantelpiece to a low, polished table where everyone could see it.

"Now, we wind the box three times, no more," she always said, speaking especially to the children. "We never turn the key while the music is playing. We never pick up the box while the music is playing. And we never close the lid until the music has stopped."

Then she'd lift the box, turn the key three times, put the box down again, and open the lid. The chiming music would begin — soft, sweet, and strange. And when Leo was little, it always looked to him as if the tiger shadows were moving and the painted people were dancing to the tune.

"Why can you only wind it three times?" he remembered whispering to his mother the first time he went to one of Aunt Bethany's afternoon teas, the first time he saw the music box.

"I suppose it might break, if it's wound too far," his mother had whispered back. "We wouldn't want that to happen, would we?"

And Leo had shaken his head solemnly.

But little Mimi Langlander, who was also visiting Aunt Bethany for the first time that afternoon, had said in a loud, piercing voice, "How do you *know* that three times is all you can wind it, Auntie Bethany?"

Aunt Bethany's blue eyes widened. "Well, my uncle Henry told me so, dear," she said.

"But how did *he* know?" Mimi persisted, as her mother suppressed a sigh and her brothers and sisters made faces at one another and rolled their eyes.

"Well, I'm not — " Flustered by this startling break in her usual routine, Aunt Bethany eyed Mimi nervously. Then she seemed to recover.

"Uncle Henry left the music box to me because he knew I'd take care of it," she said. "He told me the rules. They're even written down. I'll show you, in a minute."

They all waited awkwardly while the music box ran down. When the last chime had struck, Aunt Bethany carefully shut the lid.

"The tune didn't end," said Mimi. "Three winds aren't enough."

"Mimi!" her mother murmured, in a tired sort of way.

"But the tune played all through, then it started again, but it stopped before it finished," Mimi insisted.

What's she talking about? Leo remembered thinking, staring at the small, skinny girl who had put her hands on her hips and was frowning quite fiercely. *She's so* weird.

Her cheeks very pink, Aunt Bethany lifted the box high so everyone could see the yellowed strip of paper stuck to the bottom, just above the key. The paper was covered in cramped, faded writing.

"Important!" read Aunt Bethany impressively.

Turn the key three times only. Never turn the key while the music is playing. Never pick up the box while the music is playing. Never close the lid until the music has stopped.

"So there you are."

With a mildly triumphant air, she carried the music box back to the mantelpiece and put it down exactly where it had been before.

Mimi looked mutinous, but before she could say anything else her mother got up hurriedly and started saying that they really had to go.

Leo had seen Mimi Langlander a couple of times a year since then — whenever his mother's family got together.

Though they were the same age, they hardly ever spoke to each other at these events. Mimi's brothers and twin sisters, who were all much older than she was, were very friendly, but Mimi herself just skulked at the edges of the crowd looking superior and bored. Sometimes you'd even see her reading a book in a dim corner, her thin shoulders hunched, her knees drawn up to her sharp little chin.

Mimi played the violin, Leo's mother said. It had been discovered that she had an extraordinary musical talent. *As if that makes it okay to act like she's better than anyone else,* Leo thought sourly.

This year, he hadn't seen Mimi Langlander since what turned out to be the very last of Aunt Bethany's afternoon teas. He scowled at the thought of it.

As usual, Aunt Bethany had rambled on happily about Langlanders of the past, including Rollo Langlander the world traveler, and glamorous, scandalous Alice Langlander, who had played the harp and ended up joining a circus, while everyone else fidgeted, smiled politely or stared into space. When at last she lowered her voice and moved on to her wicked uncle George, however, most of the children, including Leo, started paying attention. They all liked hearing about Uncle George, the family disgrace.

Wicked Uncle George was the eldest of three brothers. The middle brother was Henry, the famous Uncle Henry who had left Aunt Bethany the music box. The youngest, born twelve years after Henry, was John, Aunt Bethany's father.

George was a charming, handsome boy, and his parents' favorite. "They *doted* on George," Aunt Bethany said, shaking her head.

"He could twist them around his little finger." She spoke as if she'd seen it all, though she hadn't even been born at the time.

Uncle George grew up selfish and lazy, Aunt Bethany said, her gentle voice shocked and disapproving. He spent money like water, began to gamble on horse races, and couldn't keep a job. There were even rumors of trouble with the *police*! Soon after his father died, George ran away, leaving a trail of debts, and was never seen again.

"He broke his poor mother's heart," Aunt Bethany sighed. "She passed away not long after that. My father was just a boy then, still at school. But his brother Henry promised to look after him, and he did."

She paused and stared mistily into space. With all his might, Leo willed her to forget about Uncle Henry for once, and start talking about something else.

For a long moment it seemed that his wish would be granted. Then:

"Your uncle Henry put your father through school, and then university, didn't he, Aunt Bethany?" prompted Mimi Langlander, her air of innocent interest totally at odds with the malicious, sidelong glance she shot in Leo's direction.

And, her eyes suddenly clearing as if she'd been freshly wound up, Aunt Bethany nodded, smiled, and launched into the tale of Wonderful Uncle Henry.

Thanks, Mimi, Leo thought, as he sat through the depressing story of Henry working selflessly to care for his brother John and pay all his wicked brother George's debts, never marrying but being a kind uncle to John's children (especially Bethany herself), then tragically drowning just three days after receiving an engraved chiming clock for working twenty-five years at the bank.

Aunt Bethany sighed sentimentally and reached for the silver-framed photograph of Uncle Henry as a child that stood with dozens of other ancient family photographs on the cabinet by her chair. Leo's gloom deepened.

"There," said Aunt Bethany, holding up the photograph and nodding placidly. "Even when he was young, you could see what sort of man he was going to grow up to be. A true gentleman. And Leo is the image of him. The spitting image." She beamed at Leo approvingly.

Leo's cousins tittered and nudged each other. Leo squirmed and felt his face grow hot. He didn't think he looked anything like that long-ago boy staring seriously out from his oval frame in old-fashioned buttoned-up clothes, his ears sticking out a little and his slicked-down hair parted in the middle. He certainly hoped he didn't. But as usual his mother murmured that perhaps there was a similarity, and Aunt Bethany insisted there was a strong likeness.

"It's the eyes," she said. "The steady, responsible eyes."

Mimi Langlander gave a harsh yell of laughter.

Leo groaned softly, just thinking about it. Why did he have to look like poor old Uncle Henry, who'd obviously never had a moment's fun in his life? If he had to look like someone, why couldn't he look like handsome, charming Uncle George?

Yet he knew in his heart that he and Uncle George had nothing in common. It wasn't just a matter of looks. Leo knew that he *was* steady and responsible, just like Uncle Henry. He worked fairly hard at school. He never missed soccer training. He wasn't impulsive or reckless. People were always saying how mature and sensible he was.

Either he'd been brought up to be like that, or he was like that naturally. Either way, he couldn't help it.

That was why he'd always found Uncle Henry's story so depressing. He knew how he would have felt, if he'd been in Henry Langlander's place: He would have felt trapped. But he would have acted exactly as Uncle Henry had, all the same. Except for the getting drowned part, he hoped.

Naturally, Leo had never said a word to Aunt Bethany about all this. He'd never protested when she compared him to Wonderful Uncle Henry. She wouldn't have understood his feelings at all.

Aunt Bethany had never had a job, and she'd never married. She didn't have any pets, because looking after a pet might worry her. She'd never learned to drive. She'd never been interested in travel. She didn't read books, because reading made her head ache.

Leo's father said her life would drive a normal person crazy, but Aunt Bethany was clearly quite content to spend her days looking at old photograph albums and watching game shows on television.

It was while she was watching television, in fact, that she had quietly stopped breathing, aged ninety-four, her plump little hands peacefully folded on her lap, and tea growing cold in a cup on a table beside her.

Aunt Bethany had had the quietest, most boring life that it was possible to imagine. She'd never taken a risk, or allowed herself to be worried by anything. Leo's mother said that was why she'd lasted so long, outliving both her brothers, though she was the eldest of the three. She said that Aunt Bethany hadn't so much died, as just rusted away.

So there was no reason for Leo to think that anything that had been owned by his great-aunt Bethany would be in any way dangerous or surprising. He knew everything about her, so he thought the same applied to the music box she had left him.

But, of course, it didn't.

CHAPTER 2

Mimi Langlander arrived just after lunch on Sunday with her violin case and her little mustard-colored dog clutched in her arms, and her mother hurrying behind her with two bags and a pillow.

Leo's father wasn't home. He was on his way to speak at an interstate conference. Usually he complained about having to go to conferences, especially when he had to give a speech, but Leo suspected he wasn't so unhappy about it this time. Home wouldn't be nearly as comfortable with Mimi and Mutt around.

He'd left for the airport early and this was fortunate, because he missed seeing Mutt and Einstein's first meeting.

Einstein appeared in the hall to greet the guests, his tail very upright. Mutt, who looked like a fluffy toy with teeth, burst into an explosion of ear-splitting yaps.

Einstein arched his back and hissed. Every hair on his body stood up, so that he looked twice his normal size. Mimi screamed and shrank back against the wall, holding Mutt high as if Einstein were a ravening panther. Struggling to free himself and fly into the attack, Mutt began to make high, hysterical gargling sounds that were apparently supposed to be growls.

"Leo! Put Einstein in the kitchen," Suzanne ordered distractedly. "Shut him in!"

"I'm so sorry, Suzanne," Mimi's mother shouted over Mutt's yaps and snarls as Leo scooped up the outraged Einstein and backed away with him. "I'm terribly sorry. This is so awkward for you, I do appreciate that. Mutt should have gone to a boarding kennel, but it was honestly just impossible with Mi — with things as they are. You know." She jerked her head in her daughter's direction and rolled her eyes helplessly.

By this time Mimi was visible to Leo only in flashes because Einstein's tail was thrashing in front of his eyes like a fluffy windshield wiper. Mimi was clutching her little dog tightly, her face absolutely rigid.

She heard what Carol said, Leo thought. *She saw Carol roll her eyes. But she doesn't even look upset. She must be used to it.*

And suddenly, unwillingly, he wondered what it would be like to have grown used to your parents talking about you as if you were a problem no normal person could solve.

Mutt saw Leo and Einstein looking at him and his yaps suddenly doubled in volume.

"Mimi!" Carol snapped, scarlet with embarrassment. "This is ridiculous! He's *your* dog! Make him stop!"

"He'll stop if you take that cat away," Mimi said flatly, and pressed her lips into a hard straight line.

Suddenly furious, Leo turned on his heel and stomped toward

the kitchen. Mutt went on yapping till Einstein was out of sight. Carol apologized some more.

It wasn't the best start to a visit that was going to last a whole month.

After she'd wearily given Suzanne a long list of things that Mimi wouldn't eat, a list of Mimi's appointments for the next month, and notes about all Mimi's allergies while Mimi stared silently at the huge, shabby sneakers that encased her feet, Carol went home to finish packing.

Just before she left she suddenly became tearful and hugged Mimi tightly, murmuring things about calling often and being back soon. Mimi, her face expressionless, said nothing except "Okay" and "Yes, Mom." As soon as the car had driven away, she turned and went upstairs to her bedroom with Mutt still clutched in her arms.

She climbed the stairs, her head high and her back very straight. Her legs looked pitifully thin poking out of her pale pink shorts, which flapped hugely just above her knobbly knees.

Leo didn't usually notice people's clothes much, but he couldn't help thinking that Mimi Langlander was the last girl in the world who should wear shorts like that. The bright pink jacket with kittens and bows on it was a big mistake as well. Mimi wasn't a kittens-and-bows sort of person.

Mimi reached the top of the stairs and started along the short corridor that led to the bathroom and her and Leo's rooms. Just before she disappeared from sight, Leo saw her duck her head and bury her face deeply in Mutt's soft hair. Perhaps she was murmuring something, because the little dog licked her hand.

Quickly Leo looked away. Instinctively he knew that Mimi would hate it if she thought she was being watched.

The phone began to ring. Einstein yowled and scratched at the kitchen door.

"Go up and talk to Mimi, Leo," Suzanne whispered distractedly, heading down the hall. "Don't make a big thing of it. But see if you can make her feel better."

The last thing Leo wanted to do was talk to Mimi Langlander. She was weird and stuck up and her little dog was horrible. Besides, he knew that nothing he could say would make her feel better. She obviously didn't like him any more than he liked her.

Then his conscience got the better of him. He thought how bad *he* would feel if his parents had just left him in a strange house, with people he hardly knew. So on his way upstairs he rehearsed a few things he might say as he passed Mimi's room on his way to his own. Something like, "How's it going?" or "Anything you need?"

They all sounded lame, so he was relieved to find that Mimi's door was shut. That was a clear sign that Mimi wanted to be left alone.

He went on into his own room and sat down at his desk with the vague intention of finishing his math homework. He found himself staring at the music box instead.

It was beautifully made. Leo ran his fingers over the smoothness of its shining black lid. He wondered how long it would take to learn to make something that fit together so perfectly.

He would have loved to try. He liked the idea of making things out of wood, though he didn't talk about it much. His father and mother were bored by the very idea, none of his friends were interested, and there were no woodworking classes at school.

Leo saw that his fingers had made smudges on the lid's shining black surface. He wiped the marks away with his sleeve, and turned his attention to the painted parts of the box.

The little figures on the front of the box fascinated him. The more he looked, the more of them he could see. It was like looking at stars in the sky. You saw the biggest, brightest ones first, then gradually you became aware of the thousands — the millions — of smaller, dimmer stars that studded the blackness beyond them.

The front of the music box was like that. There were larger figures in the foreground, men, women, and children walking down the cobbled main street, going in and out of shops and stopping at stalls. Beyond them there were others — hundreds of others, many so tiny that Leo could hardly see them.

The artist must have used a magnifying glass to paint them, he thought, squinting at the box. Then he remembered that he had a magnifying glass himself — a strong one, which his father had given him. He found it at the back of one of his desk drawers and peered through it at the box.

Now he could see all sorts of details that he hadn't been able to see before. He could see the expressions on some of the distant people's faces, he could make out the goods on display in the shops, he could see cats sitting on windowsills, vegetables growing in kitchen gardens . . .

And there was more — so much more.

Leo shook his head in amazement, moving the magnifying glass slowly across the surface of the box. He couldn't imagine how long it must have taken to paint a scene as detailed as this. Months — maybe years — using a brush so fine that it could paint in the green eyes of a cat as small as a freckle. Maybe it had even been painted in layers — one layer on top of another, and another . . .

He was so absorbed that he jumped when his mother called his name and Mimi's, her voice echoing from the downstairs hallway. Leo left his room, went to the top of the stairs, and peered down.

Suzanne looked frazzled. She'd thrown on her coat, and was clutching the car keys and a large handbag. "Leo," she called, as soon as she saw him, "that was your father on the phone. He got all the way to the airport and found he'd left his speech behind. Can you believe it?"

Yes, Leo could believe it. Easily. He grinned. "Are you going to take it to him?" he asked, walking down the stairs.

"I have to!" Suzanne said. "He gives the speech tomorrow. And the copy on his laptop's no good. He's worked on the hard copy by hand — written all over it. You know."

Leo knew. He'd seen his father's speeches many times before. They were always covered with corrections. Sometimes whole paragraphs were crossed out, with arrows pointing to notes scribbled in the margins.

"I'll just make it if I leave now," his mother said. She glanced at her reflection in the hall mirror and pushed rapidly at her hair, making no difference to it that Leo could see. "The back door's locked. Lock the front door after me. Where's Mimi?"

"In her room," Leo said. "Don't worry. I'll tell her."

"I'll be back as soon as I can," Suzanne gabbled. Now, you be careful, and be — "

Nice to Mimi. "Don't worry," Leo repeated dutifully. "We'll be fine."

He followed his mother to the door but didn't wait to wave good-bye, because he knew from experience that she would prefer to see the door closed, and hear it locked, before she left.

He heard the car start up and back out of the driveway as he began to walk up the stairs and back to his room. Suddenly the house seemed extremely quiet.

The door of the spare room was still shut. He debated whether to knock and tell Mimi that his mother had gone out. Then he decided against it. Almost certainly, Mimi had heard Suzanne shouting up the stairs, and knew everything already. She just hadn't bothered to come out and say good-bye.

Leo went back into his room, sat down at his desk, picked up the magnifying glass, and continued his examination of the music box.

Soon he was fascinated once more. Everywhere he looked, there was something new to see. He was certain that Aunt Bethany had never looked at the box this closely. If she had, she'd have mentioned some of the things Leo was seeing now — and probably made everyone look for them, too.

Here was a wedding party in the garden of what looked like a palace — guests were gathered around a long table and holding up glasses to toast the bride and groom, who were both wearing gold crowns. There a house was on fire, and firefighters were spraying the flames with hoses while other people ran to help with buckets of water.

Leo turned the box and scanned the forest side. In fact, the forest only covered the bottom half of the scene. Above it was a brown road, thin as string, running from the front of the box to the back, where it ended at a little bridge. On the other side of the road was a winding river, surrounded at first by farms and tiny villages, then, closer to the bridge, by scattered clumps of trees. Leo looked with appreciation at the largest farm — at the red-roofed house and barn, the haystacks, windmill, orchard, and neat white fences.

He was just about to turn the box again, to look at the back, when he noticed for the first time that narrow paths wound through the forest, and that every now and again there was a cottage nestled in a tiny clearing. Wondering afresh at the artist's loving attention to detail, Leo peered closely at one of the cottages.

It had a thatched roof, and red roses grew around its green-painted door. At the side, in the shade of an old apple tree, a young woman in a red dress sat on a tartan rug, playing with a black-haired baby.

A man was stacking firewood nearby. He was looking over his shoulder and laughing, as if at something the woman had said. In the shadows of the trees beside him there was something gray. Leo squinted at it. At first he thought it was a huge, shaggy dog. Then he realized that it was a crouching wolf. The wolf's hungry yellow eyes were fixed on the baby.

Feeling suddenly sick, Leo put down the magnifying glass.

The baby was in danger. The wolf was stalking it, waiting patiently for its chance to spring. The moment the father finished stacking the wood and went to do something else . . . the moment the mother turned her back . . .

Leo felt strangely angry and betrayed. Why had the painter put a horrible thing — a tragedy waiting to happen — in a scene that should have been only pleasant and happy?

Then he shook his head. *I'm being stupid,* he thought. *A house fire isn't pleasant or happy. There are probably lots of things on the box that aren't. Bad things sometimes happen in real life, so the artist painted bad things as well as good ones, to make the world he was painting seem as real as possible.*

But he still felt uneasy. Trying to put the memory of the wolf's hungry eyes out of his mind, he lifted the box and turned the key three times, then put the box down again and opened the lid. The familiar music began, sweet and strange.

He pulled his math book toward him and began to work. Gradually the music box slowed, and finally stopped. He'd just picked the box up to wind it again when he heard a small sound behind him and turned quickly around.

Mimi Langlander was standing just inside his door.

"I heard you got that," Mimi said, pointing at the music box. "You got it because Aunt Bethany thought you looked like her uncle Henry, and because at her place you were always so go-od."

The way she stretched out the word "good" made her scorn very clear. Leo felt his face grow hot, but he didn't say anything.

"The last time you played it, it stopped at the end of the tune, for once," Mimi said. "Next time, wind it four times. Then it'll finish at the right place again. Otherwise it's really irritating."

Leo shook his head and turned back to his math problems, hoping she'd go away. But she didn't. She moved farther into the room and stood right behind him, so close that he could hear her breathing.

"Dad got money, in the will," she said. "That's why he and Mom can have a vacation in Greece. Your mom got money, too. All the nieces and nephews did."

Leo felt stupid sitting with his back to her. He twisted around in his chair again.

Mimi blinked at him owlishly. Her eyes looked much too big for her thin, pale face. She'd unzipped her pink jacket and the frilly, lemon-yellow shirt she was wearing underneath gave her a sickly look. Her mouse-brown hair was cut very short at the back and over her ears, but her bangs were so long that they reached her eyebrows.

Leo couldn't help thinking how different she looked from her brothers and sisters. They all had thick, glossy, dark-brown hair, and they were tall and healthy-looking. Also, their faces were sort of . . . open, and full of confidence. They were always talking or laughing. Mimi's face was still and closed.

"You don't look like the rest of your family," Leo said, without thinking.

Mimi's expression didn't change. "Everyone says that," she said. "I'm the ugly duckling."

Leo felt terrible. He hadn't meant it that way — or maybe he had. Anyway, it had been a stupid thing to say. He racked his brains for a way of changing the subject.

"What did Aunt Bethany leave you?" he asked desperately. That was a safe question. His mother had told him that none of the great-nieces and nephews had been forgotten.

Mimi shrugged. "The twins and I got a box of old jewelry," she said. "We were supposed to share it among us, but they got most of it."

She must have seen Leo's face change, because she added quickly, "I only wanted one thing, anyway."

She pulled at a chain hanging around her neck and drew out a silver pendant that had been hidden beneath her shirt. "See?" she said. "It's an antique. It's probably really valuable."

Leo looked at the pendant. Maybe it *was* valuable, but he thought it was quite ugly. It was a small oval of murky glass, thinly edged in silver. Beneath the glass, pressed against the pendant's silver back, you could just see a little wisp of silky brown threads.

"What's that stuff inside it?" he asked curiously.

"It's hair," said Mimi. "Probably the hair of someone who died."

She looked down at the pendant and touched the glass with the tip of her finger. "They used to do that in the olden days — put bits of a dead person's hair in rings and brooches and things. That's why I wanted this. It's interesting. Maybe it's lucky."

Interesting? Leo thought. *Lucky? A pendant with a dead person's hair in it? It's* gross. *She's so* weird! And just then, Mimi looked up and saw the expression on his face. She flushed pink, and turned away.

"I didn't —" Leo began, feeling bad all over again.

"Forget it," she said curtly. "You just go on playing with your pretty music box."

Suddenly Leo felt an overwhelming desire to shock her, as she'd shocked him.

He picked up the magnifying glass. "It's not all pretty," he snapped. "Look at this!" He pointed at the small, blurry spot where he knew the wolf crouched among the forest trees.

Mimi took the glass sullenly, but obviously she was curious. She peered at the spot Leo's finger was pointing to, and frowned.

"So what am I supposed to be seeing?" she asked at last.

"The wolf!" said Leo impatiently. "The wolf, hiding in the bushes, watching the baby. Can't you —?"

Mimi sighed. "There's nothing there," she said, and rolled her eyes.

Leo snatched the glass from her hand and looked at the clearing himself.

There was the mother and the baby. There was the father, looking over his shoulder at them and laughing. And in the shadows beside him . . .

Nothing. Nothing but leaves and earth and pale, bent blades of grass.

Leo's jaw dropped. "But — but it was *there!*" he stammered. "Right there. A big gray wolf. I *saw* it!" He pushed his chair away from the desk and stood up, shaking his head in angry confusion.

Mimi smiled a superior smile. And at that moment, as if she'd been waiting for her chance, she bent forward, picked up the music box, and quickly twisted the key. One, two, three, *four.*

"*Hey!*" Leo shouted furiously as the music began to play.

"See?" squealed Mimi. She skipped out of his reach and ran to the door. "It was *fine* to wind it more than three times!"

"Get out of my room!" Leo shouted, beside himself with rage.

Mimi screeched with laughter, and went.

Leo heard her bedroom door shut. He strode to his own door and slammed it. Still gripping the doorknob, he pressed his hot forehead against the wood and just stood there, breathing hard.

The music box kept playing. It played on and on, for much longer than usual.

But it hadn't broken. It hadn't. And somehow that fact made Leo even angrier, because it made him feel like a timid idiot.

Don't be stupid, he told himself, forcing his breathing to slow. *You should be glad that everything's okay. And it's that girl who's the idiot. How did she know that the music box wouldn't break? That fourth turn really might have made the spring snap. Then she'd have been in big trouble!*

He turned away from the door. His room was full of moving light and shadow as the sun filtered through the leaves of the tree that grew outside the window behind his desk. Two small, bright-blue butterflies with black spots on their wings were fluttering above the music box. They danced in the air as though attracted by the music, which was slowing down at last.

Leo looked at them curiously. They seemed oddly familiar to him, though he'd never paid much attention to insects, despite his father's urgings.

"How did you get in here?" he said.

The butterflies fluttered aside as he went to the desk. He leaned over and pushed the window up as far as it would go. But by the time he'd straightened up and stepped back, ready to shoo the butterflies out through the gap, they were nowhere to be seen.

Leo looked around, frowning. *They've hidden somewhere*, he thought. *Well, at least my door's closed so they can't leave my* room. *They'll start flying around again eventually. I'll get them out then.*

He shut the window and sat down at his desk. The music box had stopped playing long ago, but he didn't even think of winding it up again.

Mimi could hear the music through the wall. If he only wound the box three times, she'd know. If he wound it *four* times she'd know that, too.

Either way, she'd get that infuriating, superior look on her face. The same look she'd had when she said she couldn't see the wolf. Just the thought of it filled Leo with rage.

But he hadn't been able to see the wolf either, the second time he'd looked. Could he possibly have imagined it?

No! Leo thought. He closed the music box's glossy black lid with a little snap and picked up the magnifying glass. He frowned through the glass at the place where he knew, he just *knew*, the wolf had been — in the trees right behind the man stacking firewood.

For a long moment he could see nothing but bushes and shadows. Then he moved the glass a little to the left.

And there it was! The crouching, shaggy gray body, the gleaming, hungry eyes. The beast wasn't as close to the man as he'd thought. It was, in fact, nearer to the baby and its mother.

Leo fought off a creeping feeling of dread. He also fought off the urge to go and get Mimi Langlander, and make her see the wolf for herself. He wasn't going to let that girl into his room again.

Determinedly he moved the magnifying glass away from the clearing, catching glimpses of other scenes as they became visible.

There were the firefighters battling the flames. There were the wedding guests drinking from their silver cups, while the bride and groom stood together at the head of the table.

Farther on, seven white swans glided serenely on a small lake edged with flowers. Beside the lake, a man in an embroidered robe sat beneath a tree. The ends of his long, pencil-thin moustache dangled all the way to his chest. A gray pigtail hung down his back. His face was very peaceful and his hand was cupped to his ear as if he were listening to something.

Leo suddenly remembered an old story he'd read about an emperor who loved listening to the song of a nightingale. The scene he was looking at reminded him of that story.

On impulse, he began searching the tree branches that stretched above the richly dressed old man. Moving the magnifying glass in and out, he strained his eyes to see between the leaves. Finally he spotted a small bird sitting on a twig near the top of the tree. The bird's head was tilted up, and its beak was open as if it were singing.

"Yes!" Leo whispered. This surely couldn't be just a coincidence! The artist who had painted the music box must have known the story, and had put the emperor and the nightingale into his picture.

Maybe the artist painted characters from other *stories, too,* Leo thought, fascinated. *Maybe they're tucked in all over the place — the artist's private little jokes.*

The idea pleased him very much. It would be like a treasure hunt, finding other storybook characters on the box.

In quick succession he discovered some possibilities: a knight riding a white horse, a green dragon snoozing on a hill, seven small, bearded men tramping through a forest with picks and shovels over their shoulders, and a house so dark and dilapidated that he was sure it must be haunted.

The strain of peering intently at such tiny details was making his eyes water. Impatiently he wiped them with the back of his hand and moved the glass away from the distant scenes at the top of the picture, down to the larger figures at the bottom.

These were familiar, and also much easier to see. Quickly Leo scanned the street, the shops, the stalls, the bustling figures, looking for anything that reminded him of a story.

There was the man with the curled black moustache standing outside his art gallery. There was the large building labeled TOY FACTORY. Beside it, just past a dark little laneway, the happy landlord of the Black Sheep was carrying a tray of foaming tankards to guests grouped around a table outside the tavern.

A little farther along the street, a thin, rather mournful-looking man in a long white apron was sitting on a stool behind a tray on legs. The tray was heaped with pies. Leo remembered a rhyme about a pie man who refused to give his pies away, and looked at the pie man's customers carefully. None of them looked in any way unusual.

An old man with a short white beard was standing at the edge of the small crowd around the pie man. He was holding two little girls by the hand. The girls were dressed alike, as if they were twins, and each of them was holding up a shiny coin. The old man was smiling indulgently at them as they jumped around in excitement, waiting to be served. Behind him, a man in a checked coat had stopped to tie his shoelace . . .

Leo gave a short, shocked laugh. The man in the checked coat was stealing the old man's wallet! He was pretending to tie his shoelace, but all the time he was easing the wallet out of the old man's back pocket.

There were lots of stories about thieves and pickpockets, but Leo couldn't think of any one in particular. He moved the magnifying glass on.

The pie man was standing near a small flower stall with a red-and-white-striped awning.

Leo had often noticed the flower stall when he'd looked at the music box at Aunt Bethany's place. The stall was near the middle of the street scene, in front of a narrow gap between two buildings. It was half-hidden by hurrying passersby, but it made a splash of bright color because of the buckets of flowers arranged on a shelf behind the flower seller, and clustered around her feet.

Leo told himself that there was no real need to look at it again. But it was in his nature to be thorough, so he moved the magnifying glass over it anyway.

He was mildly surprised to see that there weren't nearly as many flowers as he had remembered. He'd always thought that the stall was packed with bunches of blooms, but in fact many of the buckets were empty, as if the flower seller had been doing a brisk trade.

Leo shrugged. After all, until now he'd only seen the music box once a year, and he'd never studied it through a magnifying glass before. Then he noticed something else, and frowned in puzzlement.

He was sure that the last time he'd looked at the flower stall, the customer had been a woman — a tall black woman in purple, buying a mass of pink lilies.

But the woman wasn't there. Instead, the flower seller was handing a bunch of daisies wrapped in green paper to a bashful-looking young man with curly hair.

Leo's skin prickled. Then he shook his head. *I'm just remembering wrong,* he thought. *The woman in purple must be somewhere else on the street.*

He saw a bunch of pink lilies standing in a bucket toward the back of the flower stall. *There,* he thought. *That's what happened. My memories got mixed up. I saw the woman carrying pink lilies, and I saw pink lilies at the flower stall, and —*

Then he froze.

Above the lilies hovered a cloud of small, bright-blue butterflies with black spots on their wings.

Leo's mouth went dry. He dropped the magnifying glass with a clatter.

"No," he muttered to himself. "No, no, no!" Distractedly, he ran his fingers through his hair. Then he stood up and began walking around his room, examining every surface, waving his arms in every corner.

But no blue butterflies fluttered out of hiding. And, really, he'd known all the time that they wouldn't.

Because now he knew why the butterflies he had seen over his desk had looked familiar. And he knew that they were no longer in his room.

They were in the music box. They were *back* in the music box.

CHAPTER 4

Leo stood motionless in the middle of his room, his heart beating very fast. He'd seen the butterflies fluttering above his desk. And he'd seen the same butterflies at the flower stall on the music box. There just couldn't be any mistake.

Calm down, he told himself shakily. *Think it through, step by step.*

He took a deep breath. *Okay*, he thought. *You claim that these butterflies came out of the music box. Leaving aside the fact that this is* impossible, *why haven't they ever come out before? Did you ever see blue butterflies flying around at Aunt Bethany's place? No! Were there blue butterflies in your room yesterday? No! So why should they suddenly come out today?*

Because today they had time to come out. Because today, for the first time in at least eighty years, the music box key was turned four times instead of only three.

The answer struck Leo with the force of simple truth. He plumped down on his bed and sat there, thunderstruck.

There was a tap on his door. He barely heard it.

"Leo!" called a small, serious voice. "I'm sorry. I mean — I was sure the music box wouldn't break, but I shouldn't have . . ."

Slowly Leo got up. He walked to the door and opened it. Mimi stood in the hallway. She was clutching Mutt in her arms, hugging him to her chest.

"It's all right. You didn't have to open the door," she said, her lips barely moving. "I just wanted —"

And suddenly Leo knew what he had to do. He had to find out once and for all if this — this thing he thought he'd seen — was true or not. He needed a witness, right now. And Mimi Langlander was the only person in the house.

"Come in, quickly," he said, pulling the door wider and beckoning her into the room. "Something's happened — something really strange — to do with the music box."

Mimi's eyes widened. "You mean — it *did* break?" she whispered. "Just because I wound it —"

"No, no!" said Leo impatiently, closing the door behind her. "I don't think the rule about only winding three times has anything to *do* with breaking the spring. It was made for another reason."

Mimi gaped at him. "What reason?" she asked.

Leo led her over to his desk. "I'll show you," he said rapidly. "But first you've got to swear that whatever happens you won't tell anyone."

"I can't swear that!" Mimi said, recoiling. "What if you're a serial killer? What if you show me a jar of ears you've cut off all your victims?"

Leo stared at her, then shook his head to clear it. "Look," he said. "Just swear that you won't tell anyone if — if you don't think you really *have* to. I'm going to do an experiment, and I need a witness. Okay?"

"I suppose so," said Mimi, eyeing him doubtfully.

She carried Mutt to the bed and put him down on the quilt, as if placing him out of harm's way. "Stay, Mutt," she said. The little dog yapped defiantly, then suddenly seemed to decide that the bed was comfortable, and curled up to sleep.

Mimi came back to the desk. Leo noticed that she was fingering her horrible pendant. *Maybe she thinks it will protect her if I make any sudden moves,* he thought, and had a wild desire to laugh.

"All right," he said. "Now, all you have to do is watch the music box. Don't take your eyes off it while the music's playing — especially at the end."

Mimi's lips thinned. "What am I supposed to be looking for?" she asked in a flat voice.

"I can't tell you that," said Leo. "It'll spoil the experiment."

Mimi made a disgusted sound and turned away from him.

"What's wrong?" Leo exclaimed in surprise.

Mimi looked around, peering at him from beneath her heavy bangs. "This is all just some sort of joke to make me look stupid, isn't it?" she said. "So you can tell all your friends all about it at school tomorrow. I know how it works."

"This isn't a joke, I swear!" Leo said. "Something happened, before, while the music box was playing — or at least I think it did. I need to know if it was real, or if I was just seeing things. That's why I want you to watch with me."

He thought he saw a flicker of curiosity in her eyes. He nodded vehemently. "Probably nothing will happen," he said. "Probably I *was* just seeing things. So that means that if anyone's going to look stupid after this, it's me."

Mimi seemed to consider this for a moment. Then she shrugged and turned back to the desk.

Leo picked up the music box and wound it. One, two, three, four times. Then he put the box down again, and opened the lid.

The sweet, chiming music began. Leo stood rigidly, waiting. Once he glanced at Mimi. She was standing as still as he was, her eyes fixed on the box.

The music went on and on. Nothing happened.

Leo's eyes began prickling. He heard Mimi sigh, as if she were very bored, and suddenly the whole experiment seemed ridiculous. His face grew hot.

Probably nothing will happen, he'd said. Well, of *course* nothing was going to happen. He'd had some sort of waking dream, that's all. And then he'd lost his head and told Mimi about it — Mimi Langlander, of all people! Why hadn't he kept his mouth shut?

Mimi's arm moved and she made a small sound, like a squeak. *She's yawning now*, Leo thought sourly, glancing at her again.

Mimi's hand was pressed over her mouth, but she wasn't yawning. She was staring, wide-eyed, at the music box.

Leo's stomach lurched. He looked back at the box and his own jaw dropped.

A scrap of bright blue was peeling away from the box's painted surface. It was as flat and flimsy as a shape cut out of paper, and was colored on both sides. As it curled away from the box, it grew larger, till Leo could see that it was painted to look like a blue butterfly with black spots on its wings.

"I don't believe it!" Mimi squeaked. "Is this —?"

"Yes!" Leo whispered. His heart was thudding wildly.

The butterfly shape separated itself from the surface of the music box, leaving no trace behind. It wavered in the air for a split second. Then, abruptly, the black body thickened, the blue wings moved . . . and there before their astonished eyes was a real, living butterfly.

Mimi gave another muffled squeak.

Leo felt numb. *This is true*, he kept telling himself. *This is real.* But his mind just couldn't accept what his eyes were seeing.

The butterfly fluttered up to the top of the box and settled on the edge of the open lid, gracefully opening and closing its wings.

"It's one of those butterflies that hang around the flower stall in the middle of the street," Mimi murmured. She didn't sound numb. She didn't sound scared. She just sounded deeply fascinated.

Leo glanced at her. Her eyes were startled and shining. Her cheeks were flushed bright pink. She drew a sharp breath. "Look!" she breathed.

Leo looked. More flat, black-spotted blue shapes had begun peeling from the music box like large flakes of paint. In moments a second butterfly was flying up to join the first. A third and a fourth soon followed it. And others were on their way.

"How many came out last time?" Mimi whispered.

"Two," said Leo.

"So they're learning!" Mimi clapped her hands softly.

"*Learning?*" Leo shook his head in confusion. Then, suddenly, he thought of an answer to everything. Immediately he felt better.

"They must be holograms — you know, 3-D images," he said. "There must be a laser beam in the box, triggered by the music —"

"Don't be crazy!" Mimi snorted, as he started peering into the polished interior of the music box, looking in vain for tiny holes and lights. "Those butterflies aren't holograms! You can see they aren't. And anyway, how could there be a laser beam in something that's hundreds of years old?"

She paused. "Unless it was left on earth by aliens," she said thoughtfully. "That would make sense."

Leo closed his eyes. This was too much. This had to stop. He opened his eyes and stretched out his hand to the circling butter-flies. His stomach turned over as a soft wing brushed his fingers. He snatched his hand back hastily.

"Okay, they're not holograms," he said. "You can touch them. They're real."

"Told you," said Mimi smugly.

By the time the music box began to run down, nine butterflies were fluttering around the lid like flower petals tossed by the wind. There were only three painted butterflies left hovering over the pink lilies at the flower stall on the front of the box. And Leo's mind had begun working again. The terrible, paralyzing numbness had lifted.

I guess this proves you can get used to anything, he thought, watching the butterflies dance. *Once the shock has worn off . . .*

"The music's slowing down," Mimi said. "Quick! Wind it up again."

Leo shook his head. "I have to see what happens when the music stops," he said. "I have to see if —"

At that moment, the last chime struck. Instantly, the butterflies plummeted downward as if they were being sucked by a vacuum cleaner. Before the sound of the chime had faded away, they had flattened themselves against the front of the box and disappeared beneath the painted surface.

It was almost as shocking as seeing them appear in the first place.

Leo closed the box's lid. He noticed that his hands were trembling slightly, and clenched his fists.

Mimi wet her lips. "Imagine!" she said after a moment. "Aunt Bethany had the music box for all that time, and she never knew. . . ."

Leo nodded. "Because she never turned the key more than three times," he said slowly. "I suppose her uncle Henry knew she wouldn't. That's why he left the music box to her. He knew she'd follow the rules."

"Same reason *she* left it to *you,*" said Mimi.

Leo winced, but she didn't notice.

"I wonder how long this has been going on?" she mused. "I mean, Uncle Henry didn't sound like the type to break rules, either. He was the really steady, responsible one who always did the right thing. Like you."

"Yes," Leo said shortly.

She glanced at him. "Don't be mad," she said seriously. "Be glad. If you *hadn't* been good and responsible and everything, Aunt Bethany would never have left you the music box in the first place. Then today would never have happened!"

That's one way of looking at it, Leo thought. *A weird sort of way.* Suddenly he grinned. "I'm going to try it again," he said. "Maybe this time we can get all twelve of the butterflies to come out."

"Yes," Mimi agreed, nodding vigorously. "Try turning the key *five* times. Or maybe even six! That would make the tune play three times exactly, and three's a magic number."

Leo thought about it. "I don't want to break the spring," he said at last.

Mimi snorted. "You won't. Just don't force the key to turn further than you think it wants to go. You'll feel it, when it's time to stop. Do you want me to —?"

"No, it's okay," Leo interrupted. He picked up the music box. He turned the key. One, two, three, four, *five* times. Gently, his heart in his mouth, he began a sixth turn and, feeling no resistance, completed it.

"Now we'll see," he said, putting the box down again and opening the lid.

The strange, sweet music began. Leo waited breathlessly.

"Now!" Mimi said. And as she spoke, the first two butterflies began peeling from the box.

A little irritated, Leo glanced at her.

She blinked at him. "You can tell by the music," she said simply.

Leo looked back at the box. The first butterflies were already fluttering around the lid, and five more flimsy blue shapes were flaking away from the painted surface.

"It's happening faster this time," he said, excitement driving away his irritation. "They *are* learning. And — oh!"

A different shape had begun peeling from the surface of the box. It was small, round, and brown, with a thin ribbon of a tail.

"It's a mouse!" Mimi hissed. Nervously she glanced behind her at Mutt, but the little dog slept on.

In seconds the smallest, cutest mouse Leo had ever seen was crouched beside the music box. It was furry and plump, and its tail was very long. It had tiny pink paws and round pink ears. Around its neck it wore a fine gold chain from which dangled a white square of what looked like folded paper.

The mouse sat up on its hind legs and blinked expectantly at Leo and Mimi. After a moment, it put its head on one side and twitched its whiskers in a puzzled sort of way.

Mimi and Leo stood, staring. The mouse made a small, huffing sound, plucked the white square from the gold chain, and put it on the desk. It nudged the square forward with one of its paws. Then it turned around and scuttled rapidly back to the music box, flattening out just before it hit the painted surface and quickly disappearing from sight.

"What was *that* all about?" Leo exclaimed. He reached out to pick up the little white square, but snatched his hand back with a yell.

Something else had begun peeling from the surface of the box — the shape of a woman in a long blue dress, growing as he watched.

Leo stumbled back. He heard Mimi gasp, and Mutt begin to yap.

The woman-shape, flat and flimsy as a cardboard cutout, separated from the box and drifted free, flapping slightly in the air.

Leo and Mimi backed away as far as they could without actually falling onto the bed. Mimi snatched up the yapping Mutt and held him tightly.

And the next instant, the flimsy shape had thickened into life, and a beautiful, richly dressed woman was standing on the rug in front of the desk, looking around the room with interest.

Her eyes stopped at the frantically barking dog. "Be still," she said softly.

Mutt fell abruptly silent. The sweet, slow chiming of the music box filled the room. Leo and Mimi stood frozen, staring.

Gems and gold glimmered at the woman's throat, in her ears, and on her long fingers. The wide skirts of her dark-blue gown rustled as she moved. Her hair, so fair that it was almost white, was swept up into an elaborate arrangement of coils and ringlets encircled by a jeweled crown.

And Leo knew who she was. He'd seen her dozens of times, standing on the drawbridge of her castle on the back of the music box. This was the woman he had always thought of as the Blue Queen.

CHAPTER 5

THE KEY

The queen raised her eyebrows at Mimi and Leo. Her pale green eyes were amused. "I fear I have startled you," she said in a low, musical voice. "Were you not expecting me?"

Then, as if she'd suddenly remembered something, she glanced behind her at the music box, which was now surrounded by a butterfly cloud. She turned around and closed the lid.

The music was cut off abruptly, but to Leo's astonishment the butterflies continued fluttering around as before, and the Blue Queen didn't disappear, either. She remained bent over Leo's desk, staring down at the music box.

"So it is true," she murmured to herself. Her slim fingers tapped the desk and her rings flashed in the sunlight.

"Why is she still here?" Leo whispered to Mimi. "The music's stopped!"

"It's been stopped, but it hasn't run down, has it?" Mimi whispered back. "The lid was shut while it was still playing. Remember the fourth rule?"

Never close the lid until the music has stopped.

Leo swallowed and nodded. He couldn't speak.

"I think it works like this," Mimi said as calmly as if she was explaining a math problem to a rather slow friend. "The music unlocks the gate of the music box world. Four turns are enough to make the gate swing open — wide enough to let things like the butterflies out. Five or six turns open it enough for — for anything."

Anything. Leo took a deep breath, trying to pull himself together.

He turned back to look at the Blue Queen and felt a tiny chill. "And the gate stays open until the music runs down," he muttered. "That's why she shut the lid."

"That's right," Mimi said. "While the box stays shut, she can stay here for as long as she wants."

"Indeed I can, my dear," the woman said, swinging around with a rustle of silken skirts. She was smiling, but to Leo the smile had a false look, as if she'd pasted it onto her face just a moment before. She was holding the small white square of folded paper that the mouse had left on the desk.

Mutt had begun struggling violently in Mimi's arms. "Mutt, stop it!" hissed Mimi, holding on to him with difficulty.

Slowly, keeping her eyes on them, the Blue Queen began to unfold the paper. She remained with her back to the desk, which was completely hidden by her billowing skirts.

That's what she wants, thought Leo with a shock. *She's blocking the music box deliberately so we can't get to it.*

And suddenly he wanted to reach the box very badly. He wanted to open the lid and let the music play till it slowed and died away.

He wanted the Blue Queen and the butterflies to go back where they came from. He wanted all this weirdness to stop!

Frantically he tried to think of a way to make the woman move away from the desk. He doubted he'd be able to push her aside, even if he dared to try it. He needed a distraction.

The woman finished unfolding the paper, and glanced down at it.

Mutt was still wriggling, ignoring Mimi's whispered pleas and commands to be still.

"Put him down," Leo muttered.

Mimi shook her head.

"You're holding him too tightly," hissed Leo. "Let him go!"

He pulled at Mimi's arm, taking her by surprise. Her elbow jerked upward, her grip loosened, and Mutt seized his chance. As Mimi squealed he ducked his head, slithered under her arm, and half-fell, half-leaped to the ground.

If Leo had been hoping that Mutt would create the distraction he needed, he was disappointed. Mutt just crouched where he had fallen, watching the Blue Queen intently. And the queen didn't move. She merely looked up, and suddenly her face changed.

Her green eyes widened and brightened. The false, pasted-on smile broadened and became real.

She crumpled up the scrap of paper and tossed it on the floor. She smiled at the little dog.

"So you are Mutt," she said gently. "Come, Mutt."

She stretched out her hand. Mutt whined softly and crawled forward on his belly till his front paws were touching the hem of her dress.

"Mutt, come here!" Mimi called, her voice sharp with surprise.

The woman laughed softly. "Let him be," she said, fixing Mimi with her strange, pale green eyes. "He merely wants to be sure we will take him with us when we return to Rondo together. And so we shall."

Leo's stomach lurched.

"Rondo," Mimi said faintly. "Your world is called . . . Rondo?"

A tiny, puzzled crease appeared between the Blue Queen's perfect eyebrows. She put her head to one side and studied Mimi thoughtfully. "Rondo is the name of my world, indeed," she said, after a moment. "I am surprised you do not know it, for it is your world, too, to wander as you wish."

Mimi swallowed. "You mean — *we* can go into the music box?" she almost squeaked. "Now?"

"Of course!" The Blue Queen shrugged her shoulders elegantly. "Why should you wait? You have denied yourself for far too long already. And that is why I am here — to be your guide to Rondo's wonders."

"Wonders," Mimi murmured.

"In Rondo you can be anything you want to be, my dear," the woman said. "You can be rich. You can be beautiful . . ." She paused, and suddenly her eyes, fixed on Mimi, seemed to flash and her voice softened, becoming as smooth and sweet as honey. "You can be admired. You can have friends — as many as you wish. You can have anything your heart desires."

Leo realized that he had been holding his breath. He let it out with a little gasp and drew fresh air into his lungs.

"We're very happy in our own world, thanks," he said. He'd meant to sound firm, but the words came out in a childish, squeaky rush.

Mimi said nothing. Small, thin, and awkward, she stood with her arms folded tightly across her chest. Mutt was lying motionless at the visitor's feet, looking up with adoring eyes.

"You do not understand, I think," the Blue Queen said in her honey-sweet voice. "This is a great gift that others — members of your own family — have tried to prevent you from receiving."

She saw Leo frown, and her lips curved in amusement.

"You did no wrong by breaking rules made in jealousy and spite," she said. "And there is nothing to fear in entering my world."

"It's not going in I'm worried about so much," Leo muttered, though this was not quite true. "It's getting out again."

The queen laughed musically. "You do not seem to understand how special you are," she said. "Others of your kind are in danger, certainly. If *they* were foolish enough to enter the box, with the help of someone from Rondo, they would quickly discover they were trapped, because return by the same means is impossible. *You* are different. While you carry the Key, you can come and go as you please, as so many other Langlanders have done in their time."

"Key?" Leo repeated blankly.

"You can't take the winder out of the base of the music box," Mimi said at the same moment. "It's fixed in place. It's —"

The woman's smile grew wider and she clapped her hands. "Ah, you have been kept quite in ignorance, then!" she exclaimed. "Ah, how amusing! How *foolish*!"

She realized that Mimi and Leo were staring at her, and shook her head. "I am sorry," she said, the smile still tweaking the corners of her mouth. "I was taken by surprise when I found you did not know. The thing we call the Key is not a real key. It is a magic object . . . a talisman, which allows you to enter and leave Rondo at will."

She studied their bewildered faces for a moment. Then, smiling, she drew a ring from the little finger of her left hand. The ring was gold, set with small, glittering black stones.

"This is the Key," she said, holding the ring out to Mimi. "This is your birthright, lost to you for far too long. Take it and come with me now, Bethany Langlander!"

Mimi took a step forward.

"*No!*" Leo shouted, grabbing her and dragging her back. Mimi struggled furiously, but he held on.

"You must not interfere, dear boy," said the Blue Queen calmly. "Your sister must do as she wishes."

"He's not my brother!" shrieked Mimi.

"And she's not Bethany Langlander!" Leo shouted. "Aunt Bethany died. This is *Mimi* Langlander. And she can't —"

"Shut up, you idiot!" screeched Mimi. Making a final, violent effort she twisted herself out of Leo's grip. Trembling all over, rubbing her arms as if Leo's fingers had bruised her, she eyed the Blue Queen fearfully.

The woman had grown very still. After a moment she slowly lowered her hand.

"That explains it," she murmured. "Of course — I was forgetting how quickly time passes in this world."

She closed her eyes, then opened them again and smiled at Mimi, ignoring Leo completely. "So poor, timid Bethany was cheated of her destiny after all," she said softly. "I am glad that you have not made her mistake, Mimi Langlander."

Again she held out her hand. The ring lay on her palm, its black stones glittering.

Mimi frowned very slightly, then her lips firmed. She turned to Leo, looked straight into his eyes, then turned back to face the Blue Queen and moved forward.

Do something, Leo told himself. *Stop this!*

But he hesitated. There had been such a strange expression in Mimi's eyes — an intent, pleading look, as if she were urging him to understand something she couldn't say aloud.

Maybe I don't have the right to stop her, Leo thought dazedly. Maybe . . .

And at that very moment, Mimi ducked smartly under the woman's outstretched hand, grabbed Mutt, and threw herself to one side, out of reach, with the little dog clutched in her arms.

The queen cried out in shock and anger. With a swirl of blue silk, she twisted and sprang at Mimi, both hands outstretched, the fingers curved like claws.

"Now!" Mimi screamed. But Leo was already moving. The

moment the queen stepped away from the desk, he had known what he had to do, what Mimi expected him to do.

He snatched up the music box and the butterflies scattered in panic. He flipped the box lid open. The slow, sweet chimes signaling the end of the tune began.

The Blue Queen spun around. Her face was no longer beautiful. It was a mask of rage, with narrowed eyes and teeth bared in a snarl.

Holding the chiming music box close to his chest, Leo grabbed his desk chair with his free hand and pulled it after him as he stumbled backward toward the door.

Never pick up the box while the music is playing . . .

The words of the third rule flashed into his mind, but he knew he'd had no choice. The Blue Queen lunged at him. He shoved the chair forward on its casters, jabbing it at her, keeping it between them.

The music was slowing, slowing. How long did it have to go? He backed, thrusting the chair forward with his left hand, gripping the box so tightly with his right hand that his fingers were white.

The door was behind him, but he couldn't open it. He didn't dare let go of the chair, or the music box, either. The chimes were even slower now. The tune had nearly finished playing for the third time. He could hear it.

The Blue Queen could hear it, too. Hissing, she seized the seat of the desk chair and violently tipped it sideways. Leo lost his grip and the chair crashed onto its side, its casters spinning uselessly.

The Blue Queen sprang, reaching for the box, but jerked back with a shriek of rage. Mimi, still clutching Mutt, had grabbed a handful of her skirt. The woman spun around and kicked at Mimi viciously, at the same time trying to pull her skirt free.

There was the sound of tearing silk. The queen staggered as she was abruptly released. Mimi fell backward, a ragged triangle of blue fabric in her hand. Her elbow hit the corner of the bedside table and she yelled in pain. Mutt yelped and struggled and she let him go. He scrabbled to his feet and shook himself.

The music was ending. There was one chime and a pause, two chimes and a longer pause . . .

We've done it, Leo thought, dizzy with relief. *We've —*

"Mutt!" shrieked the Blue Queen, bending toward the little dog. And as the third and last chime of the music sounded, Mutt whined piteously and leaped into her arms.

"No!" Mimi screamed.

But it was too late. Already the Blue Queen had become a flat shape flapping in the breeze from the window. Suddenly she was just a flimsy, cutout picture of a woman — a woman holding a tousled, mustard-colored dog.

Rigid with shock, Leo saw flashes of blue in front of his eyes. The butterflies, flat as paper, were being sucked back into the box. Then the woman-shape was rushing toward him. Its painted face was grinning horribly. Leo screwed up his eyes and turned his head away. He felt a sort of jolt. The lid of the box fell shut with a snap.

And then he and Mimi were alone. The Blue Queen had gone. And Mutt had gone with her.

"Mutt!" Mimi shrieked. "Oh, Mutt!" She burst into hysterical tears. Blood was oozing from a cut on her elbow and running down her arm. She took no notice of it.

Feeling dazed and helpless, Leo carried the silent music box to the desk and put it down. His eyes slid over the desk's familiar objects — his computer, his math homework, his pens, the magnifying glass . . . They seemed like things belonging to another life. The music box, gaudy and alien, seemed more real than any of them.

He picked up the magnifying glass and turned the box around. The castle rose proudly on its smooth green hill, its fairy-tale towers and turrets gleaming in the sunlight.

The fair-haired queen in the rich blue dress was standing at the end of the drawbridge. She was holding Mutt in her arms.

Quickly Leo turned the box around again so the back couldn't be seen. His teeth had begun to chatter.

It's shock, he told himself, as if putting a name to what he felt would help him deal with it. And, strangely enough, it did. He turned away from the music box and went over to Mimi.

She was still huddled on the floor beside the bed, her whole body shaking with sobs. Leo kneeled down beside her and cautiously touched her shoulder. She shook his hand off.

"It's your fault!" she gasped. "It's all your fault!"

The injustice of this took Leo's breath away.

"I don't know how you work that out," he said coldly. "We both —"

"You made me put Mutt down in the first place!" Mimi sobbed. "You shook my arm, and *made* me. And now — and now —"

Leo had forgotten that. He felt the blood rush into his face.

"I was trying to get to the music box, to open it," he said, talking to himself as much as to Mimi. "I thought Mutt would be a distraction, jumping around and barking and everything. How was I to know he'd just sit there and let the Blue Queen —"

"It wasn't his fault!" screamed Mimi. "She bewitched him! She's some sort of sorceress! Don't you know that?"

"I . . ." Leo sat back on his heels. The blood was still pounding in his head. He forced his numbed mind to work.

"You didn't act as if you were scared of her," he said slowly and carefully. "You were going to take that ring and go with her. If I hadn't grabbed you —"

"I was trying to get to Mutt, you idiot! I had to get him away from her!" Mimi screeched, scrambling to her feet and wiping her eyes with the backs of her hands so that blood streaks mingled with the tears on her cheeks. "As if I'd go with her! I knew what she was the moment she started making all those promises. That's what witches *do*. They tempt you. They promise you things — impossible, secret things that they know . . . they know you really want."

Her voice trailed off. Abruptly she turned away so Leo couldn't see her face.

The honeyed words of the Blue Queen echoed in Leo's mind.

You can be admired. You can have friends — as many as you wish.

Those promises hadn't really meant anything to Leo. They'd gone right over his head.

But the queen wasn't talking to me, he thought, numbly getting to his feet. *She was talking to Mimi. She was looking at Mimi all the time. She was talking about things Mimi wants — things Mimi doesn't have.*

"I didn't really listen to all that stuff she said," he lied, walking to the fallen chair and pulling it upright, as if tidying up his room was the only thing on his mind. "I was thinking about how to get her away from the desk."

Mimi didn't say anything, but her hunched shoulders seemed to relax a little.

Leo pushed the chair back to its place at the desk. "I didn't think about her being a sorceress, or anything like that," he said, to fill the silence. "I just thought she was the Blue Queen off the music box. That was scary enough for me."

To his amazement, Mimi gave a wild snort of laughter. "I suppose it would be scary enough for anyone," she said.

"Anyway, as well as being scared of her, I didn't like her," Leo went on. "And I didn't trust her. Her smile was fake. And when she'd finished reading that note she just dropped it on the floor.

You could tell she didn't care about anyone or anything but herself."

Mimi nodded listlessly. Then Leo realized what he'd just said.

"The note!" he exclaimed.

He looked quickly at the floor. There was no sign of any little ball of paper on the polished boards showing around the edges of the rug, so he began pacing around, scanning the rug itself. The rug's squiggly pattern, which included lots of little white patches, made the search difficult.

Mimi watched for a while, then halfheartedly joined him. After a moment she gave a muffled exclamation and crouched down, but when Leo glanced around she was already straightening up, shaking her head.

"Just a bit of fluff," she murmured.

"Maybe the note got sucked back into the music box with everything else," said Leo.

And as he spoke, he saw a little white ball lying right beside his foot. He snatched it up and smoothed the paper out, being careful not to tear it.

Mimi came to look as he spread the note on his desk. She was breathing hard, as if she'd been running.

Together they read the message, which looked as if it had been scrawled in a great hurry.

BEWARE! SHE IS YOUR ENEMY.

DO NOT TAKE HER HAND.

DO NOT TELL HER YOUR NAME.

"Someone sent a note to warn us," Mimi whispered.

Leo's scalp was prickling. Because he'd had no choice, he'd managed to make his mind accept the fact that the Blue Queen had come out of the music box, had tried to tempt Mimi to follow her inside, then had stolen Mutt away. He hadn't read any fantasy over the last few years, but when he was younger he'd read stories about genies who lived in bottles. He'd almost decided that the Blue Queen was something like that.

Now he held in his hand the proof, in black and white, that it wasn't so simple. Other people lived and breathed in the world of the music box — people who thought, and worried, and . . . and wrote warning notes.

His knees felt weak. He slumped onto his chair, staring at the bright, busy surface of the box. He remembered those times in Aunt Bethany's dim front room, when he'd been sure he saw the painted figures of the people moving as the music played.

It looked as if he'd been right.

The thought made his stomach churn. He read the note one more time, struggling to make himself analyze it calmly.

"I don't get the last sentence," he said. "Why was it important not to tell her our names?"

"If a sorceress knows your true name, it gives her power over you," Mimi said impatiently. "Well, that's what I've read, and obviously the Blue Queen gets power that way. I used Mutt's name a couple of times before I realized that she was dangerous. That's how she bewitched him so easily."

She moved restlessly. "Leo, my arm's bleeding. Could you go

and get me something to put on it? I don't want to get blood all over the floor, walking around."

"Sure," Leo said, jumping up so fast that his chair nearly toppled over again. "There's a first-aid kit in the bathroom. I'll get it."

He was very glad that Mimi hadn't burst into a storm of tears again when she'd mentioned Mutt. Her crying had made him feel so helpless, so guilty, so *useless*.

He stole a glance at her. She was gnawing her bottom lip. Her fists were clenched and she was still breathing hard. But her eyes had lost that awful wild, glazed look.

She's trying to be brave, he thought. *She's trying to accept what's happened, and deal with it. That's sensible. That's exactly what she should* do.

He was relieved, but rather surprised as well. He wouldn't have expected Mimi Langlander to see things the way he did.

He hurried to the door, but as he reached it he thought of something and turned back.

"That name thing," he said. "That's why you tried to stop me from telling her yours, earlier."

Mimi nodded wearily. She was holding her elbow, frowning as if the cut were hurting her.

Leo paused. "But I *did* tell her, so why didn't she get power over you, like she did over Mutt?" he asked at last.

"You told her the wrong name," Mimi said simply.

As Leo looked at her in confusion, she gave one of her humorless snorts of laughter. "I'm not surprised you don't know that. For a minute I even forgot it myself," she said. "My real name's Marion.

My family started calling me Mimi when I was a baby, and they've just gone on doing it, whatever I say. I'm even called Mimi at school."

She lifted her chin. "But when I'm older — when I'm a famous violinist — I'll be able to *choose* what I'm called. Then I'll be Marion Langlander. Or maybe I'll be Anne Langlander — Anne's my middle name. Anyway, I won't be Little Mimi anymore."

"Mimi does suit you, though," Leo said awkwardly. "I mean —"

Mimi tossed her head slightly and turned away. "Could you get that stuff for my arm?" she muttered. "It's really hurting."

Leo left the room and walked along the hallway toward the bathroom. He made himself stop thinking about Mimi and her problems. He thought instead about the note the mouse had brought.

The music box had run down, but the note was still lying on the rug. That meant that *objects* didn't have to return to the box when the music ran down, as living things did.

The Blue Queen had said that some of his and Mimi's ancestors had visited her world. Had those ancestors brought back jewels, and gold?

While you carry the Key, you can come and go as you please, as so many other Langlanders have done in their time. . . .

For a fleeting moment, standing by the bathroom door, Leo felt a strong regret that he would never be able to test that promise.

Then he shook his head. Nothing, he told himself, would persuade him to wind that music box more than three times ever again. In fact, just now, the thought of winding it up at all made him feel sick.

The bathroom was dim and cool. He turned on the light and went to the cabinet where the first-aid kit was kept. There was a large mirror above the cabinet. His reflection almost frightened him. He looked like a haggard stranger.

Quickly he bent and pulled from the cabinet the blue plastic box that held the bandages, the antiseptic, and all the other things his mother thought might be needed in an emergency. Carrying the box, he left the bathroom again, flicking off the light as he went.

And it was then that he heard the faint, sweet chiming of the music box.

For a split second he couldn't believe it. Then, cursing himself for being such a fool, for allowing himself to be tricked, for not trusting his instincts, he raced for his room.

The door was shut. He threw it open. Mimi was standing at the desk, leaning over the music box.

She glanced over her shoulder at him, her eyes defiant, and snapped the box lid shut. The music stopped.

"What are you *doing*?" Leo yelled, storming into the room.

"I'm going to get my dog," Mimi said calmly.

Two thoughts flashed into Leo's mind. The first was that Mimi Langlander had gone crazy. The second, immediately following, was that somehow, some way, Mimi Langlander meant exactly what she said.

But she can't mean it, he thought. *She can't —*

Then Mimi pushed her bangs out of her eyes. Something gleamed on her middle finger. It was a ring set with small black stones.

Leo thrilled with horror as he understood. The Blue Queen had dropped the ring. Mimi had found it while looking for the note. She hadn't told him, because she knew he'd try to stop her. . . .

Mimi looked back at the box. "Let me in!" Leo heard her whisper.

Instantly she was encased in a swirling cone of misty rainbow light. She gasped and crossed her arms over her chest.

"No!" Without a thought, Leo sprang forward, reaching for her, reaching through the light.

His hands touched her shoulders. A tingling feeling ran up his arms. His ears filled with chiming music — loud, so loud! He opened his mouth to yell, but he could make no sound. Multicolored light was all around him, rippling around him like water, and somehow he knew that the light, too, was the music. He felt himself losing balance, falling forward into a tunnel filled with chiming rainbows . . .

Then there was darkness.

CHAPTER 7

Leo woke slowly. He lay with his eyes closed, wishing that the fly that was tickling his face would leave him alone. Not that he was going to be able to get back to sleep — not with all the noise outside his bedroom window.

There must be a party going on at the house next door, he thought, listening lazily to the babble of chattering voices and the bangs and crashes that sounded as if furniture was being dragged around.

It was strange that the noise seemed so loud — almost as if it were in the room with him. His window was open, of course. It was open so wide that he could actually smell the flowers in the garden. But still . . .

The flower perfume, in fact, was almost too strong for comfort. It was so sweet, so heavy . . .

Leo wrinkled his nose, sneezed, and opened his eyes.

A mass of battered pink lilies, their stamens heavy with bright yellow pollen, lay on the ground right in front of him. Two small blue butterflies with black-spotted wings were fluttering around not far from his nose.

Leo's mouth went dry. He lay very still.

Rondo.

"Here's another bunch ruined," grumbled a voice somewhere very near. "Look at the poor things. Bruised to billy-o!" A brawny arm reached down and the lilies were lifted up, showering Leo with pollen. He sneezed again.

"Bless my bluebells!" exclaimed the voice. "Who's that?"

There was a clatter of buckets. The broad brown face of a woman peered down at Leo. The woman's head was wrapped in a scarf covered with red and white tulips. Green earrings shaped like leaves swung from her ears.

It was the flower seller, large as life.

Leo stared up at her, unable to say a word.

The woman's face broke into a gap-toothed grin. "Took a tumble, did you?" she said. "I'm not surprised. That was a bad one, wasn't it? But don't just lie there in the wet, blossom. Up you get!"

She held out a hand covered in bright yellow streaks of lily pollen. Not knowing what else to do, Leo took the hand and let himself be hauled to his feet.

He realized he'd been lying on one side of the flower stall, toward the back. Metal buckets lay on their sides all around him, the flowers they had contained spilling out onto the ground. The cobblestones beneath his feet were swimming with water and strewn with petals, leaves, and broken flower heads.

People were hurrying past, talking in excited voices, some helping other people who were limping or nursing bandaged arms. The parts of the street he could see looked very untidy. As well as voices, he could hear banging, clanging, the tinkling of broken glass being swept up, and a baby crying.

The flower seller stuck the lilies into one of the few buckets that remained upright, put her hands on her hips, and looked at him in concern. "Bump your head, did you, blossom?" she asked.

Leo cleared his throat. "I might have," he said feebly. "Um — could you tell me, please — have you seen a girl anywhere around here? A smallish girl, wearing a pink jacket?"

"Can't say I have," the flower seller said. "Your sister, is she?"

"My cousin," Leo said. "We came here together . . . I mean, we both —"

"Came to town to see the sights, did you?" the woman said sympathetically, wiping her hands on the bib of her green overalls. "What a day to choose, eh? Bless my bluebells, Rondo hasn't had a quake since — oh — since before the Dark Time!"

Quake. Earthquake . . .

Never pick up the box while the music is playing.

Leo's face grew hot. Again he looked around, and this time he realized what he was seeing. He realized why the street looked messy, why windows were broken and stalls had been overturned and people were upset and nursing injured limbs.

There had been an earthquake — or what the people in this place thought of as an earthquake. And he had caused it, by grabbing the music box while it was playing and running with it to his bedroom door.

The idea of telling the flower seller where he'd come from was suddenly very unappealing.

"Never you mind, blossom," the flower seller said, seeing the stricken look on his face. "We'll find your cousin. Can't be far away, can she? Come out to the front and keep a lookout for her."

She took Leo's arm and led him to the front of the stall. She looked up and down the street.

"Hoy, Crumble!" she shouted to the pie man, who was slumped over his upturned tray, staring glumly down at the smashed remains of at least two dozen pies. "Hoy! You seen a girl, just a little thing, wearing a pink jacket?"

The pie man stirred. "I might have," he said grumpily. "Or then again, I might not. I've got no time to worry about girls in pink jackets. Look at this!" He waved his hand at the mess on the ground. "Ruined! Five best meat, seven apple, three peach, ten turnip-and-chili . . ."

"Pull yourself together, you miserable old crabapple!" bawled the flower seller, scowling and nodding so that her leaf earrings swung wildly. "All you've lost is a few pies, and I know for a fact you've been trying to sell those turnip things for two weeks! This boy's lost his *cousin*."

"A few pies, indeed!" grumbled the pie man. "That's all very well for you to say, Posy. Pies don't grow on trees, you know — Hey! Get out of it!" He kicked angrily at three small, flat, golden-brown creatures that had crept out from beneath his stool and were trying to drag away a large piece of pastry covered in gravy.

The creatures dodged his foot and ran away, tittering in high-pitched voices.

Leo gaped at them as they dived headfirst into a crack between two paving stones. They looked — it was crazy, but they looked *exactly* — like the gingerbread men that were always served at Aunt Bethany's afternoon teas — right down to the two currant eyes, and the three currant buttons.

"Pesky dots!" muttered Posy the flower seller. She raised her voice again and shouted at the pie man. "You'd better get that mess cleaned up, Crumble. Those dots'll be back, and with all their friends, too. The street'll be teeming with them, next. Love a nice bit of flaky pastry, dots do."

"You tend to your own affairs, you sticky old jam bun," the pie man said rudely. But he got up from his stool and slowly reached for a broom.

"Dots," Leo murmured stupidly.

Posy shook her head. "Get into everything, don't they?" she said, pulling a couple of buckets upright with a clatter and peering into them suspiciously. "They should keep away from me for a while, anyway, with all this water around. If their feet get soggy, they just keel over, you know. Are they bad out where you live?"

"Um — not really," said Leo.

"That's a bit of luck for you, then," said Posy comfortably, picking up a huge jug and pouring water into the buckets. "I've heard that in some parts they're so thick on the ground you can hardly walk without one running up your trouser leg." She grimaced in distaste.

Leo searched around for something sensible to say. He couldn't think of anything.

To cover his awkwardness, he put his hands behind his back and looked casually up at the sky. A glittering green shape was sailing through the blue.

His skin prickled. "Dragon!" he gulped, before he could stop himself.

"Oh yes?" Posy said absentmindedly. "Quake must have disturbed it. Never mind. It'll soon settle." She put a few sad bunches of daisies, the remains of the pink lilies, and some tattered roses into the newly filled buckets, put a sign reading HALF PRICE! in front of them, and straightened up with a groan.

"I should be grateful," she said. "I didn't have much stock left to lose, really. Not like some."

Leo felt another sharp pang of guilt. Posy looked at him and her forehead wrinkled in concern. "No sign of your cousin yet?" she asked.

Leo shook his head wordlessly.

Posy peered up and down the street and suddenly her face brightened. She pointed to a tall blue figure striding toward them from the right, towering head and shoulders above the rest of the crowd.

Leo's heart jumped into his mouth. A policeman!

"There you go, blossom," Posy said, beaming. "Officer Begood. Just the man you want."

Oh no he's not, Leo thought in panic. He knew that the first thing the police officer would ask him was where he lived. If he told the truth . . . if anyone found out he was the one who had caused the earthquake . . .

I'll end up in jail, if the shopkeepers don't lynch me first, he thought. In horror he saw Posy begin to wave vigorously at the approaching blue figure.

"Oh!" he exclaimed, in an excited voice that sounded very fake even to him. "There she is! I see her! My cousin! Just down there!"

He waved his hand vaguely to the left. As Posy turned to look, he edged quickly away from her. "I'd better hurry," he gabbled. "Don't want to lose her again. Thanks for everything, Posy. Bye."

He shot off into the crowd, leaving the flower seller staring after him in puzzlement.

Leo walked as fast as he dared without actually running. At first he was worried that his clothes would mark him as a stranger, but there were people in all sorts of clothes on the street, and anyway everyone was too busy cleaning up to look closely at anyone else. No one took any more notice of his jeans and T-shirt than Posy had.

He hurried along, keeping his head down and stealing glances left and right. Everywhere he looked he saw evidence of earthquake damage — shattered shop windows, collapsed stalls, people sweeping up broken china and glass.

A bald man he recognized as the street's balloon seller was standing at the very top of a ladder, vainly trying to catch the trailing strings of a huge bunch of balloons that had floated up out of his reach.

And everywhere the little creatures Posy had called dots were scampering around, giggling, dragging stolen food away, tripping people up, and generally making nuisances of themselves.

At last Leo reached the tavern called the Black Sheep. The familiar swinging sign of a dancing black lamb dangled crookedly, trailing a long piece of broken chain. The benches and tables that usually stood in front of the tavern had been overturned. A wet mess of food scraps, broken glass, and smashed china littered the ground. The landlord, now looking very glum, was sweeping up.

Mimi, where are you? Leo thought desperately. *We've got to get out of here!*

He risked a glance behind him. He could see a blue police cap over the heads of the crowd. It was right beside the striped awning of the flower stall and it wasn't moving. It looked as if Officer Begood had stopped to talk to Posy. Leo's stomach flip-flopped unpleasantly.

"Here!" The soft call seemed to come from right beside him.

He jumped and looked wildly around. A tiny, chubby woman wheeling a vast wheelbarrow of squashed bananas squeaked a warning as she nearly ran into him.

"Sorry, sorry!" babbled Leo, jumping out of her way. As the barrow trundled past he could see dots peeping from between the bananas. Some of them were gobbling slimy banana scraps greedily. Others, black currant eyes gleaming with mischievous delight, were throwing skins down onto the road, probably hoping to make passersby slip and fall.

The chubby little woman couldn't see what they were doing. She had her head down, pushing the wheelbarrow. She was wearing a brightly striped cap and matching mittens. Stubby orange wings stuck out through holes in the back of her duffle coat.

Leo's jaw dropped.

"Over here!" The low call came again, and this time, when Leo looked around, he caught sight of Mimi peering at him from the mouth of the dim, narrow alley that ran between the Black Sheep and the toy factory next door.

Mimi looked nervous and excited. She beckoned to Leo urgently.

He hurried over to her. "Where have you been?" he demanded fiercely.

"*Sshh!* Where have *you* been?" Mimi retorted, just as fiercely. "If you *had* to come with me, why didn't you hold on to me, so we stayed together? I've wasted ages looking for you!"

"I didn't want to come!" yelled Leo. "It's the last thing I wanted! We've got to go back, right now! You —"

"Now, now, young people!" broke in a smooth voice from the shadows behind Mimi. "No need to argue! No need to fuss! We're all together now, and that's what matters. Come in, my boy. Come in!"

A man's arm reached out of the alley, and soft, damp fingers, glittering with rings, fastened on Leo's wrist.

CHAPTER 8

Leo was drawn firmly into the shadows. As his eyes adjusted to the dim light, he saw that the person who had pulled him into the alley was a man in a checked coat. The man had wavy brown hair that shone with oil, a dimpled chin, and a toothy smile. He looked vaguely familiar to Leo, who disliked him on sight.

Mimi, however, seemed perfectly comfortable in the man's company.

"He knows all about it," she announced breathlessly. "He knows where we come from, and he wants to help us find Mutt. He can take us to the Blue Queen's castle. He knows the way. Oh, if only I'd gone straight there! I meant to, but I was staring at the tavern when I asked to come in and I suppose —"

"Mimi —" Leo began, but the man in the checked jacket interrupted, as smoothly as before.

"We have to keep it all very quiet," he said, tapping the side of his nose. "I gather you picked up the box while the music was playing, my boy. Carried it around, too. *Not* a good idea, if I might say so. It caused a lot of damage. People wouldn't like it if they knew."

Leo glanced nervously back at the street. The man nodded, and pulled him a little farther into the shadows.

"You're safe for the moment," he said reassuringly. "But as I was explaining to our little friend here just before you came along, we should make ourselves scarce as soon as possible. She wouldn't leave without you. She wouldn't even move away from the street, out of sight — never mind the danger if anyone realized who she was. Loyalty like that's a fine thing, isn't it? But now you're here . . ."

"I think a policeman might be following me," Leo said rapidly.

The whites of the man's eyes gleamed in the dimness as his eyes suddenly widened.

"Begood?" he snapped, in quite a different voice.

"Yes," Leo admitted. "I was talking to Posy the flower seller, and she —"

The man swore under his breath. "That's torn it," he muttered. He looked at Leo. "How far behind you is Begood?" he demanded. "Did he see you come in here?"

"I don't think so," Leo said uncomfortably. "He was still at the flower stall, talking to Posy. But other people might have —"

"Right," the man interrupted, frowning. "So. I'd been hoping to get some supplies together before we left. There's a window that leads into the Black Sheep kitchens just along here. And old Jolly, the landlord, you know, won't be keeping an eye on his storeroom for a change. He's too busy cleaning up out front. But with Begood coming . . ."

He smacked his lips regretfully. "It's a pity. A chance like this doesn't come every day. Old Jolly keeps excellent brandy. And a particularly good, spicy sausage . . ."

He saw Mimi and Leo exchange glances, and hurriedly cleared his throat. "Naturally I'd have squared it with old Jolly later on," he said heartily. "Oh, we're great friends, Jolly and me. But never mind, never mind. We'll forget all that. The important thing now is to get you out of trouble. We'll go through the side door of the toy factory. It's down there on the left."

He pointed down the alley. Leo and Mimi squinted through the gloom, but could see nothing.

"It's hard to see from here, but it's there all right, trust me," the man chuckled. "Dolly and Teddy always leave it unlocked, the silly old ducks. It makes a nice, quiet shortcut through to the back streets. Very handy for a quick getaway. I've used it hundreds of times. Now —"

"Are the people who run the toy factory really called Dolly and Teddy?" Leo interrupted suddenly.

"Yes," said the man, looking surprised. "I told you!"

"And the tavern landlord's called Jolly, and the flower seller's called Posy, and the pie man is Crumbles and there's a policeman called Officer Begood?" Leo went on, his voice rising in disbelief.

Mimi gave a snort of nervous laughter.

"Ah!" said the man, his face clearing. "You mean the names suit the people? Yes. Quite a coincidence, isn't it? Happens a lot around here, for some reason."

"So what's *your* name?" Leo asked abruptly.

"My —" The man hesitated. Then he gave his big toothy smile again. "Oh, my name's — uh — Tom. Plain old Tom. Sorry. Didn't I say?"

"No," Leo said. He was certain the man was lying.

"We'd better be off," the man said hastily, backing further into the alley and beckoning Leo and Mimi to follow. "Begood will be here any minute. You don't want him to catch you, do you?"

The toy factory door was about halfway down the alley, on the left. An enormous, overflowing black trash can stood outside it, almost invisible in the dim light.

Tom dropped Mimi's arm and gripped the doorknob with both hands. "Got to take this ve-ery slowly," he muttered. "Otherwise the hinges squeak."

Leo seized his chance to draw Mimi aside. "Mimi, what are you doing?" he whispered in her ear. "You don't know this guy. You can't just go with him. I'm sure his name's not Tom, for a start, and —"

"Don't be silly!" Mimi flashed back impatiently. "If he works against the Blue Queen, of course he'd keep his real name a secret. I didn't tell him yours, did I? Not that it would probably matter. He's on our side. He's helping us escape from the police, isn't he? And he's going to help me find Mutt. He promised! Oh, and I didn't tell you. *He* was the one who sent us that warning note!"

Leo stared at her in confusion. This changed everything. If Tom had written the warning note, he really *was* a friend. And yet . . . He frowned, thinking furiously.

"Mimi," he said suddenly. "Did Tom mention the note first, or did you?"

"Oh, *I* don't know." Mimi sighed. She turned to watch Tom easing the door open, little by little. "He said he'd been looking for me everywhere, and was so glad he'd found me. He knew where I'd come from. He knew about Mutt being taken by the Blue Queen — they call her the Blue Queen here, too, because no one knows her real name."

She broke off. She looked up at Leo and for the first time her eyes held a trace of doubt. "So then I asked him if he'd written the warning note," she murmured reluctantly. "And he said yes, he had."

Leo groaned.

Mimi wet her lips. "You think he just said that to make me trust him," she said in a low voice.

Leo nodded.

"You don't think he wrote the note at all," Mimi said, even more quietly.

Leo shook his head.

They both glanced at the man who called himself Tom. He had the door almost half open now. Any minute he'd turn and beckon to them.

"Come away," Leo urged. "Now. While he's not looking."

In dismay he saw Mimi's mouth straighten into the stubborn line he'd learned to know only too well.

"No," she whispered. "If Tom did lie about the note, maybe he had a good reason. I've *got* to go with him. He knows how to get to Mutt — I just know he wasn't lying about that. And, besides, if we don't use his shortcut through the toy factory we're sure to get caught by that policeman who's after us."

Leo glanced nervously back at the main street. And there, to his horror, he saw a tall blue figure. Officer Begood was standing right in front of the alley, with his back toward it. He was nodding, talking to someone, but Leo couldn't see who it was.

Maybe it's the landlord of the Black Sheep, Leo thought, his heart pounding. *Did Jolly notice me outside? Did he notice Mimi? Did he see us come in here?*

Mimi squeaked with fright as she, too, saw the policeman.

Tom swung around. He darted a sharp look toward the main street, and stiffened. "Come on!" he whispered urgently, gesturing at the half-open door. "Squeeze in!"

But at that moment, Officer Begood moved, and the person he'd been talking to became visible. It was an old man with a white beard, who looked very annoyed. On either side of the old man, clinging tightly to his hands, were two little girls dressed alike in pale blue overalls and frilly white shirts.

Leo gasped and gripped Mimi's arm. No wonder the man who called himself Tom had looked so familiar!

"Come *on!*" Tom whispered fiercely from the door. "Do you want to get caught? Do you want to go to jail? If you do, you'll never find your dog!"

Mimi struggled to tear herself away from Leo, but he wouldn't let her go.

"You're a thief!" he said, glaring at Tom. "You stole that old man's money!"

"What?" spluttered Tom, his eyes darting left and right. "Why would you say a thing like that?"

"I saw you!" Leo insisted. "You took the old man's wallet out of his pocket, while he was waiting at the pie stall!"

"What does that matter?" Mimi hissed. "I don't care if he's a *bank* robber! I just want —"

A flash of inspiration struck Leo.

"And that's why you don't want Officer Begood to find us here!" he exclaimed. "It's not because of us at all! You're scared for yourself!"

"That's — that's very, very hurtful, my boy," the man said, fingering his moustache nervously. "You're upset, I understand that, but that's no excuse for insulting people who are trying to help you."

"You're not trying to help us!" said Leo, more convinced than ever that he was right. "People who are trying to help you don't tell you lies."

Tom bared his teeth in what was probably supposed to be a charming smile, but in fact was more like a lopsided snarl. "Let the girl go," he said sharply. "She wants to save her dog, and she knows I can help her. She needs me. Don't you, Mimi?"

Mimi's eyes were very wide. She looked at Leo, then she looked at Tom, then she looked back at Leo again.

Leo swallowed. His heart sank to the soles of his shoes. He knew what he had to say.

"You don't need him, Mimi," he mumbled. "I'll help you find Mutt."

"Really?" Mimi asked seriously. "Don't say it if you don't mean it."

"I mean it," Leo said, forcing himself to sound firm. "I'm with you. We're Langlanders aren't we? And Langlanders stick together."

Mimi looked at him for a long moment, then nodded. She turned to Tom. "Thank you," she said primly, backing away until she was pressed against the big black trash can. "But I think I'll just stay here for now."

Tom's eyes narrowed. "Suit yourself," he said curtly. "I'll just —" He broke off and, without any warning, hurled himself at Mimi, clawing at her like an animal.

Mimi screamed, and tried to beat him off. Leo, horrified, launched himself at the man, punching and kicking wildly. Tom yelled and swore. The trash can rocked dangerously.

"Oi!" Officer Begood shouted from the mouth of the alley. "Who's that?

"Thieves!" roared the old man with the white beard. "A nest of thieves, fighting over my wallet! There they are! Get them!"

Instantly the man who called himself Tom whirled around and plunged into the toy factory, pulling the door closed behind him. There was the sound of a bolt sliding into place.

Officer Begood began to run toward Leo and Mimi, his heavy boots pounding on the stones. The old man tottered after him, still hand in hand with the two little girls, who were both squealing, "Get them! Get them! Get them!" in high-pitched voices.

Mimi and Leo looked at each other, then, without a thought, they dodged around the trash can, and ran.

There was nowhere to go but farther down the alley. Hearts pounding, the voices of their pursuers echoing in their ears, they ran blindly through the dimness.

Brick walls rose high on both sides of them. There was nowhere to hide.

We shouldn't be running, Leo thought wildly. *That just makes us look guilty. We should stop, turn around, explain . . .*

But somehow the squeals of the girls, the angry shouts of the old man, the sound of Officer Begood's thundering feet, were making it impossible to stop. His legs just kept moving as if they had a will of their own.

Behind them there was a crash and a furious yell. Leo and Mimi glanced over their shoulders. Through the shadows they saw Officer Begood sprawled on the ground. He'd collided with the trash can, which was rolling on its side, its contents spilling all over the paving stones.

Hope flared in Leo's heart. What a stroke of luck! Maybe he and Mimi could get away after all. Maybe . . .

Then his stomach turned over as he saw, blocking the way ahead, another wall as blank and high as all the rest. He heard Mimi's sobbing cry of despair as she, too, realized that the alley was a dead end.

Together they reached the wall. Together they spun around, pressing their backs to it, frantically looking for a way out.

But there was no way out. They were trapped.

CHAPTER 9

THE HIDEY-HOLE

"Psst!" The hissing sound seemed to come from right beside Leo's ear. He jumped violently and looked around, meeting Mimi's startled eyes.

"What was that?" she whispered.

Both of them thought of snakes at the same time. Nervously they looked down, shifting their feet, but nothing was moving on the slimy paving stones — or nothing they could see.

They could hear clanging and bumping as the trash can rolled on the stones. They could hear Officer Begood grunting with pain as he clambered to his feet. They could hear the old man furiously complaining, and the piping, excited cries of the two little girls.

"Don't you worry, Master Whitebeard," they heard Begood say, between moans. "They can't get away. They've got nowhere to go. You'll have your wallet back in no time."

"He didn't see Tom escape into the toy factory," whispered Mimi. "He thinks we're all here together."

"We shouldn't have run," Leo groaned. "We shouldn't have —"

"I'll teach them to try to escape from the law," said Officer Begood angrily. "Oh, my back!"

There was a dull clank, as if he'd given the trash can a final kick. Then his boots thudded on the paving stones as he began to stride down the alley again.

Leo and Mimi stood paralyzed, their minds numb.

"*Psst!*" The hissing sound came again, and this time there was no doubt where it had come from. Mimi and Leo jumped away from the wall as if they'd been stung. Cautiously they turned, and froze in shock.

A large black blob had appeared among the dingy bricks. It looked like a huge blot of ink shaped like . . . like a huge mouth. As they gaped at it, the mouth moved.

"Hurry up!" it said. "I can't stay here all day."

Mimi gave a muffled shriek. Leo felt hairs rise on the back of his neck.

"Well?" said the mouth in the wall irritably. "Are you getting in, or aren't you?"

"Where —?" gasped Mimi.

"What —?" gasped Leo at the same moment.

The mouth pursed in annoyance. "Oh, save me from beginners!" it snapped. "You wanted a hidey-hole, didn't you? I distinctly heard —"

"Yes," squeaked Mimi, before Leo could say a word. "Do we just —?"

"Just get in," the mouth sighed. "I'll do the rest."

The heavy footsteps were growing louder. Any minute . . .

"Last chance, folks," said the mouth in the wall. "Here, I'll make it easy for you." It opened wide, as if it were yawning.

Leo felt Mimi grip his hand and tug. He had a wild urge to laugh. This was impossible! This was insane! "All right," he heard himself saying. "Why not?"

And he and Mimi ran to the wall and plunged headfirst into thick, warm darkness.

It was rather like sinking into a bath of half-set Jell-O — Jell-O that was black as the blackest ink. Mimi and Leo didn't know where they were. They certainly weren't in the alley anymore, but they weren't on the other side of the wall, either. They were in a soft, black place that was . . . nowhere.

Cautiously Leo stretched out his hands. They slid smoothly through the thick blackness and his fingertips touched cold, rough bricks. It's as if we're *inside* the wall, he thought. But how can that be?

"Sit still!" The grumbling voice seemed to come from all around him. "Where are your manners?"

"Oh — sorry," Leo stammered, pulling his hands back.

"How will we get out of here?" Mimi quavered.

"It's a bit late to start thinking about that now," Leo snapped. He was feeling sick again. He'd never liked enclosed spaces very much.

"*Sshh!*" the darkness hissed. "They're coming!"

Mimi and Leo huddled together and waited. It was impossible to see anything at all, but soon they heard the muffled sounds of Officer Begood stamping and swearing on the alley side of the wall. Then they heard the furious, cracked voice of the old man complaining bitterly, and the piping voices of the two little girls.

"Where are they?" Officer Begood cried in frustration. "They ran down here, I know they did. I heard them! And they didn't creep back and get through the tavern window, because I was expecting that and I was keeping my eye on it all the time. But they couldn't have climbed over this wall. That's impossible!"

"Nothing's impossible, Begood!" the old man snapped. "You're only young, but surely you've learned that by now!"

"Well, I —" spluttered Officer Begood. But the old man interrupted him.

"Spoiler was their leader, remember!" he said furiously. "I heard his voice distinctly. I just wish I'd noticed him hanging around me at the pie stall. I'd have held on to my wallet more tightly if I had."

"We don't actually *know* that Spoiler was your pickpocket, Master Whitebeard," said Begood, obviously trying to sound sensible and firm. "Just because he was seen walking away from —"

"Of course it was him!" snorted the old man. "He's a villain and a twister. He's a liar, a cheat, and a thief. Everyone knows that. I can't understand why you let him run around loose, Begood! You heard what Jolly said about the tavern storeroom. If he doesn't watch it every minute, dots take half of what's in there, and Spoiler gets the rest."

"People are always saying things like that," the policeman burst out in injured tones. "And it's true that somehow someone has always seen Spoiler lurking around just before something goes missing. But there's never any proof he's responsible, and I can't just clap him in jail on suspicion, can I?"

"I don't see why not," grumbled the old man. "There's no smoke without fire. Anyway, what was I saying? Oh, yes. Spoiler was one of the gang, so they probably *did* get over this wall, whatever you say."

Spoiler, Leo thought. *Not Tom — Spoiler.* And he was very glad he'd convinced Mimi not to go with the man in the checked coat, whose real name probably revealed far more about him than he would like.

"Oh, yes," the old man was saying crossly. "Spoiler managed it somehow. That slippery villain is capable of anything."

"Well, now, I think that's a little bit of an exaggeration, Master Whitebeard," said Officer Begood cautiously. "Spoiler's not capable of *anything* anymore, is he? I mean, he *used* to be capable of anything, but that was . . . stopped, wasn't it? That wizard broke the Blue Queen's power, and ended the Dark Time, and —"

There was a sharp banging sound, as if Master Whitebeard had pounded his stick on the paving stones. "That's the trouble with you young fellows," he roared. "You think happy endings are forever!"

"Well, now —" Officer Begood began.

"Yes, you do!" Master Whitebeard insisted, banging his stick again. "You think that once a villain's been defeated, he'll stay defeated and you can relax! Poppycock!"

"Poppycock! Poppycock!" chanted the two little girls.

"Master Whitebeard, I —" protested Officer Begood.

"Do you think Spoiler *likes* sneaking around picking pockets and raiding storerooms for a living, when he used to get anything he wanted just by snapping his fingers?" raged the old man. "Do you think that he and that evil woman aren't plotting night and day to get their power back?"

Leo's heart gave a great thud, and he heard Mimi draw a quick, startled breath.

Officer Begood cleared his throat, but didn't seem to be able to think of anything to say.

"Well, there's no sense in staying here," grumbled the old man. "The thieves have got clean away, and my wallet's gone with them. Come on, girls. Let's go home."

Leo heard the sound of footsteps moving away. He was just about to sigh with relief when Officer Begood suddenly spoke again.

"They couldn't — they couldn't possibly — have found a hidey-hole, could they?"

The footsteps stopped. Leo held his breath.

"Hardly!" the old man said scornfully. "Why, I haven't seen or heard of a hidey-hole around here for years! There are still some running wild out in the country, they say. But right in the middle of town? I don't think so."

The jellylike darkness enclosing Leo rippled and heaved a little. "Heh, heh, heh!" it chuckled softly. "A lot you know, fathead."

The footsteps began to move again. They grew fainter and fainter till at last Leo couldn't hear them any more.

"They're gone," he whispered.

"Sounds like it," the hidey-hole whispered back. "Still, you'd be amazed how tricky people can be. You know, they pretend to give up and leave, then they creep back, the sly things. But I've been in this game too long to be fooled. Hold on and I'll have a squiz."

A tiny chink of dim light appeared beside Leo's shoulder. It was too small for him to be able to see anything through it, but the hidey-hole seemed satisfied.

"All clear," it announced.

There was a sort of *pop*, and Leo and Mimi shot out of the darkness, landing painfully on the damp paving stones beside the wall. The hidey-hole had spat them out like cherry pits.

They clambered to their feet, blinking and rubbing their eyes. Even the dimness of the alley seemed bright after their long minutes in complete darkness.

The mouth in the wall smacked its lips and grinned at them. "All right then?" it said jauntily. Clearly it was quite proud of itself.

Mimi found her voice first. "Yes," she said politely. "Thank you very much for helping us."

"A pleasure!" said the mouth. "I enjoy my work, and I've been a bit bored lately, to tell the truth, with nothing to do. Folk around here are a law-abiding lot. Call me anytime."

With that, it shrank to a tiny black blob, and sank back into the wall. A whisper floated out to them as it vanished.

"I'll be seeing you. But you won't be seeing me. Heh, heh, heh!"

Leo and Mimi looked at each other. They had so much to talk about that it seemed impossible to begin.

"Let's go," Mimi said abruptly. "While we just stand here, Mutt could be —" She bit her lip and spun around to face the bustling street.

"Mimi, no!" Leo burst out.

Mimi turned back to face him. "What?" she demanded, pushing her bangs out of her eyes. The black-and-gold ring winked on her finger.

"Mimi, we can't do this. We've got to go home," Leo said in his firmest, most mature-sounding voice.

Mimi's mouth tightened. In silence, she zipped up her jacket all the way to her chin, as if she were putting on armor, and thrust her hands into the pockets. Then she shook her head.

"I'm not going anywhere till I get Mutt," she said.

"Mimi, you can't —" Leo broke off, fighting down the wave of fear, anger, and frustration that was threatening to choke him. He made himself take a deep breath, then another.

"All right," he said, forcing himself to sound reasonable and even cheerful. "Then take me home, and come back by yourself. I won't try to stop you."

"I don't believe you," Mimi snapped. "The moment we got home you'd hide the box — lock it up somewhere, or something."

As this was exactly what Leo had been planning to do, he was for a moment lost for words. Then guilt made his anger flare again. "Are you calling me a liar?" he spat.

"Yes," Mimi said simply. "You *are* a liar. You stopped me going with Tom by promising you'd help me find Mutt. You swore it. 'Langlanders stick together,' you said."

Leo's face grew hot at the memory. What an incredibly stupid, melodramatic thing to say!

But it's true, a voice said in his mind. *It really is true. Langlanders stick together. Like in the old stories, it's one for all, and all for one.*

Not when one is crazy! he argued with himself. *Not when sticking together means* everyone *goes under.*

"I said that to stop you going with Tom!" he hissed furiously. "Spoiler, I should say. And it's a good thing I did, isn't it? It turns out he works for the Blue Queen!"

Mimi shrugged. "That's not the point," she said. "The point is, I believed you, and you were lying. I'm not stupid enough to believe you again. I'm here now, and I'm staying."

Leo lost his temper completely. "But what about me?" he shouted. "You have to take me back. You can't make me stay here against my —"

"Keep your voice down," snapped Mimi, glancing toward the main street. "Listen, Leo, I didn't ask you to come with me. I didn't even *want* you to come. You did it all yourself, trying to stop me from doing what *I* wanted to do. Now you're stuck with it."

He glared at her, breathing hard. It crossed his mind that he could tackle her — force her hand out of her pocket, pull the ring from her finger, and . . .

She'd scream, he thought. *She'd scream the place down. People would hear . . . come running to help . . . that policeman . . .*

"You can wait here — in a safe place," Mimi said. "I'll come back for you when I've found Mutt."

Leo stared at her, speechless. She lifted her chin defiantly.

She's really going to try to do it, he thought dazedly. *And there's nothing I can do about it. Not here, anyway. Not now.*

"No," he muttered, trying not to think too hard about what he was saying. "I'll come with you."

Mimi's eyes flickered, whether in relief or irritation he couldn't tell. "Yes, well, I don't suppose you want to let the Key out of your sight," she jeered.

"It's not just that!" Leo protested hotly.

And strangely enough, it wasn't. Certainly he didn't want to lose sight of the Key. But just as strong was the feeling that he couldn't — just couldn't — hide himself away somewhere while Mimi hurled herself into danger all alone.

Mimi gave a thin, disbelieving smile. "All right," she said. "Then let's go." She turned and began walking up the alley toward the street.

Well, now I've done it, thought Leo. *Now I'm well and truly trapped.*

And, glumly, he thought of Uncle Henry.

CHAPTER 10

CONKER

Mimi was disappearing into the shadows of the alley. Leo hurried to catch up with her. "Mimi," he said urgently, putting a hand on her arm. "Wait a minute! We have to —"

Mimi scowled and shook off his hand. "Leo, I *told* you —" she began.

"I'm not trying to stop you," Leo said quickly. "I'm just . . . I just want us to have some sort of plan. I know we've got to get out of this alley. It's too dangerous for us to stay here, because there's no escape route. But it'd be stupid to just go rushing off into that crowded street with no idea what we're going to do next. That policeman might be still hanging around."

Mimi's eyes narrowed suspiciously, but at least she was listening. Leo hurried on.

"We've got to find a safe place where we can talk calmly, and work out what to do next," he said. "Maybe find someone who can give us some advice. That makes sense, doesn't it?"

Mimi hesitated, then nodded slightly. "I suppose," she said in a flat voice. "But I know what you're doing, Leo. Maybe you're right that we should make a plan and try to get help. But you're trying to delay things, too. You're hoping I'll change my mind and forget about Mutt. But don't you understand? I'll never forget about him. I can't!" Her lips quivered, and she pressed them together angrily.

Leo felt a painful stab of pity and guilt. He looked quickly aside and pretended to brush some dirt from his sleeve. "I'm not trying to delay things," he said untruthfully. "But I'm not going to rush into anything, either. There's lots of stuff about this place we don't understand. We've got to find out a bit more about it."

"So what will we do?" Mimi asked miserably. "Where can we go that's safe?" She thought for a moment. "I suppose we could call the hidey-hole back," she suggested, without very much enthusiasm. "It might be able to tell us a few things."

Leo couldn't think of anything he'd like less. The idea of trying to have a sensible discussion inside a dark, claustrophobic blob of nothing was horrible. "If only Spoiler hadn't locked the toy factory door," he muttered. Then he remembered something.

"The tavern!" he exclaimed. "One of its windows opens onto this alley. Spoiler and Begood both said so."

"I didn't see any window on our way down here," said Mimi dubiously.

"Neither did I," Leo admitted. "But we were running. We must have just missed it."

They crept cautiously up the alley, keeping close to the left-hand side. Far ahead, in the little rectangle of light that was the alley's entrance to the main street, people bustled to and fro like figures on a TV screen.

Suddenly, when they were least expecting it, they came upon a dingy, half-open window set deep into the wall. Its broad, greasy sill was about level with Leo's chin. The mingled smells of spices, unwashed dishes, and boiled cabbage drifted from the dark room beyond.

"This must be it," Leo whispered.

He put his hands on the windowsill. Briefly, he wondered what he was doing even *thinking* of sneaking through a strange window like a thief. Then he put the thought aside and hoisted himself up, keeping his head low.

He slithered through the window and found himself lying face-down on the draining board of a huge stone sink. The basin yawned beside him. The other side was stacked high with dirty dishes.

Across the room he could just see a thin line of dim light, which he guessed was light seeping through the crack beneath a door. It was so dark that he couldn't see anything else. But he could hear a sound — a faint, furtive, scuttling sound, which seemed to be coming from the floor.

Cockroaches, Leo thought in distaste. *Or mice. Or even rats! Whatever they are, it sounds as if there are hundreds of them.*

He realized that his feet were still sticking out of the window. He struggled to pull them in after him without slipping and falling off the sink. The idea of crashing down onto a floor crawling with cockroaches was very unappealing.

Awkwardly he curled himself around and poked his head into the alley again. Mimi anxiously raised her arms. He leaned out and hauled her up. She scrambled over the windowsill, her shoes scrabbling on the wall behind her.

They crouched precariously together on the cold draining board, catching their breath. The stealthy, scuttling sound, which had stopped for a moment while Mimi was being dragged inside, began again.

"What's that?" Mimi breathed.

"I'm not sure," Leo whispered back. "Maybe —"

He broke off in a strangled gasp as lanterns popped into blazing life all around the kitchen walls and the room was flooded with light. He just had time to see with amazement that the floor was seething with the creatures called dots, when the door burst open, and a very short, broad man hurled himself into the room.

The man had a wild brown beard, exactly the same color as his skin, and a mass of frizzy brown hair that stuck up all over his head like a wiry halo. His eyes were small and black under tremendous, bushy eyebrows. An earring that seemed to be made of a long white fang dangled from one of his ears, and in each hand he brandished what looked like a large flyswatter.

"Aha!" he bellowed, slamming the door behind him. "Got you!" And with that, he began dancing around, beating the floor with the flyswatters, his arms flailing up and down like pistons. "Take that!" he roared. "And that! And that!"

The dots squeaked and scattered. Black currant eyes gleaming and stubby little legs pumping, they skittered into hiding below cupboards or into cracks in the walls. Dozens were smashed into crumbs by the furious man's flyswatters or crushed beneath his big black boots. None of the others took the slightest bit of notice. As soon as they were safe they poked their heads out of their hiding places, making rude, jeering noises and sticking out their tongues.

"It'll be your turn next time, you little brutes, don't you worry about that!" panted the man, turning on his heel and going to the door. "Pesky dots! Arrrr!"

He pulled the door open. "Your turn," he called, beckoning to someone outside.

A large brown duck waddled into the room, its flat yellow feet making ominous slapping sounds as they hit the floor. The long, narrow black markings around its glittering eyes made it look as if it were wearing a mask.

It looked around and snapped its beak. The dots stopped jeering and withdrew their heads hastily. The duck nodded with satisfaction and then set about gobbling up the crumbs and currants that were all that remained on the floor after the small man's rampage.

The man shut the door after her, turned around, and finally noticed Leo and Mimi perched on the sink. He jumped in shock. His jaw fell open.

Leo began rapidly calculating how long it would take them to turn and escape back through the window. Would this terrifying stranger be able to reach them before . . . ?

"Hello," Mimi chirped brightly. She edged Leo aside and jumped carefully down from the sink. "I'm Mimi Langlander," she said,

with great composure. "My cousin and I are strangers here. And —
and I hope you don't mind — but we really need your help."

The stranger gaped at her. His arms dropped limply to his sides.
The flyswatters, thick with dot crumbs and squashed currants,
fell to the floor. The duck looked up briefly, gave what sounded
like a snort of disgust, and returned to its work.

The man's brown face swelled and darkened. He plunged his
hands into his wiry hair and tugged at it as if he was trying to pull
it out by the roots.

"You're — you're here!" he bellowed at Leo and Mimi, his voice
cracking with dismay. "She got you into Rondo after all! Oh, my
glory! Oh, my heart, liver, and lungs!"

His eyes bulged. "Don't say it was *you* making all that fuss in the
alley?" he breathed. "Jolly said it was Spoiler with a gang of
pickpockets!"

"Spoiler escaped into the toy factory," Mimi said. "He tried to
grab us before he went, but we got away from him — and Officer
Begood, too."

The man stared at them open-mouthed. He seemed completely
flabbergasted.

"We didn't steal the old man's wallet," Leo added quickly.
"Spoiler did that earlier. We didn't have anything to do with it."

"Oh, of course you didn't, of course you didn't," gabbled the
man, flapping his hands. "But — but I still can't understand how
the Blue Queen got you here! Didn't you get my warning? Didn't
you read it?"

Now it was Mimi's turn to stare. "*You* sent that note?" she breathed.

The stranger nodded, swallowing. "I thought you'd get it in time," he said in a choked voice. "I sent it by the first available mouse, the moment I heard she was on the move."

The duck snorted again. The stranger glanced at it. "Freda's right," he said. "The mouse *did* take forever to come. Half the fleet was off duty, it said, and the other half . . . there was a wedding, apparently — one of the Crystal Palace princesses — lots of greetings to be delivered, and —"

He broke off, grinding his teeth. "I always said it was a mistake to agree to the mice having official cheese breaks, whatever they threatened to do if we didn't," he muttered. "What if there's an emergency, I said, while half the communications system is having a tails-up in the tearoom? But no one listened to me, oh, no. No one listened to Conker. Paranoid old Conker, they said. Conker the worrywart, they said. And now look what's happened! Disaster!"

Mimi glanced desperately over her shoulder at Leo, who was still crouched on the sink. Leo made himself move. Carefully he climbed down to the floor, feeling as if his legs and arms didn't belong to him. The dot-eating duck watched him narrowly but didn't make any aggressive moves.

"It's a miracle you got away from her," said Conker, shaking his head. "It was the quake, I suppose. It shook up her power, cracked the enchantment or something. Yes . . ."

Suddenly his small black eyes widened and he darted a look at the open window. "Where is she now?" he asked urgently. "She's not prowling around out there looking for you, is she?"

"No. She went straight back to her castle," said Mimi, and Leo realized that Mimi must have checked the music box from the moment he left his bedroom to get the first-aid kit.

Conker heaved a sigh of relief. "Well, that's one good thing, anyway," he said.

"No it's not," Mimi exclaimed. "She took my dog! She's got Mutt!"

"*What?*" Conker clapped his hands to his hairy cheeks, his face a picture of dismay. "Oh, no!" he groaned. "Oh, my heart, liver, lungs, and — *gizzards!*"

Freda the duck flapped her wings, her fierce, masked eyes gleaming.

"I've got to save him," Mimi rushed on. "Somehow I've got to find my way to the castle and make the Blue Queen give him up."

Leo waited for Conker to burst into loud protests — to tell Mimi that what she wanted to do was terribly dangerous and absolutely impossible, and that anyway it would be just absurd to take such risk for the sake of one little dog. To his enormous surprise and dismay, however, the little man nodded seriously.

"Of course!" he said. "Captives have to be rescued, don't they? That goes without saying. Ah, well." He glanced at the duck and shrugged. "Our break didn't last long this time, did it, Freda? Still, I can't say I'm sorry. Being a dot-catcher has its exciting moments, but it's a feeble sort of job for a hero to do full time, in my opinion."

"You mean — you'll come with us?" gasped Mimi. "You'll help us save Mutt? You and — um — Freda?"

"Well, naturally!" said Conker. Then suddenly his face went blank. "Unless you think we're past it?" he added stiffly. "Too old and out of practice to assist?"

Freda closed her beak with a snap.

"Oh, no!" cried Mimi. "Of course not!"

"Not at all," Leo mumbled, trying to gather his wits.

Freda gave them a hard look, and went back to eating. Conker's face broke into a broad, relieved grin. "That's all right then," he said, scratching his beard vigorously.

He picked up his dot swatters, tapped them hard on the floor to clean them, and tucked them into leather holsters dangling from each side of his belt.

"So! When do you want to start out?" he asked. "Dawn is the traditional time for beginning a quest, of course, but . . ."

"There's no time like the present, in my opinion," the duck said with her beak full.

"My sentiments exactly, Freda," Conker agreed. "My sentiments exactly!"

CHAPTER 11

Things were moving much too fast for Leo. He felt as if he were on some crazy ride and were unable to get off. Had he actually heard a duck speak?

If he had, why should he be so surprised, considering where he was, and everything else that had happened? In a way, he should have expected it. He watched in a daze as Conker cautiously opened the kitchen door and peeped out.

"All clear," the little man whispered, beckoning.

Mimi ran to join him. Leo followed slowly, trying to avoid the flattened golden-brown blobs and trails of crumbs that Freda hadn't yet had time to swallow. The idea of squashed dots sticking to the soles of his shoes made him feel queasy.

"Now, follow me and be as quiet as you can," said Conker. "If anyone sees you we'll have to tell a whole bunch of complicated lies and that will mean delay."

Delay sounded a very good idea to Leo, but Conker seemed to have taken charge and he was clearly even more impulsive than Mimi.

"First, we'll find you some different clothes," Conker went on. "That will make it harder for the Blue Queen to locate you. Then we'll pick up some supplies. Freda can stay and finish up here. She'll be ready to leave whenever we are. She travels very light."

He ushered Leo and Mimi through the doorway. "Back in ten minutes, Freda," he whispered, pulling the door shut behind him.

Freda made no answer. The only sound from behind the door was the steady slapping of her feet on the kitchen floor.

"She's a duck of few words," Conker said affectionately. "But in a scrape, you couldn't have a better partner by your side, believe me."

Leo groaned quietly to himself. No wonder Conker didn't think it was madness to risk everything for the sake of a dog, when he worked and went on quests with a talking duck!

Outside the kitchen there was a broad passage, dimly lit by a single glowing lantern hanging from the ceiling. The walls of the passage were paneled in dark wood and bristling with brass hooks from which hung coats, cloaks, scarves, and hats of many different sizes, kinds, and colors. To the right, the passage was blocked by a door of smoky gray glass through which drifted the buzz of chattering voices and the clinking of bottles and glasses.

"Jolly's opened up again," muttered Conker. "Excellent! That'll keep him busy for a while." He lifted a well-worn backpack from one of the hooks and gave it a friendly pat. "Hello, old fellow," he said to it. "Told you I wouldn't be long."

He turned left and, with Leo and Mimi close behind him, hurried along the passage till he reached a large cluster of hooks that were painted bright red. Unlike the brass hooks closer to the glass door, the red hooks supported what looked like dozens of garments each. Bunches of boots and shoes with their laces tied together hung from the hooks closest to the floor, like oddly shaped fruit.

"Take whatever suits you," Conker ordered, gesturing at the red hooks. "There's bound to be something here."

Mimi began rummaging enthusiastically through the clothes at once, but Leo held back, frowning. "We can't just take other people's things!" he protested.

Conker clicked his tongue impatiently. "These don't belong to anyone!" he said. "Well, they did once, but now they're red hooks. *You* know!"

Seeing that Leo *didn't* know, he gestured at the red hooks again. "They're mistakes, unwanted gifts, lost clothes that have never been claimed, clothes that don't fit anymore, and so on," he explained rapidly. "People put them here so they can find new homes. Just go through them till you find something that feels right. Get to it! Quick-sticks!"

Leo began to go through the clothes dangling limply from the red hooks. A dusty, musty, sad sort of odor hung around them. He didn't like the thought of putting any of them on.

Then, suddenly, his hand tingled. He snatched it away from the clothes, thinking that something had bitten him. The tingling disappeared instantly, however, and when he examined his hand, he could see no mark on it at all.

"You found something," Conker said encouragingly. "Good! Take it, Leo, take it!"

Tentatively, Leo reached out again. Almost at once he felt the tingling begin. He saw that his fingers were touching a brown leather jacket.

He freed the jacket from the hook and the tingling in his fingers stopped as he held it up to look at it more closely. It was the sort of leather jacket that motorcycle riders wore in old movies. The leather was soft, and a wonderful, rich brown. It was exactly the sort of jacket he'd secretly always wanted. It didn't smell musty, either. It smelled of old leather, fresh air, and warm grass. It smelled of adventure!

It probably won't fit, he thought, preparing himself for disappointment. When he slipped the jacket on, however, he found it fit perfectly. He wished he had a mirror so that he could look at himself, and immediately felt embarrassed.

"That suits you, Leo," said Mimi from the other end of the red-hook cluster. Leo saw that she already had several garments draped over her arm. She'd obviously caught on to the red-hook system much more quickly than he had.

Or maybe she always chooses clothes that make her fingers tingle, Leo thought darkly. *That wouldn't surprise me at all.*

"Keep going!" said Conker, glancing in agitation at the smoky glass door.

Now that Leo had gotten the idea he worked more efficiently. He didn't bother to look at the clothes anymore. He just ran his hands through them and took out anything that gave him a little shock when he touched it.

In a very few minutes his arms were full. He had a pair of rough pants in a murky green color, a soft white shirt, a broad brown belt with a large brass buckle, and a pair of long brown boots.

He looked at the garments doubtfully. But Conker was nodding with satisfaction, and Mimi, a neat bundle tucked under her arm, and small black shoes dangling by their laces from her fingers, also looked approving.

"All right," Conker said briskly. "That's that! Now, follow me!"

He scurried away. Clutching their bundles, Leo and Mimi followed him.

At the end of the passageway, beside a narrow staircase that twisted up into darkness, there was a door marked STOREROOM in black letters. Beneath the black letters someone had pinned a large notice written in purple ink: NO ADMITTANCE EXCEPT ON TAVERN BUSINESS. TRESPASSERS WILL WISH THEY HAD NEVER BEEN BORN. THIS MEANS YOU!

Ignoring the notice completely, Conker turned the door handle and pushed. The door swung open and he ushered Leo and Mimi inside. "Jolly never locks the door," he whispered. "He can't be bothered, because he's in and out of here all day. He thinks his notice will scare thieves off, but of course it doesn't. Only honest people get scared off by notices."

"What does that make us, then?" Leo muttered, as Conker closed the door silently behind him.

"We're heroes about to go on a quest!" said Conker indignantly. "Heroes have a right to supply themselves with food for their journey. It's traditional. And anyway, Jolly hired Freda and me to get rid of some of his dots and promised us a fat purse for our trouble. He's not going to mind if I take food instead of gold."

It was very cool and dark inside the storeroom, which smelled strongly of garlic, onions, and spices. Leo heard the familiar scuttling of dots and winced as he felt something run over his foot.

"Pests!" Conker growled. Leo heard the scratching sound of a match. Light flared briefly, then brightened as Conker lit a candle.

Shadows leaped on the walls, which were stacked high with bags of flour, rice, and potatoes, racks of brown bottles, and labeled boxes of provisions. Long, strong-smelling sausages, nets of onions, ropes of garlic, and legs of ham and bacon swung from hooks attached to the ceiling. At floor level, hundreds of dots dived into hiding.

"Change your clothes," Conker ordered. "I'll collect some food."

As he began bustling around, filling his backpack, Leo moved to a shadowy corner and began changing into the things he had taken from the red hooks. With every piece of new clothing he put on, he felt freer and more alive. By the time he was fully dressed, he could almost feel the blood fizzing in his veins.

"I'm done," he said simply. He turned around, and gasped.

Mimi Langlander was standing on the other side of the storeroom — but she was a Mimi Langlander transformed!

The frilled lemon-yellow shirt, the pale pink shorts, and the pink zip-up jacket with its bows and grinning kittens were gone.

The enormous, grubby sneakers were gone. And the sulky, snooty expression had gone as well.

The Mimi Langlander who faced him stood tall, with her shoulders back. She was wearing slim black trousers, soft black shoes, and a strange green-and-gold jacket with a high, Chinese-style collar. She looked exotic, poised and, really, Leo thought, quite beautiful. He could suddenly imagine Mimi standing on a concert platform with her violin, accepting the applause of a huge audience.

Color flared in Mimi's cheeks. "What are you staring at?" she snapped.

"You look amazing," Leo said, startled into speaking the plain truth. "Those clothes suit you a lot better than — um . . ." His voice trailed off as Mimi glared at him.

"Well, naturally they suit her," put in Conker, busily strapping up his bulging pack. "They *chose* her, didn't they? I mean, would *you* want to be worn by someone who'd make you look ugly?"

The color in Mimi's cheeks grew brighter. Then the corner of her mouth tweaked into a wry smile. "My sisters' clothes have probably been miserable ever since I started wearing them, then," she said, gesturing at the tangle of pink and yellow lying on the floor. "I'd better put them on the red hooks so they can find new homes."

"Afterward, maybe," Conker said absentmindedly. "For now, you'd better hide them in here. We don't want to leave the Blue Queen any clues. Speaking of which . . ."

He began feeling around in his pockets. "I've just thought . . . before we do anything else, I'd better write a report." He pulled out a very short, very blunt pencil and a grubby little notebook. He bent closer to the candle, stuck out his tongue, and began writing laboriously.

When he had finished the note, he tore the page from his notebook and passed it to Mimi and Leo. "That explains things pretty clearly, don't you think?" he said with satisfaction.

Leo took the note, and he and Mimi read it.

BQ HAS TAKEN LANGLANDER HOSTAGE.

QUEST TO RESCUE IN PROGRESS.

PASS IT ON.

CONKER

"Who are you writing to?" Leo asked, bewildered.

"The others, of course," said Conker, taking the note back and folding it small. "The old team! I don't suppose you were planning for us to do this all on our own?" He laughed, as if he'd made a very good joke.

"Well, yes, I thought . . ." Mimi began.

Conker looked up quickly. When he saw that Mimi was serious, the amusement died from his face and was replaced by a look of embarrassed pride. He squared his shoulders. "Well, I'm very flattered," he mumbled. "And Freda will be, too, when I tell her. My word, she will!"

He rubbed his beard, and his eyes began to shine. "What if the four of us *did* face the Blue Queen on our own?" he breathed. "Oh, *that* would be a story for the minstrels to sing about, and no mistake . . . Think of it! Courage and sacrifice — a gallant struggle against tremendous odds . . ."

The glow faded from his eyes. He shrugged. "But I have to admit it would probably be a story with a very sad ending," he said. "You know — with everyone dying? And I hate those."

"Me, too," said Leo fervently.

"I don't mind them," said Mimi. "But I wouldn't like to actually be *in* one," she added quickly, as Leo glared at her.

"Yes," sighed Conker. "It was a lovely thought, but I really think it's impractical. Six isn't the *ideal* number for a quest, but it's a lot better than four. I speak from experience. Besides, the others would never forgive us if we left them out of this. Our last quest was a bit of a disappointment — swamp lurgies aren't much of a challenge."

He turned to Mimi. "But I thank you for your faith in me, Mimi Langlander," he said, bowing low. "It means a lot." He straightened, sniffed, and hurriedly turned away, wiping his eyes.

"The others —" Leo began.

"No, no, don't you worry about that. I won't say a word about it to them," Conker snuffled. "I wouldn't want to hurt their feelings. But I'll know, in here" — he punched his chest in the vague position of his heart — "and I'll never forget it."

After that, it seemed impossible to question him about the mysterious "others." Neither Leo nor Mimi could face telling Conker the truth — that Mimi had assumed Conker and Freda were to be their only companions because she hadn't had the faintest idea that there were any "others" who might help.

Leo shook his head in frustration. He loathed the feeling that he was being swept along, out of control, but there wasn't a thing he could do about it. For the moment he just had to follow where Conker led, and hope for the best.

CHAPTER 12

Conker gave a last, tremendous sniff and cleared his throat noisily. "Well," he said with forced heartiness, "enough of that! Here — have a lemon drop."

He felt around in his pocket and pulled out a handful of large yellow candies shaped vaguely like flattened lemons and covered with a dusting of dot crumbs and fluff.

"Help yourself," he said grandly, holding the lemon drops out on the palm of his rather grubby hand.

Not wanting to offend him, Leo and Mimi each took one of the dingy candies, murmuring insincere thanks.

"Take two!" Conker urged.

"Oh, no. One's plenty, thanks," Leo assured him, surreptitiously rubbing the lemon drop between his fingers to get off the worst of the fluff. He would have liked to throw the thing away, but Conker was watching him eagerly. Trying not to think about the dot crumbs, he pushed the lemon drop into his mouth.

"Delicious," he said. And it was true that the lemon drop tasted good, if rather gritty.

"I might keep mine for later," Mimi said hastily, pushing the lemon drop deep into her pocket. "I'm not hungry just at the moment."

Leo wished he'd thought of that.

Conker took a lemon drop himself and put the rest away. "All right," he said, chewing with relish. "We'd better get on. You hide your clothes while I get this report on its way."

He bent and knocked sharply three times at the base of the nearest wall. He straightened up and looked around expectantly, but nothing happened. He sighed deeply and began tapping his foot.

Mimi and Leo rolled their old clothes and shoes into tight bundles and hid them behind a box labeled CRABS' ANKLES. As they turned around again, there was a scuffling sound from the back of the storeroom and a brown mouse appeared from behind a sack of potatoes.

It was even smaller than the mouse that had brought the message to Leo's bedroom. It sauntered up to Conker, sat back on its hind legs, and held out a tiny paw in a bored sort of way.

"About time!" said Conker tightly, handing over the folded note. "Take this to Tye in Flitter Wood, please. It's very urgent."

"Oh, they're all *urgent*, aren't they?" sighed the mouse, fussily clipping the note to the gold chain around its neck. "Why you people can't plan ahead, I do not know. It's one emergency after another with you. We were just saying in the cheese room earlier —"

"Just deliver the message, will you?" Conker roared, suddenly losing his temper.

"Well, *really*!" said the mouse. It sniffed and stalked away, its tail held out very stiffly behind it. At the potato sack it stopped and combed its whiskers, deliberately taking its time, before finally disappearing into the shadows.

"Something's got to be done about those mice," growled Conker. "Once upon a time they couldn't do enough for you. Now they act like they're doing you a favor by carrying the mail."

He shook his head. "In my opinion, the trouble started when they stopped wearing caps. Discipline went out the window after that. They said the caps kept getting knocked off in low tunnels. Well, why didn't they just tighten their chin straps, I'd like to know?"

He glared at Mimi and Leo as if waiting for an answer.

"Chin straps can be a bit uncomfortable," Mimi said cautiously. "I had a hat once —"

"*Uncomfortable?*" Conker exploded. "What does that matter? Why, in my day mice were *proud* to wear messenger caps, and the more uncomfortable they were the better they liked it! Young mice *dreamed* of getting their first caps. They half-strangled themselves regularly, they wore their chin straps so tight. But this young generation — bah!"

"Are they paid?" asked Leo curiously.

"Of course they're paid!" snorted Conker. "Paid far too much, in my opinion. They've got a monopoly, that's the trouble. They're the only ones small enough to run between the layers —and they know all the Gaps, too. Old Wizard Bing over in Hobnob once tried to train lizards to do the job, you know. But the lizards kept getting lost, and having nervous breakdowns. Bing had to give it up."

"Oh well," Mimi murmured, before Leo could ask any more questions. She glanced at the door. "Are we ready to go now, Conker? Only — I'm worried about Mutt."

"Oh, of course you are, of course you are!" exclaimed Conker, his scowl disappearing instantly. Hoisting his loaded bag onto his shoulder, he went to the door, opened it, and peered out.

"All right," he whispered, beckoning.

They all crept out of the storeroom. The muffled sounds of laughter and singing drifted through the glass door at the other end of the hallway.

"You wait there," Conker whispered, pointing at the staircase. "Keep out of sight. I'll go and get Freda."

Leo and Mimi scuttled to the staircase. They climbed up to the fourth step and crouched there in the dark.

"What if someone comes down?" Leo whispered.

"Oh, we'll just say we're waiting for our parents or something," Mimi said confidently. "That usually works."

Leo bit his lip. He hadn't thought about his mother and father since he and Mimi had climbed through the tavern window, but suddenly he couldn't think of anything else. What was his mother going to think when she got home and found Mimi and him missing?

First she'd be puzzled. Then she'd be annoyed. Then she'd get worried. Then she'd panic.

He sighed and shook his head.

"What's the matter?" Mimi hissed.

"Mom," Leo said. "She'll worry. She doesn't know where we are."

"If she *did* know, she'd worry a lot more," Mimi said reasonably.

Leo nodded gloomily. This didn't make him feel any better.

"Anyway, who knows how time works in this place?" Mimi went on. "It mightn't be the same as at home. If it's like some of the stories I've read, it isn't. For all we know, a day here is like a minute in our world, and we'll be back before Suzanne even knows we're gone."

"If we get back at all," Leo muttered.

"Of course we will!" Mimi exclaimed. "We've got the ring, haven't we?" She held up her hand, and even in the darkness Leo could see the gleam of gold. He looked at it longingly, his mind suddenly filled again with thoughts of grabbing Mimi, wrenching the ring from her finger, and wishing them both back to home and safety.

I'll just do it, he told himself. *It's up to me. I'm the sensible one. I have to think for both of us. She'll thank me later.*

But he had hesitated a moment too long. Mimi must have seen the expression on his face, because she abruptly made her hand into a tight fist and hid it behind her back.

"Don't even think about it, Leo," she said fiercely. "I've got really strong hands, from playing the violin. If you want this ring, you'll have to break my fingers to get it."

"I wouldn't —" Leo's horrified protest broke off as he heard soft footsteps coming down the passage and recognized Conker's voice.

". . . to tell the others what's going on," Conker was saying to his companion. "A bit risky otherwise, don't you think, Freda?"

"Insane!" said the duck flatly.

Just as Conker and Freda reached the staircase, there was the sound of a door swinging open and a burst of noise from the other end of the passageway.

"All right, all right!" a voice roared. "Plenty more pickles in the storeroom, ladies and gentlemen. Give us a chance!"

"Jolly's coming!" muttered Conker, scurrying up to Leo and Mimi with Freda behind him. "Quick! Up to the first floor."

Instantly, Mimi darted up the dark stairs. Leo followed, very aware that his chance to grab the ring had passed. He didn't know if he was glad or sorry.

They arrived, panting, at the first floor landing and stood aside to let Conker and the duck join them. Deserted corridors lined with doors led away from the landing to left and right.

Both corridors were littered with framed paintings that had dropped from the walls. The window at the end of the left-hand corridor was cracked, and the curtain rod had fallen down, so that the red curtains lay in a tangled heap on the floor. *More earthquake damage*, Leo thought guiltily.

Conker turned left. "Mind the paintings," he whispered as he tiptoed carefully along the corridor. "Don't tread on them, for goodness' sake. They're Jolly's pride and joy. He's been taking lessons, you know."

The paintings — those that Leo could see — were not very good, and they were all of a large pink pig.

The pig had been painted in different poses. Sometimes it was standing and sometimes it was lying down. Sometimes it was serious. Sometimes it was smiling. Sometimes it was wearing a blue-spotted scarf around its neck. Sometimes it was wearing a straw sun hat covered in flowers and tied under the chin with broad pink ribbons. Sometimes it even had a daisy behind its ear. But it was always clearly the same pig.

"Doesn't Jolly ever paint anything else?" asked Mimi in amazement.

Conker sighed. "Well, no, not at present," he said, skirting a very large gold-framed picture of the pig leaning against a fence with her front legs crossed. "He just paints Bertha. She works for his brother actually. Jolly goes out to the farm to paint her. There are lots more of her downstairs as well. We've all suggested he might try another subject. Pigs get a bit monotonous to look at after a while, as you can imagine. But he won't hear of it."

"He must really like her — Bertha I mean," Leo commented, for something to say.

Freda quacked explosively. Leo jumped in shock, then realized the duck was laughing.

"*Like* her?" exclaimed Conker. "He can't *stand* her. He says he's sick of the *sight* of her."

"Then why —?" Leo asked helplessly.

"Bertha was the first thing Jolly painted, you see," Conker explained. "He was really proud of that picture, and his wife liked it, too. Or so she said — she's a kind soul, Merry, and very fond of him. So Jolly took his picture of Bertha to Monsieur Rouge-et-Noir at the art gallery. He thought it should be hung up where everyone could see it. But Monsieur wouldn't have it. He said the subject was interesting, but the painting wasn't good enough for the gallery. He told Jolly to try again."

"Wak, wak, wak," snickered Freda.

"So Jolly *did* try again," Conker went on, shooting the duck a reproving look. "He hung the first picture of Bertha behind the bar and painted another picture of her, in a different pose, for the art gallery. But Monsieur didn't like that one either, or the next one, or the next."

He scratched his beard and sighed again. "So then Jolly got stubborn. Jolly's a very nice fellow, but he can get really stubborn when he's roused. And he swore he was going to get a picture of Bertha hung up in the art gallery if it was the last thing he ever did."

"I can understand that," said Mimi. And as she was the most amazingly stubborn person he'd ever met, Leo believed her.

"The fact remains," Conker said, "that at last count Jolly has done four hundred and eighty-two paintings of Bertha. Now, I'm not one to lay down the law to other folk, but in my view that's enough."

"More than enough," Leo agreed.

They'd reached the end of the corridor by now. The cracked window was right in front of them, and the crumpled red curtains lay at their feet. On their left was a narrow door marked STAFF ONLY, which looked as if it might open onto a broom closet.

On their right was blank wall. They seemed to have reached a dead end.

"What now?" Mimi demanded.

Conker turned to the narrow door and grasped its brass knob. He spun the knob around three times to the right. Then he spun it twice to the left, and four times to the right again. There was a sharp click and the door swung open.

Inside was swirling grayness, thick and dense as fog.

Freda made a high, quacking sound.

"In you go," Conker growled. He seized Mimi and Leo by the arms and thrust them through the door.

CHAPTER 13

FLITTER WOOD

The door slammed shut. Gray mist closed in around Leo, blinding him. His feet tried and failed to find solid ground. His hands clawed at empty air. Twisting and flailing uselessly he began a slow, drifting fall through swirling gray space. His ears were ringing with Mimi's terrified cries as well as his own.

His stomach heaved as he somersaulted, and somersaulted again. In terror he realized that he'd lost all sense of which way was up and which way was down.

Panic-stricken, he beat at the grayness around him. His mind groped frantically for an answer to what had happened, as if somehow knowing would make a difference.

Conker had made some sort of terrible blunder. Conker had impetuously pushed them through the door, not realizing what was behind it.

No. That couldn't be. The swirling grayness was clearly visible. Conker must have seen it.

And Conker had pushed Leo and Mimi into the mist, and slammed the door behind them. There was no doubt. No doubt. The memory of Conker's strong, determined grip flashed into

Leo's mind. The memory of Conker's suddenly rough voice rang in his ears. It was such a different voice from the one Conker had used before, as he had bustled around preparing his new acquaintances for . . .

For this? The thought hit Leo like a splash of cold water. He gasped, and suddenly his mind was working properly again. Suddenly he saw that everything Conker had said and done in the tavern could be understood in a different way.

Conker had warned them to keep out of sight, and to hide their clothes. Conker didn't want anyone to know they were there — or ever *had* been there. Because he was trying to protect them? Or because it wouldn't do for anyone to suspect that Conker had disposed of them?

No, Leo thought desperately. *It can't be.* But he forced himself to go on, to face the suspicion, and deal with it, as his heart grew cold in his chest.

What if Conker wasn't the Blue Queen's enemy? What if he was her ally, like Spoiler? If so, he had succeeded where Spoiler had failed, because he was clever. He'd disarmed Leo and Mimi completely with all his funny stories about mice who wouldn't wear caps, and pigs called Bertha. He'd made them think he was harmless — just an eccentric little dot-catcher and part-time hero with a duck for a partner.

Then he'd led them to this — this nowhere place. He'd pushed them in and slammed the door.

And now they were drifting, helpless. There was nothing they could do to save themselves. Nothing . . .

Leo's whole body tingled as if an electric shock had run through him.

"Mimi!" he yelled. "The ring! Use the ring! Wish us —"

His feet hit solid ground. He felt himself pitch forward. Then he was rolling on something soft, something that crackled beneath him.

He came to rest flat on his back. His nose was filled with the sharp, sour smell of sap.

He opened his eyes. Above him stretched the branches of a vast tree through which gleamed tiny patches of sky.

I'm home, he told himself dazedly. *This must be the tree that grows outside my window.*

He desperately wanted to believe it. But as he turned his head a wave of bitter disappointment rose in him, burning in his throat.

He was lying on a thick bed of ferns. A few blue butterflies danced in the air above him. Fragile, lacy fern fronds, palest green, tickled his hands, face, and neck. The light was green and dim. More giant trees, their roots hidden beneath drifts of ferns, their trunks dotted with red and yellow fungus, stood silently around like guards.

A memory stirred at the back of Leo's mind — a picture of a forest, exquisitely detailed, covering the side of the music box. Tall trees rising from a sea of lacy ferns. Shadows flickering like the stripes of tigers . . .

A shiver ran down his spine. He made himself sit up. With a start, he saw Mimi kneeling nearby, almost hidden in a deep bank of ferns. She was so still, and her green-and-gold jacket so perfectly blended with her surroundings, that at first he hadn't noticed her. Small, pale green moths fluttered around her. They were exactly the same color as the ferns, and had the same lacy appearance. It was almost as if tiny pieces of fern had grown wings.

Then Leo saw Mimi's face. She was smiling — a dreamy, delighted smile.

Leo's skin prickled. "Mimi!" he shouted.

His voice seemed shockingly loud in the forest stillness. The moths fluttered upward in a lacy green cloud.

Mimi turned her head. "Shh! You're frightening them," she whispered.

Leo scrambled up. Green fronds bent and cracked under his feet as he began to wade through the ferns toward the place where Mimi was kneeling. His legs were trembling. Rage was boiling up inside him.

"Leo, be careful!" Mimi called in distress. "You're crushing the ferns."

"Who cares?" Leo shouted. "Why did you wish us here? Why didn't you wish us home, like I told you? What crazy thing have you done to us now?"

Mimi's face froze. She lifted her chin. "I haven't done anything," she said coldly. "I didn't hear you tell me anything. I didn't wish anything."

"Why *not*?" Leo shouted, stamping his feet, beside himself with anger.

Mimi raised her eyebrows and looked him up and down.

"Actually," she drawled, "it was because I was so scared that my mind was a complete blank."

Leo stared at her, trying to take this in. Slowly his anger drained away, leaving a cold, empty feeling in its place.

"So — we just landed here without you doing anything," he said, getting it straight in his mind. "So — either we ended up here by accident, or this is where Conker meant to send us all along."

Mimi shrugged and looked bored.

Leo wet his lips. "This is the forest on the side of the music box," he went on.

Mimi looked even more bored than before, making it clear that Leo was telling her something she already knew. She turned to look at the green moths, which had begun fluttering cautiously back.

"It's all right," she said to them. "He's harmless. Stupid, but harmless."

Anger flared in Leo again. "There are tigers in this forest, Mimi," he shouted. "And wolves, however ridiculous it is for wolves and tigers to live in the same place! Are you just going to sit there and wait until one of them comes to get you?"

"The way you're yelling it's a wonder one hasn't come already," Mimi said, looking down her nose at him. "Why don't you just shut up?"

"Why don't you?" Leo retorted childishly.

Mimi gave one of her humorless snorts of laughter. "I'm going to stand up now," she said to the moths.

Slowly she got to her feet. She held out her hands and, to Leo's amazement, dozens of the moths settled on her fingers.

Leo stared at the little creatures, and suddenly gasped in shock. They weren't moths at all! They were perfectly formed little people, with green skin, green wings as delicate as lace, and top-knots that curled like the tips of new fern fronds.

"What are they?" he burst out. "Mimi, be careful!"

Mimi's mouth tightened at one corner. "They're not going to bite me," she said scornfully. "They're some kind of fairy, can't you see that? They're called Flitters."

Something tickled Leo at the edge of his mind. He knew that name ought to mean something to him, but he couldn't think why. Had he read it somewhere? Had he heard it? Or even dreamed it? He clenched his fists in frustration.

"How do you know what they're called?" he demanded, still shocked at the sight of the little green beings balanced on Mimi's fingertips and fluttering in the air around her. "Are you saying they're talking to you? I can't hear anything."

"They don't talk aloud," Mimi said, as if this were the most natural thing in the world. "They make you hear things — know things — in your mind. Can't you hear them?"

"No!" Leo snapped.

"Well, maybe you would if you stopped shouting and jumping up and down for a single minute," Mimi snapped back. "Your mind has to be quiet before you can hear. And even then it's not like ordinary talking. It's more like . . . like music, really. All I know so far is what they're called, and that they're friendly."

"Conker seemed friendly, too," Leo pointed out heatedly. "And look how that turned out!"

A shadow crossed Mimi's face. "I really liked Conker," she said. "I trusted him the minute I saw him. It just shows . . ."

Her voice trailed off. Her head drooped. Leo knew what she was thinking.

It just shows you shouldn't let down your guard. It just shows you shouldn't trust anyone. How often do you have to be hurt before you learn?

The Flitters on Mimi's fingers looked up at her with slanting emerald eyes, opening and closing their wings anxiously as if they could feel her pain.

Leo felt a pang of shame. "I'm sorry I shouted at you, before," he muttered. "I was scared, that's all. Really scared." It was amazing how difficult it was to say.

Mimi gave a small shrug. He couldn't tell if what he'd said had made her feel better or not.

He'd opened his mouth to speak again when suddenly all the Flitters rose into the air. Leo hadn't heard a sound, but clearly something had startled them.

He thought of tigers, and his heart gave a great thud. He looked quickly around, but could see nothing — nothing but trees, and ferns, and shadows.

Mimi was looking around, too. She jumped nervously as five or six Flitters flew close to her face, their fragile wings brushing her cheeks.

The fluttering green cloud of Flitters had thinned and lengthened.

Now it looked like a long trail of green smoke. The little creatures were streaming away into the trees. It was impossible to see their faces, and they made no sound at all, but fear was in the air. Even Leo could feel it.

The movements of the Flitters still hovering around Mimi became more jerky and frantic. One landed on her hair and tugged with tiny fingers.

"Something terrible's coming," Mimi whispered. "Some terrible danger. They want us to go with them." She glanced at Leo.

He nodded. "We'd better do it then," he said grimly. "Whatever's scaring them probably won't be too good for us, either."

They stumbled through the ferns, following the fleeing green cloud as it snaked rapidly through the trees. The few Flitters who had stayed with them fluttered anxiously around their heads, urging them on.

In moments Leo and Mimi had lost sight of the place where they had landed. In another minute they were hopelessly lost.

"We could have dropped a trail of bread crumbs," said Mimi. "If we had any bread."

"Or unwound a spool of thread," said Leo. "If we had a spool of thread. Not that it matters. We didn't know where we were to start with."

And then they stopped, awestruck. Ahead of them was a giant tree — the biggest Leo had ever seen, or even imagined. It stood alone in the center of a clearing thick with ferns. Ferns of a different kind hung from its branches, which spread over the clearing like a high, shaggy roof.

The Flitters were streaming toward the tree. Leo's eyes followed them as far as a clump of ferns just above the lowest branch. After that, they were impossible to see. The great tree's shade swallowed them completely.

For a moment, Leo and Mimi simply stared. Then, not far behind them, they distinctly heard a low, menacing growl.

They ran to the foot of the tree and looked up. The smooth silver trunk rose high, impossibly high. They had to tilt their heads far back to see the lowest branch.

"There's no way we can get up there," Leo said, putting what they both knew into words. "The trunk's too straight. There's nothing to hold on to."

Almost all of the Flitters had disappeared now, but a few still hung back, tugging urgently at Mimi's hands and hair.

"We can't do it," she said to them, patting the great tree's trunk, miming trying to climb, and shaking her head. "You go. Be safe. We'll hide somewhere else."

The Flitters hovered. They seemed not to understand.

"Go!" Mimi whispered. "Don't you see? We can't climb this tree. We need a ladder."

The low growl came again. It was closer now, and Leo thought he could hear the soft cracking of fern stems. He pictured a huge striped shape padding relentlessly toward them.

"Come on!" he urged. He darted to the edge of the clearing, realized that Mimi was still standing by the tree with the Flitters, and ran back to her again.

"Mimi, come on," he whispered urgently, tugging at her arm.

"Leave them. They'll be okay. We've got to find a tree we *can* climb."

"If *we* can climb it, a tiger can, too," Mimi said grimly. "Oh, if only —"

She jumped back with a muffled shriek.

A broad, thick tongue of scarlet fungus had suddenly erupted from the tree's smooth bark. It was about level with Mimi's knees, and as she and Leo stared in amazement, another appeared above it, and another.

In seconds a ladder of fungus tongues stretched up the tree's trunk, all the way to the lowest branch.

"Fungus can't possibly bear our weight," Leo said in a dazed voice.

But Mimi had leaped forward. She stood on the lowest step of the fungus ladder, and it didn't snap. As the Flitters dipped and whirled around her, clapping their tiny hands, she reached up, grabbed the edges of a higher step and began to climb.

"Come on!" she called back to Leo in a low voice.

And Leo followed. All the time he was telling himself that fungus couldn't possibly hold him. But the fungus steps were broad and strong. Their edges were smooth and steady under his hands. Beneath his feet they felt firm, but at the same time springy, so that they seemed to push him gently upward with every step.

Never had Leo climbed so high, yet never had a climb seemed so easy or so fast. It reminded him of walking up a moving escalator, though he knew that the only movement was his own.

In no time at all he was joining Mimi on the lowest branch of the great tree. The branch was so broad that they were easily able to stand side by side with the clump of ferns between them.

Feathery fronds tickled Leo's ear as, holding tightly to the tree trunk, he turned his head and looked down at the clearing below. His stomach turned over as he saw how far away it seemed. If he and Mimi had fallen, they'd have been killed for sure. If just one of the fungus steps had crumbled . . .

He glanced at the tree trunk below him, and blinked. The trunk was bare, silvery-gray again. The red fungus had completely disappeared. A cold weight seemed to settle on Leo's chest. Had he and Mimi made yet another mistake?

"Mimi, the ladder's gone!" he whispered. "We're stranded up here."

There was no answer. And when he turned his head, he saw that Mimi was no longer beside him. She, and the last of the Flitters, had vanished.

CHAPTER 14

Leo had a moment of blind panic. High above the ground, alone in the green dimness, he felt his knees begin to tremble. The silence of the forest seemed to press in on him. He went on clinging to the trunk of the great tree only by instinct, and when he heard a whispering voice close to his ear he was so shocked that he almost let go.

He gasped and steadied himself, sick and dizzy at the thought of how close he had come to falling.

"Leo!" the voice whispered again.

The sound was coming from the clump of feathery ferns growing on the tree trunk. Leo leaned cautiously toward the clump, and peered into it. He saw Mimi's face, just her face, floating deep among the ferns.

It was a weird, unsettling sight. Like something you'd see in a dream, Leo thought, and for an instant he wondered wildly if he *was* dreaming.

Then Mimi's hands appeared, pushing the fern fronds farther apart, and Leo saw her neck, shoulders, and arms. The ferns masked a large hole in the tree's trunk. The tree was hollow here, and Mimi was standing inside the hollow, looking out at him.

"Quickly, Leo!" Mimi whispered impatiently. "Don't just stand there! Come in!"

Before Leo could snap back at her she disappeared inside the hole again. Swallowing his irritation, Leo considered how best to follow her.

He edged a little sideways, so that the hole was directly in front of him. Then he took a deep breath, shut his eyes, forced his aching hands to relax their grip on the tree trunk, and launched himself forward.

For one awful moment he thought he wouldn't make it. The hole was smaller than he'd imagined and while his head went through easily, his shoulders stuck.

It was so dark inside the tree hollow that he couldn't see a thing. The air was warm and heavy with the scent of wood and crushed leaves. He felt Mimi pulling on the collar of his jacket, heard her shouting at him. He stretched his neck forward and wriggled desperately, his toes drumming on the tree branch behind him. And suddenly his shoulders slipped through the gap, and he was in.

The fall was short, and the base of the hollow was thickly padded with dry ferns, so he came to no harm. He sat up, panting and blinking in the dimness, as Mimi crouched beside him.

"The fungus ladder's gone," he gasped.

"Oh, it'll come back when it's safe for us to leave," she said confidently. "The Flitters can obviously make it appear whenever they want to."

"Maybe," Leo said grimly. "But what if they *don't* want to? What if they want to keep us here?"

"Don't be ridiculous!" hissed Mimi, glancing quickly around as if she was afraid they'd be overheard.

As Leo's eyes slowly adjusted to the dim light, he saw that the hollow was far bigger than he'd realized. It was like a round room with a very high ceiling — like a room in a lighthouse, or a castle tower.

The walls were thickly covered with what looked like little green cocoons. Then Leo saw that the cocoons were actually tiny, woven hammocks.

Many of the Flitters were already sitting on their hammocks in pairs, swinging their legs and picking seeds and specks of dirt from one another's topknots. Some were still fluttering around, making circles in the air or zooming up to the top of the hollow and down again, apparently just for fun.

"Isn't it — fantastic?" Mimi whispered.

Leo moved restlessly, the dry ferns crackling beneath him. There was a strange ringing in his ears. He felt stunned — as if he'd been hit on the head and couldn't quite get his senses back. He disliked the feeling intensely.

"Listen, Mimi," he said abruptly, "you might be able to just accept this stuff that's been happening to us, but I can't. I'm going to go crazy if I can't get at least some idea of the reasons behind all this."

The smile disappeared from Mimi's face as instantly as if it had been wiped away with a wet cloth.

"You know why we're here, Leo," she said tightly. "I wound the music box too many times. It's all my fault. Simple."

"No, no, no!" Leo exclaimed, shaking his head and clenching his fists. "That's not what I mean! Look, forget about being prickly for just one minute, will you? Listen to me!"

He glared at her. She raised her eyebrows in the haughty, superior way he loathed. He controlled his anger and took a deep breath.

"Mimi, maybe you're the reason this whole thing started," he said, forcing himself to speak in a level voice. "But that's not what I'm talking about. I'm interested in things that have happened since. Like, why did the Blue Queen want us to go with her? Why did she take Mutt? Why did Spoiler try to grab us? Why did Conker —?"

"Oh, *that*!" Mimi broke in harshly. She had become very pale. Her eyes looked huge. "Well, the only thing I can think of is that maybe the Blue Queen *needs* us — needs people from our world, anyway."

"What for?" Leo demanded.

"To make herself more alive?" said Mimi, and shrugged as Leo's jaw dropped. "After all, she was the only person to come out of the box. She might be the only one with the strength to do it. She might be some sort of vampire, who drains the life force from people of our world to give more life to herself."

Leo couldn't think of a thing to say. He couldn't even close his mouth.

"She tried to get us," Mimi went on, turning even paler, if that were possible, "and when she couldn't, she took Mutt instead."

Leo's first thought was that Mutt was so tiny that his life force wouldn't be worth much. Then he remembered the little dog's furious reaction to Einstein, and changed his mind. Mutt was small, but he certainly had plenty of determination.

"We've got to get to the castle and save him," Mimi whispered. "We've got to. I can't bear it otherwise."

Leo saw that her eyes were shining with tears, and immediately felt mean for making jokes about Mutt, even in his own mind. However unlikable Mutt was, why should he be drained of life just to make the Blue Queen stronger than she was already?

Drained of life . . . Leo felt cold. And with the cold came a bleak awareness of just how desperate Mimi and his situation was. Here they were, in the middle of a forest, high in a tree around which tigers prowled. They were depending for escape on a bunch of fairies whose language they couldn't speak and whose friendship was still, in Leo's opinion, in question. They didn't know which way to go to save themselves. They had no weapons, no food . . .

"What's happening?" Mimi interrupted, stiffening.

And at the same moment Leo realized that the ringing in his ears had suddenly grown louder, and had separated into words. At last, he was hearing the voices of the Flitters.

Danger! Danger! Danger!

The Flitters were all swarming upward. In an instant, the hammocks were empty, and the roof of the hollow was a moving mass of green. All peace and comfort had disappeared, and a terrible fear filled the air.

Almost at once, the reason became clear. A sound drifted

through the hole in the tree trunk — the distant sound of raised voices.

"Someone's come into the clearing," Leo whispered, jumping up.

Dead ferns crackling and snapping under his feet, he moved close to the hole through which he and Mimi had slid just minutes before. As Mimi hurried to his side, he stood on his toes, parted the fern fronds cautiously, and tried to peer out.

He could see nothing but ferns, leaves, and dimness. But he could hear. He screwed his eyes shut, listening intently to the sounds floating up from the ground.

"There!" a woman's voice said huskily. "I knew how it was! The Flitters heard us. They fled, and the Langlanders went with them. See? Langlander tracks go right to the Nesting Tree before moving on again. Who knows where the two are now!"

Leo and Mimi exchanged silent glances, both remembering how Leo had run to the edge of the clearing and back before the fungus had appeared and they'd begun to climb the tree. *I laid a false trail by sheer luck*, Leo thought gratefully.

"It's not my fault, Tye," the woman's companion grumbled. With a chill, Leo recognized Conker's voice.

A fresh wave of terror swept over him from above. He looked up. The Flitters were swirling in agitation.

Danger! Danger! Danger!

The voices chimed in Leo's mind like tiny, frantic bells. And his last flicker of hope that there had been some sort of terrible mistake, and that Conker was after all a friend and not a deadly enemy, went out.

"Tye was the person Conker wrote to about us," Mimi hissed.

Leo nodded grimly. *Take this to Tye in Flitter Wood*, Conker had said, when he gave the messenger mouse his note. Right under their noses he'd sent out the news that he'd made contact with them and gained their trust.

Flitter Wood, Leo thought. *Of course! That's why the word Flitters rang a bell in my mind. Why didn't I remember before? Not that it would have done us any good if I had.*

"Whose fault is it then?" exclaimed the woman called Tye. "Of all the foolish, inefficient —"

"I thought they trusted me!" Conker protested in injured tones. "And anyhow, I thought you'd be waiting for them. I thought *you'd* deal with them. I had to send them on their own. I didn't have any choice. I told you! Someone came up the stairs and nearly caught us pushing them through the door."

"Who was it?" Tye snapped.

"Pop, the balloon seller," Conker said. "He lost his balloons in the quake. The whole bunch drifted off and ended up caught on the weather vane on the roof of the Black Sheep. Pop got Jolly's permission to climb out onto the roof from the first-floor window, to try to get them. He turned up right at the wrong moment for us."

Tye made a disgusted sound.

"It's just lucky Pop's a bit nearsighted," Conker went on. "He saw us, but he didn't see what we were doing. We got the door shut just in time."

"This talk is pointless," Tye growled. "The damage is done. We will search the forest till the light fails. If we cannot secure the Langlanders by then we will have to go and explain what has happened."

"We don't have to explain in person," Conker said nervously. "We could just send a mouse."

"Have you lost your senses?" spat Tye. "Send a *messenger*? When he was depending on you? He is angry and desperate enough as it is about his own failure to contain the Langlanders. No. We must see him, so he can decide what is to be done next."

Again Mimi and Leo exchanged glances.

"Spoiler," Leo breathed, his skin prickling. "They're working for —"

He broke off as the sound of low, harsh muttering rose from the clearing. Leo strained his ears, but couldn't make out the words. The Flitters' terror was beating down on him like a stinging wind.

"The Flitters might indeed know where they went," Tye said, obviously in answer to some comment or question. "But they are hardly going to come out and inform us, are they?"

The muttering began again.

"Good idea," Conker said heartily. "Go for it!"

There was a sighing, rustling sound above Leo's head. He looked up quickly. The Flitters were shrinking even farther toward the top of the hollow, crowding closely together, their green wings fluttering rapidly, their tiny faces filled with terror.

"Get back," he gasped, pulling Mimi away from the hole.

There was a flapping sound from outside. Something slapped on the broad tree branch. The ferns that masked the entrance to the hollow began to thrash as they were pushed roughly aside.

And the next moment, a dark, narrow head poked through the hole, and glittering, masked eyes were staring straight at Mimi and Leo.

It was Freda the duck.

"Aha!" she quacked, and snapped her beak.

Leo and Mimi stumbled backward till they were pressed against the far wall of the hollow and could go no farther.

Danger! Danger!

Freda turned her head. "They're here!" she shouted. "Both of them!"

"How did they get up there?" Conker's amazed voice floated up from the clearing below.

"We will have to find out, later," Tye said shortly. "For now, the important thing is to get them into our hands. If they are not secured, the consequences might be —"

"Go away!" Mimi shouted passionately. "Leave us alone!"

The duck snapped her beak again. "Out," she ordered Mimi and Leo, jerking her head.

"No!" Mimi said defiantly. "We won't come out, and you can't make us!"

"There's no safe way down from here," Leo added, trying to sound very calm and firm. "And even if there were, we want to stay. We certainly don't want to go anywhere with you and your friends."

Freda's eyes narrowed till they were fierce black slits. "Come out," she said distinctly, "or I will come in."

No! No! No! The Flitters' cries of terror crashed down on Leo and Mimi in a mighty wave, almost making them sag at the knees.

Frightening pictures began flickering in front of Leo's eyes like images on a screen. A huge masked figure raging through a mass of ferns, wings half spread, snapping, biting, crushing. Flitters taken by surprise, scattering in panic, desperate to escape . . .

He knew he was seeing the fearful memories of the Flitters. He gazed at Freda in horror. How could he ever have thought she was harmless? To the Flitters she was a giant, a monster more fearful than any wolf or tiger. And here she was, at the very entrance of their refuge.

"Ah yes, the Flitters know me," said the duck menacingly. "They know what I am, and what I can do. They have met me before. If you value their lives you will do as I say!"

Leo turned, and his eyes met Mimi's. He could see that she, too, had seen and felt the Flitters' terrible memories.

"We'll have to go," Mimi said, her lips hardly moving. "We can't make them suffer because of us."

"Quite right!" sneered the duck.

No! No! the voices of the Flitters chimed in Leo's mind. *No, friends, do not go for our sake!*

But Leo knew they had no choice. Almost without thinking he took Mimi's hand. Together they began to move toward the hollow's entrance. Freda's eyes glinted triumphantly.

No! No! Fly away with us! Fly away! Here! Look here!

A clump of dead ferns fell softly onto the base of the hollow. A column of light streamed suddenly from somewhere near the roof. Leo and Mimi looked up, startled.

Come with us!

High above them, another hole had miraculously appeared in the trunk of the tree. Flitters were zooming through it, out into the open air.

Come with us!

An emergency exit at the top of the hollow, Leo thought in confusion. *It was hidden by a mass of dead ferns, but it was there. So the Flitters can escape! But we can't. We can't get up there. To get up there, we'd have to . . . to . . .*

Fly! Fly!

The duck quacked angrily from the hollow entrance. She had seen the Flitters escaping. She pressed forward, pushing at the ferns that fringed the mouth of the hole. Soon she would be inside.

Come with us, friends! Save yourselves. Fly! Fly!

Afterward, Leo couldn't remember whether it was he or Mimi who had first sprung upward in answer to that call. Their hands were linked, so it could have been either of them.

Whoever was responsible, the fact remained that the next instant, as Freda struggled through the entrance hole, quacking with rage, they both rose from the base of the hollow and soared upward to join the Flitters.

Once they were part of that swirling green cloud there was no turning back. Before they had time to speak, or even to think, they were rising out of the hole that was the Flitters' emergency exit and speeding away through the trees.

They were flying — gliding effortlessly in the center of a long green cloud that snaked through the maze of leaves and branches high above the forest floor. Cool wind beat against their faces. Behind them they could hear the shouts of Conker and Tye, the enraged quacks of the baffled duck.

Then the shouts died away and they could only hear the rustling of leaves, the calls of birds, and the fluttering of a thousand tiny wings.

The cries of the Flitters were ringing in their minds. At first there was joyful relief in the cries. Then there was glee, because the invading monster could not easily give chase through the tree maze. Then came a terrible sadness, because the ancient Nesting Tree had been abandoned, left for the invader to despoil.

The grief was terrible. Leo couldn't bear it.

"You had to leave, to save yourselves," he found himself calling against the wind. "But you can go back very soon. They're only interested in us. They'll leave the tree now, to come after us."

Yes, they are following as best they can, the Flitters sighed. *But the Nesting Tree is tainted now. The invader has spoiled its peace. We cannot return to it.*

"Yes, you can!" Mimi shouted, almost angrily. "If you don't claim your home back, you let them win! And hasn't the Nesting Tree sheltered you for all these years? It doesn't deserve to be left empty and alone."

There was a moment's silence. Then . . .

Perhaps . . . we will try.

There was a trace of hope in the sighing sound. *They'll go back,* Leo thought. *They'll go back, clean up, and settle down again.*

Resentment mingled with his relief. He'd talked perfect sense to the Flitters and it hadn't made a scrap of difference. Then Mimi had talked a load of garbage about trees having feelings and, lo and behold, the Flitters had listened.

"Logic doesn't always work when you're feeling bad," Mimi murmured, as if she'd read his mind.

Leo didn't answer.

The Flitters began to slow down, drifting lower and lower so that soon they were threading their way through a maze of tree trunks, and the tips of the tallest ferns were brushing Mimi's and Leo's feet. High above them stretched the green canopy of the treetops, blocking out the sky.

We are nearing the edge of our territory. The sound chimed softly at the edges of Leo's mind. *We cannot go beyond the ferns. You must fly on alone.*

Leo felt a stab of panic. Fly on alone? How could they do that without the Flitters' magic to hold them up? And which way should they go, anyway? The Flitter flight had turned and twisted so often that he'd lost all sense of direction. For all he knew they'd been flying in circles.

If only I could see the sun, he thought desperately.

That way, chimed the Flitters, pointing straight ahead. *Fly that way and you will find the sun. Farewell! Be safe! Farewell!*

With that they fell from the air, drifting down like a shower of lacy leaves, settling into the thick ferns and disappearing from view.

Alone with Mimi, stranded in the empty air, Leo hesitated, wobbling dangerously. Mimi tugged his hand, but all he could think was that he was going to fall.

Why do you wait? the Flitters called from below them, a trace of panic sharpening their tiny voices.

"Leo, stop thinking!" Mimi muttered through clenched teeth. "If we fall now we'll crush hundreds of them. We've got to keep going! Just tell yourself —"

"I can't!" Leo gabbled. "We can't fly alone. We can't —"

Fly on! Fly on!

"They say we can and so we can," Mimi snapped. "They must mean they'll help us." She tightened her grip on Leo's hand and shot forward, hauling him after her.

They flew awkwardly, losing height. Flitters sprang out of the way as the toes of their shoes trailed heavily through the ferns. They fumbled their way around one tree, then another and another. Already the Flitters' voices were chiming more softly in their minds.

Fly on! Be safe! Farewell!

The trees were thinning. The ferns became fewer every moment, shrinking to mere clusters in the deepest shade. Then, suddenly, the ferns were gone altogether. Sunlight had begun filtering through the canopy, making golden pools on the forest floor. Grass appeared, dotted with nodding flowers. Blue butterflies fluttered about.

And the voices of the Flitters were faint, so faint . . .

Through a gap in the trees ahead, Leo saw open ground. "We've reached the edge of the forest," he called excitedly.

The next moment they had sailed through the gap. The light changed abruptly from green to gold. Sun warmed their faces as they soared across a flower-filled ditch and a bare brown road.

Leo found it a huge relief to move out from under the trees at last, to see wide sky above him and land stretching ahead. It was like throwing off a heavy, shrouding cloak that he hadn't realized he was wearing. All at once he seemed to be able to breathe more freely and think more clearly, too.

Mimi obviously felt differently. "There's nowhere to hide out here," she called, and glanced longingly back at the green shade they'd left behind.

Before they could gather their wits enough to turn, they'd skimmed over a white-painted fence that was leaning over drunkenly, almost touching the road. Then the lush grass of a field was below them, and a rambling farmhouse, an apple orchard, a red-roofed barn, a windmill and several neat haystacks were ahead.

"I know this place!" Leo exclaimed. "I've seen it on the music box."

And just then, he realized that he couldn't hear the Flitters' voices anymore.

Well, that's it, he thought, bracing himself. *We're really on our own now. Any minute . . .*

His feet hit the ground with a shuddering jolt. Mimi's high scream echoed in his ears as he lurched forward and fell, dragging her down with him.

They came to rest, shocked and panting, beside a large pile of straw. The red-roofed barn loomed above them, the windmill creaked nearby, and somewhere a rooster crowed dismally.

"Leo, why did you do that?" shouted Mimi, staggering to her feet. "Why did you drag us down? We were going fine! We could have turned around and flown all the way to —"

"No, we couldn't," Leo shouted back. "The Flitters are too far back to help us anymore. And we *weren't* going fine! We were losing height every minute, and —"

"Only because you were practically a dead weight!" Mimi raged, stamping her foot. "If it hadn't been for me, you'd have dropped like a stone and broken your neck. You'd be lying dead in the forest right now, with tigers chewing on your bones. I told you to stop thinking! I told you! But oh, no!"

"I *can't* stop thinking!" Leo yelled, jumping up. "And it's lucky for you I can't! Where would you be now if it wasn't for me? With Spoiler in the Blue Queen's castle, that's where you'd be! In chains in a dungeon or something waiting to be sucked dry!"

Mimi's lips suddenly twitched. "Hanging upside down by my ankles?" she suggested dryly, looking at him sideways. "With savage rats nibbling at my fingernails?"

Leo's own lips twitched. He couldn't help it. "Dots, more like it," he said. "Thousands of savage dots."

Mimi nodded solemnly. "Sounds bad," she said.

"Lying dead in the forest being eaten by tigers doesn't sound too good, either," said Leo. "So — we'd better stay together. It looks like we need each other. You've got straw in your hair, by the way."

"So do you," Mimi said.

"Ahem!"

The cough had come from right behind them. They whirled around . . .

And met the small, angry eyes of a huge pink pig in a flower-laden hat.

CHAPTER 16

"And what are *you* doing here, may I ask?" the pig said grandly, tossing back the ribbons of her hat.

Staring at her, astounded, two plans popped into Leo's mind at once. The first, and simplest, was to run. He considered this briefly, and discarded it. Even if he could outrun an angry pig, it was unlikely that Mimi could.

That left the second plan. He hoped it would work.

"This farm is *private property*. You flew in without invitation. Therefore, you are *trespassers!*" said the pig. She frowned ferociously and pawed the ground.

"We didn't mean to fly in here," Mimi began angrily. "It was a mistake. You don't have to be so —" She broke off with a squeak as Leo nudged her violently.

"I shall now call my employer, Farmer Jack Macdonald, and he will *deal* with you!" said the pig. She took a deep breath and opened her mouth to yell.

Leo quickly stepped forward. "Lady Bertha," he said respectfully, bowing low.

Mimi gaped at him.

The pig closed her mouth, drew back a little, and fluttered her eyelashes. "Oh, you recognize me!" she simpered, glancing at her reflection in the large water trough that stood beside her and adjusting her ribbons self-consciously. "Lawks-a-daisy, how *very* embarrassing! I'm not all *that* famous!"

"How could I fail to recognize you?" Leo asked, with perfect truth since Bertha's hat, and Bertha herself, had been indelibly imprinted on his memory in the first-floor hallway of the Black Sheep.

"Oh," tittered Bertha, blushing deeply. "So — you've seen my pictures, I gather? Do you go to the art gallery often?"

"Oh, no — not really," stammered Leo, deciding that it wasn't up to him to explain to Bertha that not a single one of Jolly's portraits of her had been accepted by Monsieur Rouge-et-Noir. "Actually, I saw some paintings of you at the Black Sheep. We've just come from there, as a matter of fact."

"*Have* you!" exclaimed Bertha with great interest. "Then you know my artist, Jolly! I suppose *he* told you where I lived, the naughty boy! So — you liked my paintings and you wanted to see me in person?" She cast down her eyelids demurely.

"Oh, yes," said Leo fervently. "I knew that paintings could only be — um — pale reflections of your — your beauty. I couldn't wait to meet you!"

This was *not* the truth, but it had a very good effect on Bertha, who by now was almost wriggling with pleasure.

"Leo!" Mimi muttered in disgust. "How *can* you —"

"Unfortunately," said Leo, raising his voice, "we were so excited to see you that we intruded on your privacy. When you tell Farmer Macdonald, he'll probably call the police and have us taken straight to jail."

Mimi's indignant protests died in her throat. If Bertha told Farmer Macdonald they were here . . . if Macdonald told Officer Begood . . . Before they knew it they would be back in town, not only in deep trouble, but as far away from saving Mutt as ever.

She clasped her hands nervously, quite accidentally looking exactly like an anxious fan.

Bertha nodded to her graciously. "Don't blame yourself too much, dear," she said. "We all make mistakes. But I'm sure you understand that I can't overlook this. I have my job to do."

"Of course," Leo said, bowing his head. "But before you give us up to the law . . . could we have your autograph?"

"My *autograph*?" Bertha breathed, clearly thrilled. "Why, of course! It's the *least* I can do when you've come so far."

She wagged her head this way and that, tossing her ribbons in confusion. "But I don't think I have a pen," she murmured. "I mean, I usually carry a pen for autographs, naturally, but I just can't find it at the moment. Silly me!"

"Oh," said Leo, looking disappointed. "I don't have a pen, either. What a shame. Look, you wait here, and we'll run and get one."

Bertha frowned in thought. Leo held his breath.

"Hoy! Bertha!" roared a voice from behind the barn. "Where are you?"

Bertha jumped guiltily and looked over her shoulder. "It's Farmer Macdonald," she whispered rapidly. "Quick! Get under that pile of straw. We'll talk about the autograph after he's gone. He's — well, I'm afraid he doesn't understand the pressures of being a star."

Leo and Mimi dived into the straw, wriggling into it until they were well covered. The straw was prickly and smelled strongly of pig.

"Here I am, Farmer M," Bertha called in a lilting voice. "Here, by the water trough."

"Admiring yourself as usual, I suppose," shouted the farmer, who seemed to be in a very bad mood. "Primping and preening. Ah, I never should have let Jolly paint you. Ruined you, he has!"

Leo and Mimi heard the sound of heavy footsteps approaching and shrank farther into the straw.

"I was *not* primping and preening, for your information," Bertha said haughtily. "As a matter of fact, I was —"

Leo held his breath. Bertha was going to give them away, he knew it. Cautiously he moved a little of the straw aside. He had to see what was going on.

Bertha was looking very ruffled. Her hat was slightly askew and a red poppy was nodding over her left eye. All Leo could see of Farmer Macdonald was a large pair of mud-spattered black boots.

"Call yourself a watch-pig!" the owner of the boots roared. "The barn's crawling with dots! They got through that broken window. They've made off with two bags of wheat, a churn of milk, and a dozen eggs already. The rooster's exhausted himself trying to catch them. Now he's lying down with his feet in the air, dots are running all over him, and the hens are having hysterics!"

The black boots stamped the ground furiously.

"As if I haven't got enough on my hands with all this quake damage to see to!" the angry voice raged on. "Fences down! Windows broken! The wife's prize garden ruined! A whole batch of cider spilled and my brother screaming for more supplies in town! Dots stealing everything that isn't nailed down! And where are you? Staring at your reflection in the water trough! Bah!"

Bertha tossed back her ribbons. "I was *not* employed to chase *dots*!" she said disdainfully. "I was employed to protect the farm from *wolves*. My extensive experience —"

"Dots to your experience!" shouted the farmer rudely. "You get in there and clear out those pests, you fat, conceited lump, or I'll find a pig who can and send you packing!"

"Yoo-hoo! Jack!" a woman shrieked from the direction of the farmhouse. "*Another* mouse has come from Jolly. It's waiting for a reply. What should I say?"

The farmer swore violently. "Coming, Mary!" he yelled. The boots turned and stomped away.

"How *dare* you!" squealed Bertha as the sound of footsteps faded.

Leo and Mimi crawled out of the straw. Bertha swung around to face them, her small blue eyes filled with furious tears.

"Did you hear that?" she demanded in a choked voice. "Did you *hear* what he said to me?"

"He was only —" Mimi began.

"He wasn't very understanding," Leo said quickly, drowning her out.

"He's — a brute!" sobbed Bertha. "After all I've done for him! Why, I've made his farm *famous*! Of all the ungrateful, insensitive . . ." She broke off with a wail, and turned to gulp some water from the trough.

When she turned around again, she seemed to have herself more under control. She gave a huge sniff and pushed the red poppy out of her eye with a trotter that trembled only slightly.

"Well, that's the end," she said. "He's gone too far this time. Come on!"

She set off rapidly across the field, heading for the road that ran beside the forest. Leo and Mimi hurried after her, continually glancing over their shoulders in case Farmer Macdonald reappeared.

"Where are you going, Bertha?" Mimi panted, as they reached the half-collapsed fence.

"I'm leaving!" snapped Bertha, casually putting her shoulder to the fence and pushing it over completely. "I'm not staying here to be insulted."

She stormed out onto the road, trampling the fence flat and kicking aside a cracked sign that read BEWARE OF THE PIG.

"I'm going to town, where I'm appreciated and where my talent can flower!" she declared. "I'll go straight to Jolly. He'll be *furious* when he hears how his brother has treated me."

Leo thought rapidly. He remembered the forest side of the music box well enough to know that Bertha would have to turn right if she was going to walk to the town. He instantly decided that he and Mimi would turn left. Mimi certainly wouldn't object. Leo was sure that she didn't want to stay in Bertha's company any more than he did, and if they turned left they would be heading directly for the Blue Queen's domain.

That was unfortunate, but he told himself it didn't really matter. The Blue Queen's castle was faraway, and surely he'd be able to convince Mimi to give up and take them both home long before they got there.

"We go left," he murmured. Mimi nodded eagerly.

Before they could say anything to Bertha, however, she turned left herself and began trotting briskly toward the distant hills. Wondering what she was doing, they hurried after her.

"It's just lucky that as well as being a famous artist, Jolly also owns the Black Sheep," Bertha called back to them over her shoulder. "He'll be only too pleased to give me food and lodging in return for free modeling. It'll be just till I'm on my feet, of course. Then I'll get a little place of my own. Somewhere near the art gallery, perhaps. I'm very well-known there."

"Bertha," Leo began, running to catch up with her, "are you sure —?"

"I've never been so sure of anything in my life!" Bertha snapped, shooting a cross look in his direction. "I'm going to town, and that's all there is to it!"

"But you're going the wrong way," panted Mimi, who was having trouble keeping up.

Bertha stopped short. "No, I'm not!" she exclaimed. "Jolly *always* comes from this direction when he visits me." She frowned. "And you must have come the same way yourselves, if you came from the tavern," she added suspiciously. "Weren't you telling the truth about that?"

"Of course we were," Leo said quickly. "But we came — um — out of the forest."

"Well, of course you did!" said Bertha impatiently. "Jolly's Gap ends in Flitter Wood, doesn't it? But Jolly always moves onto the road as soon as he can. He's not keen on traveling through the forest. There are some very strange people in there, you know. And tigers. And bears. Not to mention the wolves, of course."

She pushed the red poppy out of her eye and started walking again. "It's *such* a pity Jolly's Gap ends there," she added, as Mimi and Leo hurried after her. "But, as Jolly says, it's *very* convenient to have your own, personal Gap, wherever it ends up. He always keeps the door locked, of course. Only three or four wolves and one small bear have ever got through to the Black Sheep since he's owned it. And the tigers don't really bother."

She sighed. "I daresay I'll have to knock for *ages* before Jolly hears me and lets me in. My nails will be *ruined*!"

"Oh!" Leo gasped, suddenly understanding. "The Gap! The misty tunnel in the tavern broom closet! You mean — Jolly uses it when he comes to paint you?"

"Well, of course!" said Bertha, blinking at him in surprise. "He'd hardly travel overland, would he? It would take days and days! He gets all his supplies from the farm through the Gap, too. It's *awfully* handy for him."

"Yes, it would be," murmured Leo.

"Of course, he usually keeps *very* quiet about it," Bertha went on. "He wouldn't want just *anyone* using it — turning his first floor into a bus station, as he puts it. Candy wrappers on the floor, and marks on the walls, and so on." She wrinkled her nose fastidiously. "And if someone got eaten in the forest, well, Jolly might be held responsible, mightn't he? But obviously he felt he could trust *you*, being such huge fans of mine."

"Oh — yes!" chorused Leo and Mimi weakly.

As Bertha set off again they hurried after her, darting looks at each other, their eyes full of unspoken questions.

How had Conker found out about Jolly's Gap? By accident, during a dot hunt? Or had Jolly told Conker about it, maybe when he needed help carrying a load of cider or potatoes from the farm down to the storeroom? Did Jolly have any idea that Conker was in league with Spoiler, and was using the Gap for evil purposes of his own?

And what *was* the Gap, anyway? From what Bertha had said, it sounded as if it wasn't the only one of its kind in this strange world.

Soon the white fences of Macdonald's farm were behind them. The forest loomed beside them, dark, secret, and forbidding.

Leo found himself becoming increasingly nervous. Every

minute he expected Conker, Freda, and the mysterious woman called Tye to jump out at them from the whispering darkness.

Think about something else, he told himself. *Do something useful, like working out where we are.*

He tried to remember the details of the picture on the side of the music box. He had a feeling that there was a village somewhere ahead — a small place, bright with sunflowers.

If I'm right, it'll be on the left, he thought. We should get to it soon. And suddenly he thought of the music box sitting on his desk in his room. If someone looked at it now they would see three tiny figures on the forest road — a boy, a girl, and a pink pig wearing a hat.

Not long afterward, just past a bend in the road, they came to the village. It wasn't at all what Leo had expected. Grass and berry bushes grew among the burned-out ruins of houses and sheds. Dots skittered furtively in the abandoned vegetable gardens where towering sunflowers grew wild.

"I remember this place," Mimi murmured in Leo's ear. "I remember the sunflowers. But I've never looked at it closely. I didn't realize it was a ruin."

"Me neither," Leo whispered back. He raised his voice. "I wonder what happened here, Bertha?"

"Oh, it probably happened in the Dark Time," Bertha said carelessly. "Strange that the people didn't come back and rebuild their houses, but there you are. Sometimes it's just too much trouble — as I know only too well myself."

She moved across the road to where a path marked with wagon tracks wound away into the forest. "Is this where we turn off for the Gap?" she asked.

"Ah —" said Leo. "Well, I'm not really sure. We . . ." He debated how much to tell Bertha, and decided to keep it simple. "We got lost in the forest," he went on. "So we don't know exactly where the Gap is anymore."

"*What?*" screeched Bertha, stopping so abruptly that her trotters dug deeply into the dirt of the road. "You don't *know*? But — but that was the whole idea! You were going to lead me to the Gap! Oh, I can't believe this!"

"We never said we knew where the Gap was!" Mimi broke in crossly. "We never promised to lead you anywhere! You can't blame us!"

Bertha's eyes narrowed. "I certainly *can* blame you!" she squealed, her voice rising alarmingly. "You tricked me!"

She was panting with rage. *Any moment she's going to yell for help, and Conker and Tye will hear her for sure,* Leo thought. Frantically he flapped his hand at Mimi to warn her not to say anything else.

"You — you vipers!" wailed Bertha. "I've worn my trotters to the bone walking along this horrible, dusty road because I thought I could trust you! And now —"

"Wait!" Leo said quickly. "We're a bit — confused, that's all. Look, this probably *is* the path to the Gap. It looks as though it's used quite often. Let's try it, anyway. We've got nothing to lose."

"How do you know?" Mimi muttered darkly. "What if Conker, and that Tye person, and that crazy duck are in there, waiting for us?"

But Bertha had already snorted and lumbered onto the path. Helplessly, not knowing what else to do to avoid a scene, they followed.

CHAPTER 17

The path through the forest was broad, and very winding. Tall trees rose on either side of it, their leaves whispering softly in the breeze. Flowers and blue butterflies made bright splashes of color beneath the trees, birds sang, and there was the gurgling, rippling sound of running water. Leo could hear a faint tapping noise, too, as if somewhere nearby a large bird was pecking at a tree trunk, looking for grubs.

Bertha stomped along, fuming. Leo and Mimi crept cautiously behind her, their eyes darting everywhere.

"There aren't many ferns around," Mimi murmured to Leo after they'd been walking for a few minutes. "And the stream doesn't sound the same as it did in Flitter Wood — it sounds as if the water's deeper here. I don't think this is the right path."

Leo couldn't hear any difference in the sound of the stream. But it seemed to him that the tapping noise was a little louder, and he could suddenly smell something that made his nose twitch. There was a faint trace of smoke in the air.

"Maybe we'd better turn back," he said uneasily. Smoke meant people — maybe the very people they wanted to avoid.

At that moment, Bertha rounded a bend and stopped. Snorting in disgust, she sat down heavily in the middle of the track.

"This isn't right," she said, as Leo and Mimi caught up with her. "It's a dead end!"

Sure enough, not far ahead, the path ended at a smooth green clearing in which stood a small cottage with a thatched roof. A thin trail of smoke drifted from the cottage's chimney. Red roses twined around its green-painted door.

Leo stared, a cold trickle of dread running down his spine.

He knew this place.

Like someone who was sleepwalking, he began to move toward the clearing. With every step, a hand seemed to squeeze harder on his heart.

The scene in the clearing had changed since he'd gazed at it through his magnifying glass. Petals had fallen from the roses to lie like spatters of bright blood on the ground. The grass at the side of the house was deeply scored with the marks of running feet, and covered with leaves and twigs. The tartan rug lay in a crumpled heap beneath the old apple tree.

And there was no one to be seen. No smiling mother. No laughing father. No baby.

No baby . . .

Leo's mouth went dry. His eyes moved to the bushes that edged the clearing. It seemed so long ago that he'd seen the shaggy body of the wolf crouching there, perfectly camouflaged in the shadows.

But it wasn't long ago at all, really. It was just that so much had happened to him since he'd seen the wolf's hungry yellow eyes, and the glint of its white fangs. He shivered.

Nothing might have happened, he told himself. *And even if it has, I couldn't have done anything to stop it.*

Then a horrible thought came to him. Not long after he'd seen the wolf, he'd arrived in Rondo. He could have sent a mouse to this cottage, with a message. He could have asked Conker to do it. Conker couldn't have refused.

But he'd forgotten all about the baby and the wolf. Too busy with his own troubles, he'd completely forgotten . . .

"Where are you going?" Bertha called shrilly after him. "Come back at once! I *insist* you take me to the Gap, as you promised! Right *now!*"

Leo clenched his fists. *Don't lose your temper*, he told himself. *Don't take your feelings out on Bertha. It's not her fault. She doesn't know . . .*

Mimi ran up behind him, and started tugging at his arm. "Come on, Leo!" she said impatiently. "We've got to go back to the road. We're wasting time. And Bertha's getting really mad. She'll start yelling soon."

Leo hesitated, wetting his lips. He couldn't bring himself to talk about the wolf.

"The people in that house might know where the Gap is," he heard himself saying. "I'll go and ask them."

I have to know. I have to know if . . .

He shook off Mimi's hand and began walking again. He heard her run back to Bertha to explain, and Bertha groaning and complaining in response.

His heart was in his mouth as he reached the end of the path and stepped onto the grass at the edge of the clearing. He jumped as the tapping noise came again from somewhere near. Then, as he could still see no sign of movement, he tiptoed forward.

He crept around to the side of the cottage, screwing up his courage to call out. He rounded the corner, and got a clear view of the apple tree for the first time.

Something was hanging from the tree's lowest branch. As Leo moved closer, he realized that it was a large basket. And inside the basket, wrapped in a furry gray rug, was the baby, fast asleep.

Dizzy with relief, Leo drew a deep, trembling breath.

The cradle swayed gently as the old tree's branches stirred in the breeze. The baby slept peacefully on.

It's all right, Leo told himself, turning away, hardly able to believe it. *The fallen rose petals, the marks on the grass, are just quake damage. It's all —*

Then, out of the corner of his eye, he caught a flicker of movement. He spun around, saw a blur of gray, saw snarling jaws and burning yellow eyes — saw the wolf, huge and shaggy, burst out of cover at the edge of the clearing and leap for the apple tree.

Without a thought, Leo threw himself at the cradle, wrapping his arms around it, covering the baby with his own body. There was no time for anything else. No time to snatch the baby up and run. The wolf was already upon them.

The beast's ferocious snarls filled his ears. Its hot, panting breath was searing the back of his neck. He yelled in terror. The baby moved and wailed beneath him. Someone was screaming. A man was shouting . . .

Then there was the sound of thundering feet, a harsh, blood-curdling squeal, a tremendous thump, and a high, wailing yelp.

And the snarling, the hot breath . . . the wolf itself . . . were gone.

Dazed, Leo looked up. The first thing he saw was the woodcutter, familiar in his red-checked shirt and padded vest, running from behind the cottage with a hammer in his hand.

Then he saw the wolf. It was writhing on the grass. Above it loomed a huge pink figure — Bertha, transformed, her flowered hat hanging disregarded behind her ears, her tiny eyes flashing, her blunt teeth bared. As Leo watched, astounded, Bertha lunged forward, butting the fallen wolf savagely, trying to trample it. The wolf howled, scrabbled violently, and at last managed to get to its feet.

It ran for its life, whimpering, its tail between its legs. Bertha pounded after it, squealing savagely. Pale and sweating, the woodcutter ran after them both.

"Rosebud! Oh, Rosebud!" Someone grabbed Leo's shoulders and pulled him away from the cradle. He scrambled aside as the baby's weeping mother snatched up her child and held her close.

"You saved her," the young woman sobbed, her voice half muffled in the baby's fluffy blanket. "Oh, bless you! Oh, how can we ever thank you? I was only away for a minute — just to check on Grandma. The quake upset her so. But I shouldn't have left Rosebud. I shouldn't! She could have — she could have been — Oh, Rosebud!"

"Leo, are you okay?"

Leo looked around blankly and saw that Mimi was beside him, looking up at him with a strange, scared expression on her face. He nodded and wiped the sweat from his forehead with the back of his trembling hand.

"I can't believe you did that," Mimi said in a low voice. "I've never seen anything so incredibly brave."

"I *told* you there was a wolf in the bushes," Leo said. It was all he could think of to say.

At that moment, the woodcutter came crashing back into the clearing, with Bertha trotting behind him.

"Jim!" cried the woman.

"Polly! Is she all right?" the man shouted, running over to his wife and child. Seeing that all was well, he gave a moan of relief and swept them both into his arms.

Bertha strolled up to Mimi and Leo, looking very pleased with herself.

"The beast jumped the stream and got away," she said, yawning. "I doubt it will come back. Wolves who tangle with me usually don't."

"Bertha, you were amazing," Mimi exclaimed. "You and Leo were both —"

Bertha nodded complacently. "I *am* amazing, it's true," she said.

"Could I trouble you to replace my hat? The sun is quite warm, and I have to take care of my complexion, you know."

"What's all this rumpus?" called a quavering voice. "Polly! Jim! Who are all these strangers? I'm waiting for my tea!"

Leo looked around. Standing at the side door of the cottage, leaning heavily on a stick, was a very thin, very old woman in a frilly white cap. A red fox sat beside her on the doorstep, its ears pricked alertly.

"Grandma!" Polly cried, turning tearfully in her husband's arms. "The wolf was here! It tried to —"

"What?" The old woman banged her stick furiously on the doorstep, narrowly missing the tip of the fox's bushy tail. "That beast is skulking around *again*? That's the third time this year! Doesn't it ever give up?"

"We think it has now," laughed Jim, the woodcutter. "Go back to the fire, now, Grandma, and keep warm. We'll come in and tell you all about it."

"Come in? I should think so!" quavered the old woman. "I don't know what you two are thinking of, lollygagging out there with that precious child, and a bunch of strangers, and a *pig*, of all things, while the wolf's on the prowl."

She turned and hobbled rapidly inside.

"The wolf's gone!" Bertha shouted after her, highly insulted. "Thanks to *me*, I might add!"

"Bertha is old Macdonald's watch-pig, Polly," Jim said hastily. "I've seen her often at the farm. We were very lucky that she happened along just at the right moment, weren't we?"

"Oh, yes!" Polly said, smiling anxiously at Bertha. "Please excuse my grandmother. She once had a very bad experience with that wolf."

"Who *hasn't* had bad experiences with wolves?" Bertha demanded huffily. "When I was young — that is, younger than I am now, which is very young *indeed* — a wolf who wanted to eat me actually blew down my house!"

"Blew down your house!" repeated Polly, aghast, glancing over her shoulder at her own cozy little cottage.

"Every last bit of it," said Bertha, obviously pleased at the sensation her story had caused. "That wolf had quite exceptional lungs. I managed to get away from him, but then, well, I had nowhere to live, did I? So I had to go and stay with my older brother."

She sighed. "It was very good of him to have me, and all that, but he's such a stick-in-the-mud that I nearly went out of my mind! Darts *every* Thursday night, without fail. Washing-up done just *so*, after *every single* meal. A huge fuss if there was as much as a snout hair left in the bath . . ."

She closed her eyes, shuddering at the memory. "And then our *other* brother, the middle one, came to live with us, too, and that was the last straw," she said. "He and I had to share a room and his snoring was *indescribable!*"

"Is that why you went to work for Farmer Macdonald?" Mimi asked with interest.

"Certainly," said Bertha, tossing her head. "I did a course in unarmed wolf fighting — graduated third in my class against *very* strong competition, as a matter of fact — and off I went. My older brother said I'd never make it as a watch-pig. He said I was too frivolous. But I proved him wrong, my word I did! Farmer Macdonald thinks the *world* of me."

At the mention of Farmer Macdonald's name, she became rather wistful. "I do — rather — like the farm, you know," she said, her voice trembling slightly. "Macdonald isn't a bad old stick, really, and I don't know what he's going to do without me. Perhaps I was too hasty, running away like that."

"Maybe you were," Leo agreed quickly. "It's a very nice farm. And you had a really responsible job there, too."

Bertha nodded, and flicked back her hat ribbons. "If only Macdonald didn't have this obsession with dots!" she complained. "I really *do* draw the line at chasing dots. They're so *small*. And they won't stand and fight. They run away, and hide, and poke out their tongues at you. Dealing with them is so *degrading*!"

"You should tell Macdonald to get a fox," said Jim. "Foxes are the only thing to keep dots down. Have you noticed any dots around here?"

"Why, no!" Bertha replied. Her eyes brightened. "Is that because —?"

"Because of Rufus, yes," Jim said, jerking his head at the fox. "Dots are dead scared of him. They know he's too smart for them."

Rufus grinned wickedly, his long pink tongue lolling from the side of his mouth.

Bertha's brow wrinkled.

"Not that *you* aren't clever, Bertha," Polly put in hastily. "But you're a wolf fighter, aren't you? You can't be expected to waste time thinking up ways to outwit dots!"

"Quite," said Bertha. Her stomach rumbled loudly. "Pardon," she said, patting it delicately. "Being heroic, and saving babies and so on, always makes me a little peckish." She cast a meaningful glance at the cottage door. "A hot drink wouldn't go astray either," she added.

"Oh, of course!" Polly exclaimed. "You must be starving! And Grandma's waiting, too. Let's go inside straightaway. I'll put on the kettle, and we'll all have tea."

CHAPTER 18

"THE POM-POM POLKA"

Some time later, Leo and Mimi were full to the brim with tea, toast, and little golden cakes, and Bertha was lying fast asleep in front of the fire, having eaten more than both of them put together. The tale of Leo's brave deed, and Bertha's heroic battle with the wolf, had been told in every detail. Rosebud had been admired and played with by everyone. Blue butterflies were coming to rest on the cottage windowpanes. And long, dark shadows were stealing over the grass of the clearing.

Leo's head kept drooping. Mimi was yawning and rubbing her eyes. Leo saw Polly glancing at them in surprise and smiled weakly. "We've had a busy day," he said, thinking that this was far truer than Polly could possibly realize.

"You'd be more than welcome to stay the night," Jim said heartily. "We haven't got a spare bedroom, but we could make up beds for you here, in front of the fire. You'd be snug as bugs in rugs. That is, if you don't have to go straight home."

Leo hesitated, exchanging looks with Mimi. She nodded reluctantly. Desperate to reach the castle as she was, she knew they

couldn't travel through the night — especially with Conker, Freda, and Tye on the prowl.

"We're a long way from home, actually," he said. "We'd be very glad to stay, if that's really all right."

Polly smiled. "We'd love to have you," she said warmly. "I'll just send a mouse to your parents so they won't worry, and —"

"Oh! No!" Mimi and Leo broke in together.

Polly looked confused, then a little alarmed.

"It's fine, Polly," Mimi said hastily. "It really is. Leo and I are on our own at the moment, you see. We're — traveling. Seeing the world."

"*Really?*" said Polly. "Traveling Rondo — alone? But you're so young!"

"Oh, *ppff*! Stop fussing, Polly," Grandma muttered. "In my day, young people were always going off seeking their fortunes. Happened all the time! Why, Jim did it himself, when he wasn't much older than these two." She scowled. "Mind you, he'd have done much better to stay at home. I don't know what he thought he was playing at, going off to town, working in that sinful tavern, mixing with all sorts of —"

Jim shook his head, smiling wryly.

"Oh, leave Jim alone, Grandma," Polly scolded, rising instantly to her husband's defense. "I'm *glad* he went away, and you should be, too. If he hadn't gone, he'd have been at home when — when it happened — and we'd have lost him as well. . . ."

Her voice trailed off, and suddenly tears welled up in her eyes. She jumped up, murmured something about putting Rosebud to bed, and ran from the room. Frowning in concern, Jim heaved himself up from his own chair, and followed her.

"*Hmmph!*" said Grandma. But her old eyes were filled with regret.

There was a long, awkward silence. The fire crackled. Bertha snored gently. The fox blinked his golden eyes.

Mimi and Leo glanced at each other bleakly. This cottage had seemed such a haven of peace and happiness, but clearly it hadn't always been so. Something very bad had happened to this family, and the memory of it was still fresh.

The silence went on. Unable to sit still any longer, Mimi stood up and began restlessly prowling the room. Leo sat stiffly, feeling like an intruder, trying to think of something to say to relieve the tense atmosphere.

"Who plays this?" Mimi's voice was sharp with interest. Leo twisted in his chair and saw that she was standing by a shelf, pointing to a shabby old violin case.

Oh, no, not now, Mimi, he thought. *Now isn't the time. . . .*

The old woman by the fire looked up slowly. "No one plays that fiddle now," she said flatly. "No one's played it since my Charlie died." The corners of her mouth turned down.

This is getting worse and worse, Leo thought desperately. *Maybe we should leave. Maybe I should just get up, say we've changed our minds, and —*

"Would you mind if I looked at it?" Mimi asked, staring greedily at the violin case.

The old woman shrugged.

Taking this as permission, Mimi flipped open the catches of the case, opened the lid, and stared for a moment at the instrument inside.

"Oh, it's beautiful," she said in an awed voice. "Could I . . . just hold it for a minute?"

"You play a bit, do you?" Grandma asked, with a grim sort of smile.

"Yes," murmured Mimi, her eyes feasting on the gleaming violin.

"Well, go ahead, then," Grandma said. "But don't you drop it."

Reverently, Mimi lifted the violin from its case. She plucked the strings experimentally. Then she lifted out the bow, tucked the violin expertly under her chin, and began to tune it, drawing the bow across the strings, then adjusting the pegs at the top of the fingerboard.

Bertha frowned and smacked her lips in her sleep.

"Knows a bit about it, doesn't she?" Grandma asked Leo in a low voice, looking at Mimi.

He nodded.

"Thought so," Grandma said. "Charlie always used to warm up that way. Awful racket, isn't it?"

"Was Charlie your husband?" Leo asked, wanting to keep the conversation going.

To his enormous surprise, the old woman burst into loud cackles of laughter. "Husband?" she gasped, slapping her knee. "That's a good one! Arthur wouldn't have known one end of a fiddle from the other. No, no, no, boy. Charlie was my cat!"

And while Leo was still trying to digest this startling information, Mimi began to play, and the room was suddenly filled with glorious sound.

Leo sat, transfixed. He didn't know enough about music to know what Mimi was playing. It was something classical, of course. Some piece by Mozart, maybe, or Beethoven, or someone famous like that.

It didn't matter. All that mattered were the pure notes, rising and falling, filling every corner of the little room with thrilling beauty.

I didn't know she could play like that, Leo thought in awe. He saw that Jim and Polly had come back into the room. They were pulling the door to the bedroom closed behind them, staring at Mimi, then looking over at the old woman by the fire.

She was sitting bolt upright. Her eyes were very bright. Her knotted hands were clutching the arms of her chair as her head moved slowly in time with the music.

The tune ended. The last, throbbing note died away. Mimi lowered the violin with a sigh.

There was a moment's silence, then Jim began to clap. Polly joined him, her tearstained face wreathed in smiles. Leo jumped up and clapped, too.

Mimi hunched her shoulders, suddenly self-conscious. "I'm a bit out of practice," she mumbled.

"I don't know how you'd be if you were *in* practice, then," said Jim. "That was grand."

But Mimi was looking at Grandma.

"Not bad," the old lady said, nodding. "Not bad at all. But now let's have something a bit jollier — something a person can sing along to."

"Like what?" Mimi asked in her prickliest voice, and Leo's heart sank.

"What about . . . 'The Pom-Pom Polka,'" said Grandma. "That was one of Charlie's favorites. Do you know it?"

She began to hum a rollicking tune in a cracked but surprisingly strong voice. Polly joined her, her voice high and clear. Jim rumbled tunelessly along with them.

Mimi listened, expressionless, for one whole chorus. Her lips were a straight, hard line. Then she met Leo's anxious eyes. She seemed to think for a moment. Then she began tapping her foot, tucked the violin under her chin again, and began to play vigorously along with the singing voices.

Not a note was out of place. Mimi played "The Pom-Pom Polka" as if she'd been listening to it all her life. The sound of the violin again filled the old room — not with beauty this time, but with simple joy.

Beaming, Jim seized Polly around the waist and began whirling her around the room. She laughed breathlessly. Grandma went on singing, banging her hands on the arms of her chair. The fox grinned, his golden eyes gleaming red in the firelight. Bertha woke up and stared.

"Oh, that was wonderful!" cried Polly, when the song ended and she'd thrown herself, panting, down into a chair.

"Wonderful!" Jim repeated, clapping Mimi on the back.

"Not bad at all," said Grandma, her wrinkled old face softened and wet with tears. "Oh, how that took me back."

"Me, too," said Bertha nostalgically. "My brothers and I used to dance 'The Pom-Pom Polka' when we were piglets."

"This old house used to shake with music when Charlie was alive," Grandma said, her hooded eyes shining. "People would come from all around to hear him. Gosh, he could play, that old cat! We'd dance, and we'd sing. Then we'd eat supper. And afterward we'd all sit around the fire and the old ones would tell stories."

"Family stories?" asked Leo, thinking of Aunt Bethany.

"Sometimes," the old woman said, smiling. "But mostly made-up stories — ghost stories and Langlander tales and the like."

Leo gulped.

"*Langlander* tales?" Mimi burst out incredulously.

Grandma stared at her. "*You* know," she said. "'Rollo and the Dragon,' 'Silly Billy,' 'Dorcas Wonders Why' . . . those stories about magic folk from a world called Langland, who come to Rondo and get into all sorts of . . ."

Mimi and Leo both sat shaking their heads stupidly, quite unable to speak.

"Well, glory be!" said Grandma, flapping her hands. "I knew Langlander tales were out of fashion, but I never thought I'd meet a young one who'd never even *heard* of them!"

"My favorite was 'Monty and Ida,'" said Jim reminiscently.

Polly shuddered. "I don't like Langlander tales," she said. "They used to scare me when I was a child. Don't you go telling them to Rosebud, Grandma. You either, Jim."

"They never scared me," said Grandma with relish. "I loved them. Still do. I know they're only stories, mind, which is more than some folk do. Why, I once met a woman who swore that her cousin's best friend's sister had actually *been* to Langland! Went through a secret Gap full of musical rainbows, she said. And had a cup of tea with Monty himself! Well, I ask you!"

She cackled with laughter.

The fox yawned widely. Bertha's eyes fluttered closed. Polly said something about heating up soup, and moved away. Jim drew the curtains, shutting out the night, then began to put more wood on the fire. The old woman sat staring into space, lost in her memories.

Leo felt stunned. He watched as Mimi put the violin back in its case on the shelf. Mimi's movements were stiff and jerky. Grandma's reminiscences had obviously shocked her as much as they'd shocked Leo. No doubt she was feeling as grateful as he was that she hadn't told Jim and Polly her last name.

Langlander tales.

Leo didn't want to think about this now. He *refused* to think about this now.

"How long have you lived here, Jim?" he asked, rather loudly, as Jim turned from the fire.

Jim grinned, brushing dirt and bark scraps from his hands. "Ever since I married Pol," he said. "This is Grandma's house, but Polly was living here when we got wed, and Grandma said she'd put up with my company, rather than lose her granddaughter."

"You take up a lot of room, though, big lummox that you are," mumbled the old woman. But her smile took the sting out of her words, and her eyes, as they turned to Jim, were full of love.

"Polly and I have known each other since we were kids," Jim went on. "I was born a long way away — over near the mountains — but my parents had to leave that place and we ended up here — or very near here. The village is in ruins now, but you must have passed it on the road."

"You mean the village with the sunflowers?" Leo asked.

Jim's grin faded. "That's the place," he said soberly. "Polly's parents were already living there, with Polly and her older brother and baby sister, when we arrived. My dad set up as a woodcutter, supplying folk in the district with firewood. It wasn't his trade, but it was a living, you see?"

Leo nodded. *There's another story behind this,* he thought. But clearly Jim wasn't going to go into any details about why his father and mother had left the place where he was born.

"Anyway," Jim said, "we were still newcomers — didn't know anyone very well — when one day my dad was cutting down a dead tree in the forest here and that old wolf you saw today started giving Polly and Grandma a bit of trouble."

He glanced at his wife, who was busily stirring something on the stove. "Polly had come up through the forest to visit Grandma, you see, and bring her some supplies, because Grandma was poorly."

"The rheumatics, it was," Grandma put in. "That wolf would never have got the better of me, otherwise."

"'Course not," Jim agreed amiably. "And Polly was just a little thing then. Anyhow, Dad heard the screams. He came running with his axe and scared the wolf off."

He smiled sadly. "Polly's family and mine became very close after that. By the end, we were more like one big family than two separate ones. Suki, my — my sister — married Polly's brother, Walter, and I think everyone hoped that Polly and I would make a match of it, too, one day. But of course, by the time we did, they were all . . . gone."

"Did the wolf get them?" Mimi asked, wide-eyed.

"Something worse," Grandma answered grimly.

Mimi had just drawn breath to ask more questions when there was a sharp knock on the door.

"Why, who can that be?" said Polly, turning from the stove.

Leo jumped up. He and Mimi drew close together. With a surprised glance at their frightened faces, Jim went to the door.

"Who is it?" he called.

"It's the dot-catcher!" called a voice that chilled Leo's blood. "Conker, the friendly traveling dot-catcher! May I come in?"

CHAPTER 19

GOOD ADVICE

Jim turned to look at Leo and Mimi. They both shook their heads violently, putting their fingers to their lips and backing toward the door that led to the bedrooms.

By now, everyone in the room could see their alarm. Polly and Grandma were staring at them in surprise. Bertha blinked sleepily, shook her head till her ears flapped, and lumbered to her feet.

"Hold on!" Jim called through the door. He rattled the bolt with one hand, as if he were trying to open it, at the same time waving his other hand at Mimi and Leo, signaling to them to get out of sight. Mimi and Leo slipped rapidly into the bedroom hallway, pulling the door shut behind them.

They heard the front-door bolt slide back, and the door creak open.

"Good evening," they heard Jim say heartily. "What can we do for you?"

It was dark in the bedroom hallway, but light gleamed through cracks in the old timber wall. His heart hammering, Leo put his eye to a crack. He saw Jim standing back from the door, and

Conker walking in, smiling broadly, with Freda the duck at his heels.

A third figure, tall and slim, lingered in the shadows outside.

"Don't stay out there in the cold," Jim said, beckoning.

"Jim!" Grandma muttered warningly. But Jim either did not hear, or chose to ignore her.

"Come in and warm yourself," he said to the shadowy figure. "There's a good fire in here."

The figure hesitated, then stepped noiselessly over the threshold. As it moved from the darkness into the light, Leo caught his breath.

The third visitor was a woman dressed in leggings and tunic of fine black leather. A broad belt was slung round her slim waist, and from it hung a dagger in a leather sheath. Her hair was short, spiky, and black as shreds of licorice.

She would have made a striking figure in any company. But it was her face that made her appearance really startling. It was heart-shaped, with huge, watchful, golden eyes beneath dark, slanting brows. And it was covered with soft, fine fur — fur as smooth as velvet, striped gold and black, like a tiger's.

"Tye," Mimi breathed.

Leo nodded in the dark, staring in fascinated fear as the strange woman moved closer to the fire. Her black-gloved hands hung loosely by her sides, the left very close to the jeweled hilt of her dagger. Her feet made no sound on the floor. He could almost see her muscles rippling beneath her clothes, which fitted her like a second skin.

"Well, well," said Conker, rubbing his hands and eyeing Bertha curiously. "You're very cozy here, but what a lonely spot this is! Why, we wouldn't have known this cottage was here, if your music hadn't beckoned us as we tramped through the forest. 'The Pom-Pom Polka,' if I'm not mistaken. A grand old tune!"

"Indeed," Jim agreed, smiling.

Grandma said not a word. She had turned in her chair so that she faced the fire, and only her hunched shoulders could be seen.

"You are — all — very welcome," said Polly, rather breathlessly. "But I'm afraid you'll be disappointed in your visit. We don't need a dot-catcher. Rufus sees to any dots that come here."

She gestured at the fox. He was sitting up alertly, his eyes fixed on Freda, who returned his gaze boldly, as if daring him to make a move.

"And I see to wolves," said Bertha, lifting her chin aggressively. "And any other enemies who might come my way."

"Ah," said Conker, smiling even more broadly. "I thought I recognized you! You're the famous Bertha, from Macdonald's farm, if I'm not mistaken. What brings you here?"

"I am visiting," Bertha said haughtily, showing none of her usual delight at being recognized. "The hurly-burly life of a star is so exhausting! I enjoy relaxing in the simple company of friends."

"Of course, of course!" murmured Conker. His eyes roved restlessly around the room. He cleared his throat. "Well, then," he said to Jim. "I can see you're very well protected. We'd best be off, and trouble you no farther."

Tye left the fire and prowled silently back to the door, looking at no one. The duck gave Rufus and Bertha one last, challenging stare, then went to join her. Conker bowed to Polly, turned as if to leave, then made a show of remembering something.

"Oh, I meant to ask you," he said casually. "Have you seen two young strangers around here today? A boy and a girl?"

Leo held his breath.

"No," Jim said, as Polly turned hastily to stir the soup. "Why do you ask?"

"Oh," shrugged Conker. "They're young cousins of mine, visiting from the coast. We were to meet hereabouts, but we seem to have missed one another. It worries me to think that they might be lost in the forest."

"Of course," Jim agreed, walking to the door and opening it. "Well, if we see them, we'll tell them that you were looking for them."

"Oh, no need to do that," Conker said hurriedly. "I don't want them to — to feel embarrassed. You know how easily embarrassed young ones are. Hate fuss. Just keep them here and send me a mouse. I'll come and get them. 'Conker, the dot-catcher' will always find me. The mice know my traveling ways."

Jim murmured and smiled.

Conker bowed, and then he, Freda, and Tye went out into the night.

Jim closed the door after them, and bolted it securely once more. He pressed his ear against the thick wood, and listened for a moment.

"So — now that our visitors have gone, can we eat, Polly?" he called over his shoulder, far more loudly than necessary. "I'm famished — and I'm sure Grandma is, too."

Again he listened. Then he moved away from the door, apparently satisfied that Conker and his companions were at last on their way.

Leo and Mimi waited a minute or two, just to be sure, then crept out of hiding.

Rufus, the fox, had disappeared from the hearth rug. Bertha now had sole possession of it. She was devouring the contents of a large pottery bowl, snuffling contentedly.

Grandma was sitting at one end of the table, and Polly at the other. Jim was setting out five bowls of steaming soup. He gestured to Mimi and Leo to sit down. As they slid silently into their places, he sat down opposite them and picked up his spoon.

There was a long minute's silence, broken only by the clinking of metal on china and the slurping sounds Bertha was making as she cleaned the bottom of her bowl.

The soup was tasty and thick with vegetables, but Leo could hardly swallow it. He knew that Jim, Polly, and Grandma were waiting for an explanation, and he didn't know where to begin. He knew they must feel angry and betrayed because he and Mimi hadn't told them they were in hiding from dangerous enemies.

Mimi was staring down at her soup, not even pretending to eat, but not making any effort to say anything, either. A wave of helpless irritation swept over Leo. Mimi had retreated into her shell as she always did when she felt threatened.

"Well, isn't anyone going to say anything?" Bertha exclaimed at last, looking up from her bowl with soup dripping from her snout. "If that dot-catcher is your cousin, Leo, I'm a mushroom! I want to know what's going on!"

"I think we'd all like to know that," said Polly a little sharply.

Leo felt his face grow hot. "Thank you for not giving us away," he made himself say. His voice sounded as tense as he felt.

Jim looked up at him. "I don't enjoy lying," he said quietly. "It's a sneaking wolf's trick. But you saved our daughter's life, and Polly and I would have done far more than lie to protect you, had it been necessary."

"And it's a wonder it *wasn't* necessary, Jim," Grandma burst out, scowling at him. "Letting a nasty Terlamaine under this roof! After dark, too. I'd have thought you'd have had more sense!"

"Oh, Grandma!" sighed Polly.

"Don't you 'Oh, Grandma' me, my girl," the old woman growled. "You can't trust a Terlamaine — everyone knows that. They're unnatural, the slinking, hairy things. They don't belong among normal people. And I didn't like the look of that dot-catcher, either."

"Or that duck," Bertha put in. "She gave me the creeps! Whoever heard of a duck wearing a mask?"

"It's not a real mask," Leo said, half-smiling despite his uneasiness. "It's just the color of the feathers around her eyes."

"Is that so?" Bertha retorted. "Well, since you seem to know *all* about her, maybe you'll be kind enough to explain why she and the dot-catcher and the tiger-woman are looking for you."

Mimi let her spoon fall with a clatter. "They're looking for us because they work for the Blue Queen," she said loudly.

It was as if she'd thrown a bomb into the middle of the table. Grandma looked thunderstruck. Polly reached out and gripped Jim's hand. Bertha shut her mouth with a snap.

Jim took a deep breath. "You'd better tell us about it," he said in a level voice.

So Mimi did. In a high, rapid voice, she explained that the Blue Queen had stolen her dog, and that she was determined to get him back. She told of Spoiler's attack, and Conker's deceit, and the escape through the forest with the Flitters.

But she made no mention of the music box, and didn't say where she and Leo had come from. Those things, she obviously felt, should remain secret, and Leo agreed with her wholeheartedly. It seemed to him very unlikely that Polly, Jim, and Grandma would believe them, anyway.

When Mimi had finished, there was silence around the table for a long moment.

Then, still gripping Jim's hand, Polly leaned forward. "I'm very sorry for you, Mimi," she said. "I know what it is to lose someone you love — we all do, here."

Her eyes moistened. Almost angrily, she dashed the tears away with her free hand. "But you must give up this idea of trying to get your friend back," she went on earnestly. "If the Blue Queen has claimed him, there is nothing to be done."

"Polly's right," Jim said, as Mimi shook her head passionately and opened her mouth to argue. "The Blue Queen has lost the terrible power she had in the Dark Time, sure, but she's still a sorceress. You can't possibly defeat her. It would be madness even to try."

Mimi's face seemed to close. "I have to save Mutt," she said stubbornly.

"You don't know what you're saying, girl!" Grandma snapped. "Maybe on the coast, where you come from, folk don't understand what the Blue Queen is. But we do, and we know what happens to people who try to cross her."

Mimi turned her head away.

Leo wet his lips. "We don't know very much about the Blue Queen, it's true," he said, choosing his words carefully. "Anything you can tell us will help."

Help to convince Mimi to give this up. So we can both go home.

Perhaps the other three sitting around the table read the unspoken message in his eyes, because they all began speaking at once. In the end, however, it was the old woman who began the story.

"The Blue Queen was always a bad lot," Grandma said. "Good-looking, maybe, but vain as a flamingo, and with a cold, ugly heart. She'd married the king after his first wife died. She was jealous of her stepdaughter, the young princess, and treated her badly, though the king never seemed to notice."

"He was bewitched, some said," Polly put in.

"Or just stupid," Grandma growled contemptuously. "In any case, he let the queen have her way. Over the years she got worse and worse. . . ." She glanced at Jim.

"My father worked for her, in those days," Jim said, taking up the story reluctantly. "He was a member of her personal guard. He didn't like it much, but he had my mother and me to think about and so he put up with it."

He sighed. "Then, one day the Blue Queen called him in and told him she had a special, secret mission for him. A big old forest grew around the castle then. The queen ordered my father to take the young princess into the forest and kill her."

Leo and Mimi gasped, glancing at each other, then back at Jim.

"*Your* father —?" Leo began.

"Was ordered to kill the princess, just like that," Jim repeated, nodding. "Hard to believe, isn't it?"

He shook his head. "Father talked to Mother about it, and they worked out a plan," he went on. "It would be hard, and dangerous, but anything was better than doing the young princess harm. They were both very fond of her and, anyway, Father was no murderer. He was a soldier, maybe, but a gentler, kinder man never lived."

He swallowed, and Polly tightened her grip on his hand.

"My father carried out the plan," Jim went on. "He took the princess into the forest all right. But then he told her what the queen had ordered him to do."

"So the princess ran away, deep into the forest . . ." Mimi murmured.

Jim gave her a surprised look. "Oh, no," he said. "Father couldn't have left her to fend for herself. Anything might have happened to her. No, he took her home to our cottage, by one of the forest ways, and my mother hid her. Then he went back to the queen and told her the deed had been done, and that the princess was dead."

He bent his head. "That night, we left the cottage, taking the princess with us," he said, looking down at his hands. "Father left a note for the queen, saying that killing the princess had upset him a bit, and he'd decided to try a different line of work. We crossed the river in the dark and walked for days, till my parents thought we'd gone far enough to be safe."

"It wasn't safe, though," muttered Grandma.

"No," Jim said heavily. "Nowhere in the world would have been safe, as it turned out. Because the Blue Queen found out that the princess was still alive. She realized that my father had lied to her. And from that moment on, he was a marked man."

CHAPTER 20

"How did the queen find out that the princess was still alive?" asked Bertha, who had been following Jim's story avidly.

"Maybe she had a magic mirror," Mimi suggested, glancing at Leo again.

"Maybe," Jim agreed. "She was a sorceress even in those days. Anyway, she didn't make a move against us then, and we didn't dream we were in danger. We were happy. The princess — Suki, we called her, because of course she couldn't use her real name — stayed with us. She was like a daughter to my parents, and like a sister to me.

"And to me," Polly whispered. "Everyone loved her."

"I grew up, got restless, as some young people do, and went off to find work in town," Jim said. "Walter and Suki got married and built a house of their own in the village. Then the old king died, and the trouble started. The Blue Queen had always dabbled in sorcery, according to Father, but we had no idea how powerful she'd become."

"She'd had the king fooled all right but it seemed that, even so, she hadn't dared to reveal herself while he was alive," Grandma said. "That's how it must have been, because it wasn't long after he died that the Dark Time came."

She fell silent, lost in her own thoughts.

Leo was longing to ask for more information, but he didn't dare. He was supposed to be a part of this world. He was supposed to know . . .

Surprisingly, it was Bertha who solved his problem.

"I don't know exactly how the Dark Time started," she said. "I was living with my brother at the time, and he wasn't interested in current affairs at *all*. All he ever talked about was the local darts competition. I was *completely* cut off from important news."

"The Blue Queen suddenly revealed her power," Jim said. His voice was husky, as if it pained him to speak. "She wielded it ruthlessly. She'd met Spoiler by then — actually taken him to live in the castle — and he encouraged her."

"As if she needed encouragement to do the things she'd wanted to do for years!" Polly burst out angrily. "The first thing she did was to destroy the forest that surrounded the castle. She said it spoiled her view but there was revenge in what she did, too, because Old Forest was the ancient home of the Terlamaines who had never paid her the respect she thought she deserved."

Jim nodded. "The forest vanished overnight. Thousands of Terlamaines were left without shelter, and were slaughtered by the queen's army. It was a frightful thing."

"The Terlamaines weren't the only ones to suffer," muttered Grandma. "Plenty of ordinary folk did, too. After the Blue Queen had got rid of Old Forest, she started on the farms and villages beyond it. Then she dammed up the river to make herself a lake, and all the farms around here started to die."

"Didn't anyone try to stop her?" Mimi exclaimed.

"Didn't your parents teach you *anything*, girl?" snapped the old woman. "Of *course* folk tried to stop her. Thousands died trying. But no one could stand against that army of monsters she'd created to fight for her. As fast as they were cut down, she'd make more."

"And in no time at all, she had what she'd always wanted," said Polly bitterly. "She and Spoiler ruled Rondo by fear. Whatever they wanted, they took, and whatever they disliked, they destroyed. They decked themselves in gold and jewels. They feasted while we starved. Their monsters roamed the land, spreading terror. The castle stood alone on its hill, overlooking a fine lake, with nothing but smooth green grass around it, as far as the eye could see."

That's just how it looks now, Leo thought, remembering the back of the music box. Except . . .

"There's no lake there now," he said aloud.

"Well, I'm glad you know *that* at least," snorted Grandma. "The dam was taken down when the Blue Queen's power was broken and the Dark Time ended. Everyone around here went to work on the task — everyone who was able."

"Macdonald did," Bertha said eagerly.

"So did Polly and I," Jim said with a touch of pride. "The dam came down, stone by stone, and at last the river flowed again. I only wish other evils of the Dark Time had been so easy to undo."

He fell silent. Polly stared down at her hands. Grandma looked bleak.

"The man who finally broke the Blue Queen's power was a mighty wizard," Grandma quavered. "He stood alone against her, and he won. But the battle killed his own power — burned it away to nothing, they say. He couldn't do any more for us."

Leo knew they didn't want to talk about what the Blue Queen had done to them. The memory was painful. But perhaps a real, personal story was the only thing that would convince Mimi to abandon her quest.

"What happened to your family in the Dark Time, Jim?" he asked softly. "Did the Blue Queen track your father down at last?"

Jim glanced at Polly. She tightened her lips and gave a little nod, as if agreeing that he should speak.

"The Blue Queen came to the village," he said in a hard voice. "I wasn't there, of course, because I was working in town. By happy chance, Polly wasn't there, either. She was here, visiting Grandma. But everyone else — our mothers and fathers, Suki and Walter, and Polly's little sister — were at home."

"And the Blue Queen killed them all?" squeaked Bertha, her small eyes wide with horror.

"No," said Polly, who had grown very pale. "That revenge would have been too ordinary for her. She — changed them. She turned them all into swans — seven great, white swans. And then she set the village on fire, and left them. I came home and found them wandering among the burned ruins of our homes. Everyone else had run away."

Tears were rolling down her cheeks. Leo's heart ached for her.

"The swans still seemed to half-remember what they'd been," she whispered. "But they couldn't speak to me. And, after a while, their memories clouded and they just — flew away. There was no water for them to swim in near the village, anymore. The Blue Queen had seen to that."

She buried her face in her hands. Leo felt a burning anger rise in his chest — anger such as he had never felt before in his life. He looked into Jim's eyes, and saw the same, flaming anger reflected there.

"Polly came to live with Grandma, after that," Jim said stolidly. "They sent word to me. I came home, but there was nothing I could do to change things. Later, when the Blue Queen's power was broken, we had hopes. But the wizard who had faced the queen had sacrificed his own power to defeat her. He couldn't undo what had been done, any more than he could make the great trees of Old Forest grow again."

He clenched his huge fists. "I burned for revenge, in those days. And even now, when I go to town and see Spoiler walking free, my heart feels as if it's going to burst in my chest."

"Everyone who suffered in the Dark Time must feel the same, Jim," Polly murmured anxiously. "But we've made a new life. We've been happy."

"Of course we have," said Jim, squeezing her hand. "And if ever I'm tempted to do something stupid, I think of you and Rosebud and put the thought out of my mind. Spoiler is under the Blue Queen's protection and she still has power enough to be dangerous. I might risk my safety but I won't risk yours. You're far too precious to me."

Bertha made a snuffling sound and bowed her head. Leo felt a burning lump rise in his throat and struggled to force it down. He wondered what Mimi was feeling. She was very still. Her face was unreadable.

"I'm sorry," he mumbled, and cleared his throat as everyone looked at him. "I mean, I'm sorry for what happened to you, and I'm truly sorry we came here and brought trouble on you again. We didn't know the Blue Queen was your enemy, too. We didn't know —"

Jim shook his head and held up his hands. "How could you know?" he said. "Besides, if you hadn't come here when you did, what would have happened to Rosebud? Don't forget how much we owe you."

"And if our story has convinced you not to seek out the Blue Queen yourselves, it was well worth telling," Polly put in.

Grandma gave a harsh bark of laughter. "We haven't convinced that one of anything," she said, jerking her head at Mimi. "She's stubborn as a donkey. She'll still go after her dog, and she'll drag the boy along with her."

Mimi looked down and didn't speak. There was a long silence.

Polly sighed and got to her feet. "I'm going to bed," she said, walking to the fire and putting its metal guard around it in preparation for the night.

Jim went to a closet and took out blankets, pillows, and quilts.

"In the morning we'll talk again," he said, handing the bedding to Mimi and Leo. "For now, I think we all need sleep."

A very short time afterward, Mimi and Leo were lying in comfort by the softly glowing fire. They had the hearth to themselves because Rufus was out hunting and Bertha had chosen to sleep outside in Jim's work shed.

"I'm sure you don't snore as loudly as my brother did," she'd told Mimi and Leo, "but ever since sharing a room with him, I prefer to sleep alone. I hope you understand."

They had assured her that they did.

Polly and Grandma had gone to bed. Now only Jim remained, checking the locks on the doors and putting out the last of the candles.

At last, the room was lit only by the glow of the fire.

"Good night, then," Jim said. "Sleep well, and don't worry. Rufus never strays far from the cottage. He'll bark if strangers come near."

Leo propped himself up on his elbow. Among all the things that were whirling around in his head, one thing in particular was worrying him.

"Jim," he said. "Before you go — could you tell us something about Spoiler? I mean, we've met him. He's . . . well, he's sort of ordinary, isn't he? Nothing like the Blue Queen. What made her choose *him* to share all her money and power and everything?"

Jim shrugged. "Who knows?" he said. "Spoiler came out of nowhere. No one seemed to know anything about him. He was already hanging around the town, making a big man of himself, when I first went there to work. I used to see him in the tavern. . . ."

"The Black Sheep?" asked Leo quickly.

Jim nodded. "I'd got a job there — collecting empty glasses, washing dishes, and so on. I saw Spoiler a lot. He didn't seem to work, but he always had plenty of cash. He gathered a gang of spongers around him, went in for card games, and horse races, betting for money — lots of money, sometimes."

He paused, thinking. "There was something about him. . . . He was different from anyone I'd ever seen before. Sort of — exciting. But not someone you'd like your parents to meet. You know?"

Leo was starting to feel sick. What Jim was saying sounded horribly familiar, and the vague idea that had made him ask about Spoiler in the first place was beginning to become more and more concrete.

"Was Spoiler at the tavern every day?" he asked, trying to sound casual.

Jim frowned. "At first he just came now and then. Then suddenly he seemed to be around all the time. He acted as if he owned the place. The landlord, Jolly, didn't like him, I know that for a fact. Then the Blue Queen came to the tavern to complain in person about some cider she'd ordered. She and Spoiler hit it off straightaway. The next thing we knew he was with her in the castle, acting like a king. That's really all I can tell you."

"Right," Leo said faintly.

Jim said good night again and took himself off to bed.

Leo lay down, pulled his covers up to his chin, and tried to face what he now was certain was the truth.

"This is all so strange, Leo," Mimi whispered in the dimness. "I can't — quite — believe it. Polly, Jim, Grandma, Conker, the Blue Queen — even Bertha and the wolf — they were all painted on the music box a long time ago. But somehow they didn't just stay the same, like pictures are supposed to do. They got older and moved around and went on with their lives, just as if they were real!"

"They *are* real," Leo muttered. "They're as real as we are."

"And the Langlander tales," Mimi murmured. "They're stories about people from our family, who came here a long time ago. One of them's about Rollo Langlander. And Aunt Bethany used to talk about Monty and Ida, too. They were her great-grand-parents, I think."

Leo didn't answer. He heard her moving restlessly under her quilt. Then her voice came again.

"Leo! Do you realize that we're fairy tales to these people, just like they're fairy tales to us? It's so weird!"

"I know," Leo whispered back. "But Mimi, that's not all. I think —"

"What?" Mimi asked impatiently.

Leo took a deep breath.

"Mimi," he said. "I think Spoiler — is Wicked Uncle George."

CHAPTER 21

It was very strange, and rather nice, to wake up the next day rolled in a quilt by a still-smoldering fire, with a rooster crowing outside. In a way, it reminded Leo of a school camp he'd been to once.

But the pleasant feeling ebbed away as Leo woke up fully. This wasn't a school camp, where there were teachers to tell you what to do and a whole lot of sensible, if sometimes annoying, rules to follow. This was another world, where the rules were unknown, where you never knew what was going to happen next, and where you held your future in your own hands.

A world, what's more, in which your own great-great-uncle was a major villain, and he and his gang were after you.

Leo saw that Mimi was already up. She was sitting by the window and looking out, her chin resting on her hand. Soon Jim and the others would be up and about, too. In fact, even now there were sounds of movement from behind the door that led to the bedrooms.

Reluctantly Leo crawled out of his warm nest and ran his fingers through his ruffled hair. Mimi didn't look around. Maybe she was so deep in thought that she couldn't hear him. Or maybe she just couldn't be bothered. You could never tell with Mimi.

Mimi hadn't taken a lot of convincing that Uncle George and Spoiler were one and the same when Leo had explained his theory to her the night before. She remembered Aunt Bethany's stories as well as Leo did. She remembered that Wicked Uncle George had disappeared without a trace just before the police came for him. She saw straightaway that the music box would be a perfect place for a criminal to hide.

"So George inherited the music box from his father, and came here just like a tourist at first — to have fun," she whispered. "Then, when things got hard for him at home and he needed to disappear, he just came to Rondo for good."

"And met the Blue Queen," Leo said slowly.

"Yes!" hissed Mimi, sitting up. "And that's why the Blue Queen suddenly got powerful, Leo! It wasn't because the old king died. It was because she met George!"

"The life-force thing, you mean?" Leo murmured, his heart sinking. "You think George — Spoiler — gave the queen the extra strength she needed to do all those things she did in the Dark Time? Like getting rid of the Terlamaines' forest, and moving the river. And . . . turning Jim's and Polly's families into swans?"

Mimi had nodded, and after a while, she'd silently lain down again.

They hadn't talked much after that. Leo had been sure he'd never get to sleep, but gradually his thoughts had started to mingle with dreams, and sleep had come.

Now it was morning, and he had to face his new knowledge all over again. He had to face, too, whatever this day might bring. Fighting down a flare of panic, he began to tidy up Mimi's and his bedding. That job, at least, he knew how to do.

He had just finished folding the last of the blankets when Jim came in, his hair wet and his face freshly shaved.

"Good morning!" Jim said heartily, striding to the side door and throwing back the bolt. "Sleep well?"

"Very well, thank you," Leo answered.

Mimi turned around, smiled and nodded. Her face was dreamy and very peaceful.

"It's beautiful out there," she said, glancing back at the window. "There are blue butterflies everywhere, and the sun's making tiger stripes on the grass."

"Well, let's hope they're the only tiger stripes we see today," Jim said, taking a handful of twigs and some larger pieces of wood from the basket by the door. He spoke jokingly, but his face was thoughtful as he moved to the stove. The memory of Tye the Terlamaine's black-clad figure seemed to darken the room.

"You'll be planning to leave after breakfast, I daresay," Jim said, as he fed the sticks into the stove.

It was a statement, not a question. Obviously he wanted them out of his cottage and on their way as soon as possible.

I'd feel the same in his place, Leo thought, as Jim blew on the glowing embers remaining in the stove from the previous night till the twigs crackled and caught fire. *The longer we stay, the more* we put his family in danger. If Conker and Tye come back . . . if the Blue Queen ever finds out that Jim and Polly hid us . . .

He glanced at Mimi. Her dreamy expression had vanished.

"We'll leave now," she said stiffly, edging toward the door Jim had just unlocked. "We won't wait for breakfast. I never eat breakfast anyway."

Leo felt a pang. He was ravenously hungry himself. But he murmured agreement and began hastily pulling on his jacket.

Jim pushed the larger pieces of wood into the stove, slammed the stove door, and straightened up without haste.

"Well, I'm not setting foot outside this house till I've eaten," he declared, dusting off his hands and setting a black iron pot on the heat. "And if you take my advice, you won't either. You won't get far without some good hot food in your stomachs, and I'm blessed if I'll carry you all the way to Troll's Bridge."

Mimi froze, her hand on the doorknob. "Troll's Bridge?" she asked.

"You're coming with us?" Leo burst out at the same moment.

"Polly and I decided I should," Jim said, walking back to the wood box and picking up more logs. "You were determined to go on, and we couldn't let you do it alone. It's too dangerous. I'm only taking you as far as the bridge, mind. I promised Polly that."

"You mean the bridge at the end of the road?" Mimi asked, to be sure. "The one that crosses the river into Blue Queen territory?"

"That's the one," Jim said, carrying the logs to the fireplace.

He put down the logs and lifted the fireguard aside. "I can show you a shortcut through the forest. Polly and I both thought you'd do better to keep off the road, where you can be easily seen."

He knelt down and began expertly building up the fire, this time using bellows to coax the glowing coals into life.

"Unless," he added casually, without looking around at them, "you've decided to do the sensible thing and take yourselves home after all."

"Well, *I* haven't," Mimi said immediately.

Leo hesitated. And it was then that he realized that something strange had happened to him. *He* didn't want to go home, either. Not anymore.

"I want to go on, too," he said stolidly.

Mimi flashed a surprised and grateful glance at him, and he shrugged.

"That's that then," said Jim. "Would one of you give the porridge a stir? Nothing worse than burned porridge."

Why do I feel like this? Leo thought, going to the stove and picking up the wooden spoon that lay on the table beside it. *Everything I heard last night should have made me more scared than ever. This place must be starting to affect my mind.*

He plunged the spoon into the pot of porridge and began slowly to stir, trying to make sense of his thoughts. The stories about the Blue Queen and the Dark Time had scared him, all right. The trouble was, they had made him angry, too — angry enough to want to stop the Blue Queen having her way just for once.

But deep down he knew that anger alone wouldn't have been enough to cut through his usual cautious good sense. What had done that was the terrible shame he'd felt when he'd realized that a member of his own family had shared in, and encouraged, the Blue Queen's reign of terror.

It's stupid to feel responsible, he told himself, staring down into the porridge pot. *Spoiler came here long before I was born. What he did isn't my fault!*

But he was from my world, his conscience told him. *And he was a Langlander. He once owned the music box, just like I do now. And he abused it. I can't forget that.*

Leo knew Mimi would never understand his sense of responsibility for Spoiler's actions. Mimi had had her own battles to fight, all her life. As a result, she didn't feel responsible for anyone but herself and the ones she loved.

But Leo did. He couldn't help it.

Spoiler might be just a sneaky thief now, but once he had helped the Blue Queen do terrible things to good people like Jim and Polly and their families. He had done it all just so he could live like a king. And now he was still doing the Blue Queen's bidding — still living on like a parasite on this world, still sneaking and plotting, still causing unhappiness wherever he went and spoiling everything he touched.

I can't undo what he did, Leo thought grimly. *But maybe somehow I can make him pay for it. I can try, anyway. Once we're in the castle . . .*

"Hey!" Jim called to him from the fireplace, where the fire

was now crackling merrily. "You don't have to beat the life out of it, Leo!"

Leo realized that he'd been attacking the porridge as if it were Spoiler himself. He grinned shamefacedly, and lifted out the sticky spoon.

"Is the porridge nearly ready?" Polly asked, coming into the room with Rosebud gurgling in her arms and Grandma hobbling close behind. "We're all starving!"

The porridge — thick, smooth, and sweet with honey — had been eaten with relish. Even Mimi, whose mother had written *porridge* in capital letters on the list of foods Mimi refused to eat, had scraped her bowl clean.

The dishes had been washed. Belongings had been gathered. Jim had filled a small pack with provisions, and pulled on his boots. It was time to leave.

Everyone moved out into the bright morning sun and around to the back of the cottage. Jim pointed out a narrow path leading into the forest just behind the henhouse.

"That's our track," he said. "Ready?"

But Mimi and Leo weren't ready. They were arguing with Bertha, who had suddenly announced that she intended to go with them.

"Now that I've heard your story, I can't *possibly* let you do this by yourselves!" she exclaimed, when Leo and Mimi tried to persuade her to go to town as she'd planned. "I can be a model anytime!

Besides, I've always wanted to go on a quest. This will show my brother once and for all that he should take me seriously."

"A pig's got no business going on a quest," Grandma said grumpily. "I've never heard the like! If anyone's going to face the Blue Queen with these children it should be a hero, not a great galumphing —"

"Grandma! You should have seen Bertha fight that wolf!" Polly broke in hastily. "Bertha *is* a hero!"

Bertha, who had begun to swell with rage, calmed down a little. "Heroine, actually," she murmured, nodding to Polly graciously.

Grandma hunched her shoulders. "Well, that's as may be," she growled. "Still, wolf fighting's one thing, and questing's another. A trained hero would be better."

"I had always understood that most of the professional heroes were wiped out in the Dark Time," Bertha said coldly.

"A lot of them went in the final battle, that's true," Grandma said. "But there are still a few about. There's that knight over in —"

"He's no use, Grandma," Jim said. "He's only interested in dragons, and he rusts up when he gets wet."

"And the giant-killer's retired," Polly put in. "He's got enormously fat, they say, and has trouble with his knees."

Grandma snorted in disgust. "I don't know what Rondo's coming to," she grumbled.

"We'd better be off," Jim said. He bent to kiss Polly and Rosebud, hoisted his bag onto his shoulder, and strode to the mouth of the path with such energy that he caused a great fluttering in the henhouse.

"Have you got the butter cakes, Jim?" Polly called after him. "Don't forget to give them to —"

"I won't forget," Jim called over his shoulder. "Don't worry!"

Polly hugged Mimi and Leo and curtsied to Bertha, who curtsied gracefully in return, the flowers on her hat bobbing.

"Take care now," Polly said, as they turned to go. "And don't stray off the path." She laughed and shook her head. "Oh, I'm starting to sound like my mother," she said. "She always used to tell me that. But it's good advice, believe me."

"If there are no heroes to be had, what about a handsome prince?" Leo heard Grandma mutter to Polly. "The latest crop of princes are all fools, I hear, but even a fool would be better than a *pig*, surely to goodness!"

"*Sshh*, Grandma!" hissed Polly, but fortunately Bertha hadn't heard.

"Come on!" Jim shouted.

Leo and Mimi hurried to join him, with Bertha trotting briskly after them. The moment they reached him, Jim gave Polly a final wave, then turned and set off down the path, so fast that they almost had to run to keep up with him. Obviously he wanted to get them well away from the cottage as soon as he could.

The path twisted and turned. When Leo looked over his shoulder just a few moments later, he could no longer see Polly and Grandma, the henhouse, or even the cottage itself. He could see nothing but shadows and whispering trees.

CHAPTER 22

Every now and then, the path through the forest split into two — one trail winding away to the left, the other leading to the right. Each time this happened Jim chose his way without hesitation and strode on, keeping up a great pace. Leo, Mimi, and Bertha were forced to hurry after him, afraid that if they lost sight of him they'd take the wrong turn.

By the time he stopped at last, at yet another fork in the path, Mimi was red-faced and gasping for breath, Bertha was complaining that she had a stitch, and even Leo was panting.

Jim turned as they caught up with him. He looked as fresh as when he'd started out. "Was I going too fast for you?" he inquired in surprise.

"Yes!" snapped Bertha, jerking her head to toss back her hat, which had fallen over one eye. "It was *extremely* inconsiderate!"

Leo was sure Mimi would have said much the same thing if she could speak, but fortunately she was bent over, her hands on her knees, trying to catch her breath.

"Sorry," Jim said cheerfully. "I wanted to make a good start, that's all. Never mind. We've almost reached Deep Wood, so we'll be moving more slowly from now on. We'll have to keep our eyes open. Not many people take the Deep Wood path, and there are a quite a few good reasons for that."

Casually he pulled his axe from his belt. Leo felt a shiver, like a trickle of icy water, run down his spine. He glanced at Mimi. She was slowly straightening up. Her eyes were wide and frightened. Behind her, Bertha had stopped looking irritable and had begun peering warily around instead.

"You'll be all right," Jim said, seeing their expressions. "Most Deep Wood types won't trouble you if you don't trouble them. Stay close together and keep your voices down. And if you see anything, take no notice of it. Just walk on."

Leo didn't find these words very reassuring. In fact, they made him more nervous than ever, and he was fairly sure that Mimi and Bertha felt the same. None of them said anything, however. They all merely nodded to show they'd understood.

Jim set off along the left-hand path, this time moving at a normal walking pace. His companions followed in single file, with Leo at the front, Mimi close behind him, and Bertha bringing up the rear.

Gradually the light dimmed as the roof of branches thickened above their heads. Their feet made little sound on the path, which was carpeted with dead leaves. No birds sang. A few blue butterflies fluttered sluggishly about, but they were the only moving things to be seen.

They passed a simple cottage nestled in a clearing deep among the trees. A row of white beehives stood at one side of the clearing, near a clothesline where three sets of sheets and three pillowcases had been hung out to dry. The cottage itself was very neat and tidy, and smoke rose from its chimney.

Who'd live way out here? Leo thought, slowing to look. His heart jumped into his mouth as he saw a huge, furry shape pass behind one of the windows.

"A bear!" Mimi squeaked, and clapped her hand over her mouth.

"Walk on," Jim warned in a low voice, and they hurried to obey him.

As they moved ever more deeply into the wood, the air became heavy and hard to breathe. The trees were ancient. Nightmarish faces seemed to grin from their gnarled and twisted trunks. Between the trees there were dark, looming shadows that moved with stealthy, rustling sounds.

The back of Leo's neck was burning. He was certain that they were being watched.

It's just my imagination, he told himself. But he didn't turn his head to look properly into the trees. He was afraid of what he might see if he did.

Jim walked steadily, looking straight ahead, his axe swinging loosely in his hand. He seemed perfectly at ease, but Leo could see by the set of his shoulders that he was alert, and listening.

Another fork in the path was ahead. Leo had long ago given up trying to keep track of the way they had come. He'd simply followed Jim blindly. Now they were in the depths of the forest, and for the first time Leo realized how helpless he, Mimi, and Bertha would be if for some reason Jim chose to leave them. They'd never find their way back to where they began. They wouldn't know how to get to the bridge, either. They'd be hopelessly lost.

Why am I thinking like this? Leo thought nervously. *Jim wouldn't leave us.*

At the same moment, he noticed a faint, sweet smell drifting on the air. It wasn't a flower scent. It was more like the warm, delicious smell of a bakery. He sniffed appreciatively.

"Leo," Mimi whispered, tugging at his sleeve. He looked around and saw that she was staring into the trees to her right.

Just visible through the towering tree trunks was another cottage — this time the prettiest cottage Leo had ever seen outside the pages of a storybook. The posts of the verandah looked like twists of golden toffee. The slates of the roof reminded him of shaved chocolate.

He stared at it, fascinated. He knew at once that it was the source of the delicious smell. Perhaps the owner of the cottage was baking something. Or perhaps . . .

The cottage door opened and an old woman came out. She was tall and very thin and was dressed all in black, from her tattered black shawl to the toes of her buttoned boots. Her long white hair hung raggedly around her shoulders. Her nose curved down so far that it almost met her bony chin. She looked straight at Leo and Mimi. She smiled at them and beckoned.

Walk on, Leo told himself. *Walk on!* But suddenly there was nothing he wanted more in the world than to accept the old woman's invitation.

He took a step off the path, only vaguely aware that Mimi was doing the same.

"*Ooohh!*" squealed Bertha in alarm.

Leo felt himself being roughly grabbed by the arm. Before he could do or say anything, Jim had pulled Mimi and him back onto the path.

"Walk on!" Jim ordered. And when Leo and Mimi made no move to obey, but simply looked longingly back at the pretty cottage and its smiling owner, he swore under his breath, tightened his grip on their arms, and dragged them bodily away.

Afterward, Leo was never sure how long it had taken for Jim to hustle them, fast and angrily, through the remainder of Deep Wood. Bertha said she'd been far too upset and worried to pay attention to the time, Mimi couldn't remember the journey any more than Leo could, and he'd been far too embarrassed to ask Jim.

When at last he came to himself, it was like waking from a dream. Slowly he became aware that he was sitting under a tree, his back resting against the trunk. His legs were aching. Mimi was sitting beside him, blinking dazedly. The ground in front of them was dappled with mellow sunlight, and streaked with the long shadows of late afternoon. Dots, smaller and harder-looking than the dots he'd seen in town, scuttled furtively through the long grass.

Jim was sitting against another tree, staring into space. Bertha was sprawled nearby, contentedly working her way through a bag of small, dark red apples.

We must be out of Deep Wood, Leo thought in confusion. *How did that happen?*

Thinking back, he remembered seeing the pretty little cottage, and enjoying its sweet bakery smell. Then he remembered the old woman coming out and beckoning to him. And suddenly a vivid memory of the woman's grinning face swam up at him from the dreamlike haze that still clouded his mind. Now he could see the wickedness in that grin, and the flash of those cold, hungry eyes.

His stomach lurched, and his face grew hot. What would have happened to him, and to Mimi, if Jim hadn't pulled them back onto the path?

Nothing good, that was for sure.

He ran his fingers through his hair. Jim and Bertha both looked up quickly and scrambled to their feet.

"It's all right," Leo told them.

His voice sounded husky. He cleared his throat and tried again. "I'm not going to try to escape and get back to that cottage or anything. The spell — or whatever it was — has worn off."

"Well, thank goodness for that!" Bertha exclaimed. "The way you behaved! I've never been so shocked in all my life. And do you *know* how long we've been sitting here, waiting for you to wake up?"

"It was my fault," Mimi said loudly, making everyone jump. "I was the one who stopped first. I made Leo look."

"Oh, so you've come to your senses as well, have you?" cried Bertha, working herself up into a lather of righteous indignation.

"You were keeping very quiet about it. Ashamed of yourself, I suppose. And so you *should* be! Didn't your parents teach you *anything*? Don't you know you should never *ever* stop to look at a nasty old —"

"Obviously they *didn't* know, Bertha," Jim interrupted calmly, as Leo's face grew redder and Mimi's grew stiffer and paler. "They're strangers in these parts. I should have warned them."

He bent and rummaged in his pack, carelessly brushing away the dots that were crawling all over it.

"I just assumed that problems on the coast were the same as they are here," he added. "Well, I was wrong, wasn't I?"

He straightened up with a packet of food in his hand.

"To tell the truth, I was wrong about a few things," he said. "I haven't taken the Deep Wood path for quite a while, but I'm sure there weren't anything like so many bears the last time I came through. I've never seen so many. For a while there seemed to be one behind every tree. And instead of going about their own business, they were all looking at us."

Leo's stomach churned, remembering the looming shadows, the faint, rustling sounds, in the depths of the wood. So they hadn't been his imagination after all.

"The good news is," Jim said cheerfully, handing him a chunk of crusty brown bread and a wedge of cheese, "we haven't got far to go now. The bridge is just ahead."

"But how can it be?" exclaimed Leo, astonished, as Jim turned to give Mimi her share of the food. "We couldn't possibly have come so far in —"

Jim and Bertha both laughed. Plainly, during the time that Leo and Mimi had been bewitched, they had become good friends.

"We went through a Gap!" Bertha chortled. "There are often Gaps where there are a lot of trees, you know. And Jim knew exactly where to find this one. It took us straight from the end of Deep Wood to here! It's smaller than the one that starts in Flitter Wood, Jim says, but it was such *fun!*" She rolled her eyes. "Fun for me, that is. Poor Jim had a terrible time trying to hold on to you in all that mist while you were struggling and fighting to get back to —"

"Never mind," Jim said, grinning and holding up his hand. "All's well that ends well. Right?"

Bertha broke off and shrugged. Leo nodded and tried to smile. Mimi stayed motionless, staring down at her bread and cheese.

Leo wondered what she was thinking. Was she still berating herself uselessly for falling under the witch's spell in Deep Wood? Or was she wondering, as he was, about the bears?

I've never seen so many . . . And instead of going about their business, they were all looking at us . . .

Was Mimi wondering, as Leo was, if the increased number of bears, and their interest in travelers through Deep Wood, had something to do with the Blue Queen?

CHAPTER 23

"You must be famished," said Jim. "Eat up! It'll be dark pretty soon, and I promised Polly I'd be home before midnight."

Leo took a bite of his bread and cheese, and only then realized how ravenous he was. The food tasted wonderful. The bread was brown and fresh, with a crisp, crunchy crust. The cheese was soft, pale, and tangy. He finished the snack in moments, and wished heartily for more.

"I'm not really hungry," Mimi said in a tight little voice.

Leo glanced at her in irritation, but Jim just shrugged. "Suit yourself," he said. "But you've still got a way to go, and I wouldn't want to be facing the Blue Queen on an empty stomach, myself."

He turned away and began searching for something in his pack. Mimi stared thoughtfully at his back, then slowly tore off a corner of her bread and began to nibble at it.

Jim took a bulging red napkin from his pack and unfolded it. Inside were two of the small golden cakes they'd eaten by the cottage fire the day before.

"These were all we had left after yesterday," he said. "But two should be enough."

"Ooh, they look so yummy!" sighed Bertha. "It seems such a waste . . ."

"Can't be helped," said Jim. "You wouldn't want to cross that bridge without a butter cake or two handy. You never can tell with trolls."

Leo gulped. A bread crumb went down the wrong way, and he started to cough.

"*Trolls?*" Mimi squeaked.

Jim leaned over and pounded Leo on the back. "Something wrong?" he asked.

Mimi swallowed. "Do *trolls* guard the bridge we've got to cross?" she asked.

"Oh, just the one," Jim said reassuringly, thrusting the water bottle into Leo's hands. "It's lived under the bridge for as long as I can remember. Well, that's why the bridge is called Troll's Bridge, isn't it?"

"Oh," Mimi said faintly. "Yes."

She took a large bite of bread and cheese and chewed distractedly. She seemed to have forgotten all about not feeling hungry.

Leo sipped some water and wiped his watering eyes. "So this — this troll will attack us if we try to cross the bridge, will it?" he croaked, trying to sound unconcerned.

"Well, I certainly hope not!" exclaimed Bertha. "It would be *very* unfair if it ate our butter cakes and then ate *us* as well!"

"The troll won't give you any trouble," Jim said confidently. "It's very old, and it's lost most of its teeth. All it asks these days is a decent show of fear and a butter cake or two. Still —"

He went back to where he'd been sitting, and returned carrying two stout sticks.

"I picked these up for you earlier," he said, handing one of the sticks to Mimi and the other to Leo. "If the troll gets too cranky, just give it a good sharp whack on the nose. That should fix it."

Leo weighed the stick in his hand, feeling rather sick.

"Don't you worry," Bertha assured him. "You won't need it. If that old troll gets nasty, *I'll* take care of it."

"Can't we just *swim* across the river?" Mimi asked in a small voice.

Jim shrugged. "You could, I suppose. I don't think there are too many crocodiles up this way. But I'm telling you, if you follow my advice the troll won't be a problem. Well, are you ready to go?"

Leo nodded, handed back the water bottle, and scrambled up, grasping his stick awkwardly. Mimi got up, too, hurriedly swallowing the last of her bread and cheese.

They followed Jim through the trees on the other side of the clearing. And there before them, was the road, a dusty brown ribbon with forest on one side and clumps of trees surrounding a river on the other.

To their left, the road stretched away into the distance. To their right, not far from where they stood, it ended abruptly at a bend in the river, which was spanned by a narrow wooden bridge.

The river looked deep. Willow trees lined its steep banks, their branches drooping over the water as if the trees were admiring their own reflections in the shining surface.

Leo knew that beyond the river was the vast stretch of smooth green grass that was the Blue Queen's domain, but he could see little of it from where he was standing, because the willow trees blocked his view. He couldn't see the Blue Queen's castle, either. All he could see above the trees' shaggy green heads were the misty blue mountains rising on the distant horizon.

Jim began walking toward the bridge, keeping close to the side of the road. Mimi, Leo, and Bertha followed in single file. It was so quiet that the snapping of twigs beneath their feet sounded loud. No one spoke.

Leo's heart was thumping painfully. He glanced at Mimi and saw that her eyes looked glazed. She was clutching her stick so tightly that her knuckles were white.

She felt as tense and scared as he did. Maybe she felt worse. He saw her eyes widen, and quickly looked forward again.

Jim had stopped. He was staring at some white swans that were gliding together close to the bank on the left-hand side of the bridge. Beneath the bridge itself there were only dark shadows.

Leo forced his mind away from the shadows and what might be — what *was* — lurking there. He concentrated instead on the swans. They were the only things about this scene that didn't look familiar. There were seven of them, and they all looked exactly alike.

"There aren't usually swans here," he said, without thinking.

Jim turned and looked at him. "How do you know that?" he asked slowly. "I thought you'd never been here before."

Leo realized he'd made a mistake. He felt himself blushing. "I — I haven't," he stammered. "I just — I just thought you wouldn't usually find swans here. Because of the troll. And the Blue Queen."

"Yes, well, you're right about that," Jim said, frowning and turning back to face the bridge. "I can't say I've ever seen swans this far upriver before. It's odd."

"There are seven of them, Jim," Bertha whispered, her ears twitching. "Do you think they could have come here to see you?"

Jim winced. "You mean they might be my family, and Polly's?" he muttered. "Well, they could be, I suppose. The number's right. My parents. Pol's parents. Suki and Walter. Young Lily. Seven."

He stared at the swans for a long moment. Then he rubbed his forehead angrily.

"It's stupid even to think about it," he said roughly. "Even if they are — even if they once were — Polly's and my people, they could only be here by chance. They couldn't have known I was coming."

He shook his head. "And even if they *had* known, they wouldn't have cared. They've forgotten who they are. They've forgotten they were ever human."

Leo heard the pain in his voice, and his own heart ached.

"Jim," Mimi said tensely. "Don't come any farther. We'll go on alone from here. Just in case . . ."

Jim turned to her, frowning, and she looked down, not wanting to meet his eyes.

"In case the swans are spies for the Blue Queen," she went on in a rush. "If the Blue Queen made them what they are, she might still have power over them. They might have been sent here to watch out for us, and report to her. And if they see you with us . . ."

Her voice trailed off, but there was no need for her to finish. Everyone knew how far the Blue Queen would go to gain revenge on people who helped her enemies. The swans were living proof of that.

Jim rubbed his hand over his brow again. "You might be right," he muttered. "I don't mind for myself, but I can't put Polly and Rosebud and Grandma at risk. I just can't —"

His strong face was full of anguish, and Leo felt a rush of sympathy for him.

This is what the Blue Queen and Spoiler have done, he thought. *They've made brave, decent people like Jim and Polly afraid. And they've made them ashamed. But* the Blue Queen and Spoiler *are the ones who should be ashamed — ashamed because they don't care for a single soul except themselves.*

"We'll be fine from here," he heard himself saying, with forced cheerfulness. "Thanks for everything, Jim. We —"

"Never mind about that," Jim broke in. "I was going to tell you all this at the bridge, but I'll tell you now. When you're safely on the other side, turn right, and go into the willow trees. You'll find someone there who'll help you. He's expecting you. I sent him a mouse last night."

He met Mimi's and Leo's startled eyes, and shrugged. "Polly and I couldn't let you risk your lives, after all you've done for us," he said. "So we've organized a hero for you. The best there is."

"But — but this morning Grandma kept saying —" Mimi began.

Jim shrugged again. "Grandma doesn't know this hero is still in business. Hardly anyone does. He values his privacy, you might say, and he only takes on jobs he feels like doing. But he — well, he feels he owes Polly and me a favor, and in the note I explained about Rosebud and the wolf and all, so we think he'll decide to help you if you talk to him nicely. He'll give you a bed for the night, too."

"Jim, how can we ever thank you?" Leo burst out, overwhelmed with gratitude and relief.

"How can we ever thank *you*?" Jim answered. "Now, before I forget . . ."

He handed Mimi and Leo one of the little butter cakes each.

"Put these in your pockets," he said. "You'll know when to use them. You can't risk swimming in the river now. Not with those swans around. Well, good luck."

He hitched his pack higher on his shoulder and stepped off the road, back into the trees.

"Watch out for bears on your way home, Jim," Bertha murmured. "There were so many of them in Deep Wood. A lot more than usual, you said . . ." There was a strange note in her voice. Her eyes were anxious.

"If you mean the bears might be Blue Queen spies as well, I've already thought of that," Jim said somberly. "Luckily it was quite dark, and they stayed back from the path. They didn't get a good look at me, and I won't be giving them a second chance — or leading them back to the cottage, either. I'll go back through the Gap, then cut through to the road and walk home that way."

They said good-bye and left him standing there. All their hearts were very full. Without any discussion, they moved into the middle of the road and began walking briskly toward the bridge. None of them looked back. It was important that the swans didn't realize they'd had someone with them.

Leo was certain, however, that Jim was still watching them. He could almost feel Jim's eyes on his back. The thought comforted him a little, though he would much rather have had Jim himself striding along with them, tall and capable, the axe swinging in his hand.

He caught a whiff of an awful smell, and wrinkled his nose. The smell was like a mixture of rotten meat, blocked drains, and very old garbage. With every step he took, the smell grew stronger. He realized that it was coming from the bridge.

"Troll," Bertha said, shuddering delicately. "Disgusting!"

A moment afterward, one of the swans saw them. It made a small warning sound. The other swans turned their heads to look, their slim necks twisting like white snakes.

"They were watching for us, all right," said Bertha grimly. "Be ready, in case they come at us. Swans are much stronger than they look, and these are big ones."

Leo tightened his grip on his stick, wondering how much use it would be against seven angry, enchanted swans. But the swans made no move to leave the water. They just watched as the companions moved closer and closer to the bridge. Their flat, black-edged eyes reminded Leo unpleasantly of Freda the duck.

Mimi wasn't paying any attention to the swans. She was looking straight ahead, her eyes fixed on the thick gray planks of the bridge.

"Have you seen any sign of the troll yet?" Leo whispered to her.

Mimi shook her head slightly, but didn't speak.

"It'll be underneath the bridge," Bertha said knowledgeably. "Lurking. It'll only come out when we try to cross. That's what trolls do. They're really sneaky."

"Have you fought a lot of them, Bertha?" Leo asked, to make himself feel better.

"Um . . . not exactly *a lot*," she said.

"How many?" Leo asked.

"Well, none, as a matter of fact," Bertha admitted reluctantly. "But I *saw* one once — from a distance. It was *unbelievably* ugly." She thought for a moment, and her ears twitched. "And quite big," she added.

"Very big," Mimi said dully.

Leo glanced at her. She met his eyes. "I've seen pictures," she said, her lips hardly moving. "And I've seen them in movies. Haven't you?"

Leo shrugged. He probably *had* seen trolls in movies, but he couldn't remember exactly what they'd looked like. And it didn't matter anyway. Trolls in movies were just products of someone's imagination. *This* troll — the troll under the bridge — was real.

Real. He tried to make himself believe it.

"What are moovlies?" Bertha asked with interest.

Uh-oh, Leo thought. He wondered how Mimi was going to cover up her mistake, then realized she wasn't even going to try. She had gone back to staring at the bridge. Maybe she hadn't even heard Bertha's question.

"Movies are pictures that move," he told Bertha, trying to sound very casual and unconcerned. "Haven't you ever seen one?"

"No," breathed Bertha, her eyes very round. "Why, I had no *idea* you had exciting things like that on the coast. Oh, I'd *adore* to be in a picture that moved. I must ask Jolly about it when we get back."

She sighed. "*If* we get back," she added.

They had reached the bridge. The smell drifting from beneath it was so vile that Leo felt his stomach heave. Sweat broke out on his forehead. Fighting down waves of nausea, he glanced to his left. The swans hadn't moved. Floating silently, so close together that their wings were almost touching, they were still watching the newcomers intently.

"It smells like something died down there," muttered Bertha, twitching her nose in disgust.

Mimi's eyes brightened. "Maybe it's the troll," she whispered. "I mean, maybe the troll's dead! Jim said it was very old."

"There's only one way to find out," Leo said in a strangled voice. He moved forward.

"Oh, that's the spirit!" cried Bertha warmly.

"Leo —" Mimi began.

But Leo had already stepped onto the bridge.

CHAPTER 24

The boards of the bridge were loose. They shifted and rattled beneath Leo's feet as he moved forward. It was impossible for him to walk as fast as he'd intended.

"I *do* admire a man of action," he heard Bertha say to Mimi as they picked their way along behind him.

Leo gritted his teeth, feeling like a complete fraud. Bertha thought he'd been tough and brave, leading the way onto the bridge. In fact, he'd just known that if he stayed still for a moment longer, breathing in that ghastly stench, he was going to throw up. And the thought of being sick in front of Bertha and Mimi — let alone Jim, if Jim was still watching — had been too awful to contemplate.

Anything would be better than that, he told himself. Then he reached the middle of the bridge and realized just how wrong he was.

There was a great, wallowing splash. The boards under his feet jerked upward as huge fists pounded on them from below. There was a sickening gust of the foul smell.

Choking and gasping, Leo lost his footing and stumbled backward. Bertha cannoned into him with a squeal. Mimi screamed in terror. And the next moment, a hideous, dripping figure had swung itself over the side of the bridge and was squatting before them, scowling ferociously.

"Who be daring to cross my bridge?" it croaked in a rasping voice, harsh as the sound of water running down a drain.

It was the ugliest, most terrifying thing that Leo had ever seen. Not just because its lumpy, hairless body was as pale as the underside of a fish. Or because its eyes were tiny and burning red, its huge ears stuck straight out from the sides of its head, and great clumps of black bristles sprouted from its flaring nostrils. Or because it wore the waterlogged, hairy, stinking skin of a goat, and brandished a long white bone in one huge hand.

Those things were bad enough. But what made Leo's flesh creep was the sneer of evil delight that twisted the creature's face.

The troll tapped the bone menacingly on the boards of the bridge.

A decent show of fear, and a butter cake or two . . .

Well, we're not having any trouble with the fear part, Leo thought wildly. He had managed to regain his balance, he was still gripping his stick, but his knees were trembling, and his hands were shaking, too. Mimi was cowering back, her teeth chattering. Even Bertha was looking aghast, and was making no attempt to adjust her hat, which had flopped awkwardly over one eye, its ribbons loose and dangling.

Leo forced his free hand to move to his pocket. His shaking fingers found the little butter cake, and he pulled it out. It was a bit squashed. He hoped the troll wouldn't mind.

"Please — don't hurt us," he said unsteadily. "Please — let us cross your bridge. We brought you this." He balanced the lopsided butter cake on the palm of his hand and held it out.

The troll bent forward and peered at the cake. Then suddenly it snorted contemptuously through its nose, blowing the cake off Leo's hand. The cake sailed over the edge of the bridge and fell with a plop into the river.

"Oh, what a waste!" cried Bertha.

The troll looked at her and licked its lips with a thick yellow tongue.

"Pork chops!" it croaked.

"How *dare* you!" shrieked Bertha, and took an angry step forward.

"No, Bertha, no!" cried Mimi, clinging to her in terror.

The troll grinned evilly, showing a mouthful of sharp, crooked brown teeth.

Bertha froze. "Well, if that troll's lost a single *one* of its teeth, I'm a mushroom's auntie," she murmured.

Leo stared at the grinning troll. Suddenly he felt horribly certain about something.

"You're not the troll who lived under this bridge before, are you?" he asked unsteadily.

The troll's grin widened. It shook his head. "This be my bridge now," it said. "Old troll be all gone."

"Where did it go?" asked Leo, trying to stop his voice trembling.

The troll patted its enormous belly, burped richly, and winked.

"You *ate* the old troll?" Bertha cried in horror. "How could you *do* that?"

"He were pretty tough, that's true," said the troll, scratching its bald head thoughtfully. "Took a lot of hard chewing, he did. But I got him down all right."

It considered Mimi, Bertha, and Leo, and nodded with satisfaction. "You three be tender, though," it said. "You be good dessert. Triple treat."

Run! The thought rang in Leo's mind, but he stayed rooted to the spot. They were in the very middle of the bridge. Escape was impossible. The moment he, Mimi, and Bertha tried to run, the troll would be upon them. If they jumped into the water, it would follow. Either way, they'd never reach the riverbank alive.

Then he suddenly remembered the ring. The ring! It could save them! Mimi could wish them home right now! He half-turned, taking a breath to speak . . .

And met Bertha's eyes.

Leo's chest tightened. What would happen to Bertha if he and Mimi suddenly deserted her?

You know what will happen, and it can't be helped, the cold voice of reason told him. *What's the point in all of you dying?*

But Bertha's only in danger now because she came to help us, another part of his mind argued. *We can't abandon her!*

And as he hesitated, paralyzed by indecision, he became aware that Bertha was whispering to him.

"Get behind me, grab Mimi, and run back to the riverbank,"

she breathed, her mouth hardly moving. "I'll hold the troll back for as long as I can. When I say go. Ready . . . ?"

"Aren't you going to ask us the three questions, troll?" Mimi's voice was high and trembling.

Astonished, Leo looked at her. She was deathly pale. Her teeth were still chattering. But she was looking straight at the troll.

The troll's eyes narrowed. "What questions?" it asked suspiciously.

"You ask us three questions, and if we answer them you don't eat us and we can cross the bridge," said Mimi, her voice a little stronger now. "That's how it's always done. That's the rule. Isn't it, Leo? Isn't it, Bertha?"

"Oh, yes," Leo and Bertha chorused.

The troll frowned and scratched its head. "I don't know nothing about no questions," it said sullenly. "Not my fault. I never had a bridge before. Hold on a minute."

Its tiny eyes went blank. It was obviously trying to think.

Mimi nodded slightly. This was the moment she'd been waiting for. They all began to ease themselves back, away from the troll. One step. Two . . .

Then abruptly the troll's eyes cleared. "I got it now," it said slowly. "This be my bridge. Rules be *my* rules. And my rules say dots to three questions! I hungry!"

It grinned savagely, and launched itself at Bertha.

"Run!" Bertha shouted at the top of her voice, bracing herself.

Then a few things happened at once.

Jim burst out of hiding and ran shouting toward the bridge, his axe held high. Another figure emerged from the shadowy willow trees on the other side of the river and raced toward the bridge, vigorously beating a gong. The swans took flight, soaring up and over the bridge in a loud confusion of beating white wings.

Startled, the troll veered off course. Its stubby fingers failed to grasp Bertha's neck, and fastened instead on the ribbons of Bertha's hat.

Howling, it stumbled and fell, tearing the hat from Bertha's head. The ribbons slipped from its fingers. The hat sailed over the side of the bridge, into the river.

"My *hat*!" screamed Bertha. "Oh, you *beast*!" She hurled herself at the troll, butting it in right in the middle of its bulging belly.

The troll bellowed and curled up into a ball.

"Run!" shouted the man with the gong, beckoning urgently.

"*Run!*" roared Jim from the other side of the river.

Leo grabbed Mimi's hand, dragged her over the groaning body of the troll, and ran for his life. He could hear Bertha running after them. He hoped desperately that she wouldn't stop to try to fish her hat out of the water.

They reached the other side of the bridge. The sound of the gong was deafening. The man beating the gong was tall, sinewy, and roughly dressed. His graying hair was tied back in a ponytail. He was much older than Jim, but he radiated energy and strength of purpose.

"Go!" he shouted, jerking his head toward the willow trees. "Get out of sight! Hurry!"

Leo and Mimi glanced over their shoulders and saw that the troll was staggering after them across the bridge, its huge hands clamped to its ears. They saw the dark figure of Jim on the other side of the river, making frantic gestures at them.

Gasping, hearts thumping, they reached the shelter of the trees. Not far away, right beside the river, was a dark little house almost hidden among feathery, drooping willow boughs. Someone was hammering wood behind the house, and smoke was drifting from its chimney, but they didn't move any closer. Instead, screened by the soft veil of green, they looked back.

Despite the fading light, they could see the river clearly. They could see the strange man standing very upright at the end of the bridge, apparently quite unafraid, and beating his gong furiously. Facing him was the troll, bent double, hands pressed to its ears.

"Go back, troll!" the man bawled over the clanging of the gong. "The three have crossed the bridge. They're no more business of yours!"

For a long, terrible moment the troll defied him, snarling and showing all its teeth. Then, slowly, it turned and slouched away. When it reached the middle of the bridge, it sullenly threw itself over the side, into the water.

There was a tremendous splash. Waves surged toward the riverbanks. The troll sank beneath the swirling surface, and was gone.

The man dropped his arms. The sound of the gong died away.

Bertha sighed with relief and shook her head till her ears flapped. "I forgot about trolls hating loud noises till that fellow came running," she said. "I suppose, living near that bridge, he keeps the gong handy in case of trouble."

"The swans flew away," Mimi panted, sinking to the ground.

"They saw the troll attack," Leo said grimly. "They probably thought there was no need to stay. They thought we were finished. And we would have been, too, if it hadn't been for you, Bertha."

Bertha tried, unsuccessfully, to look modest. "Mimi helped," she said graciously. "Because of her, we'd managed to move away from the troll a bit. And of course Jim and that wild-looking fellow with the gong gave the nasty creature a fright."

"The swans startled it, too, by mistake, taking off when they did," said Mimi. "I suppose they've gone to report to the Blue Queen."

"Well, that's worked out *very* well then, hasn't it?" exclaimed Bertha, nodding with satisfaction. "If the Blue Queen thinks we're dead, she won't be on her guard against us."

Leo was hardly listening. He was watching the man with the gong. The man had raised his hand to wave at Jim, who was still standing at the other end of the bridge. Jim was waving back, his grin gleaming white through the dimness.

"I'll bet that's the hero we're supposed to ask for help," he murmured, as the man gave a final wave, turned away from the bridge, and bent to pick something up from the riverbank beside it.

"Oh!" Bertha squealed. "My hat! He found my hat!"

The man began striding toward them, carrying the gong and its beater in one hand and Bertha's dripping hat in the other.

"The waves the troll made when it jumped into the river must have carried my hat to shore!" Bertha cried excitedly. "Oh, I hope it's not ruined!"

She bolted out of the trees and ran to meet the man.

"Oh, thank you kindly!" Leo and Mimi heard her say, as they slowly followed her. "I don't know *what* I would have done without my hat. My complexion is *so* delicate, you know."

"Of course," the man answered gravely. "The hat's rather wet, I'm afraid, but it'll dry nicely by the fire, I'm sure."

He paused. "Am I right in thinking I'm speaking to Bertha, artist's model and watch-pig at Jack Macdonald's farm?" he inquired, bowing slightly.

Bertha wriggled with pleasure. "Why, yes you are," she gushed, fluttering her eyelashes. "Watch-pig, wolf fighter, artist's model, and soon-to-be moovlie star, as a matter of fact."

"Really?" the man murmured. He saw Leo and Mimi move out of the trees, and waved them back with a slight frown.

"Don't come out," he said rather curtly. "We can talk more safely in the house."

"And we can dry my hat at the same time," Bertha said. She cleared her throat delicately. "And perhaps — since fighting trolls *always* makes me rather peckish — we could have a little snack?"

The man smiled at her, and his weather-beaten face suddenly looked much younger. "I'm sure I can find something," he agreed.

He led the way to the house, opened the door, and stood back as they moved gratefully inside.

The room they entered was very dim. At first, Leo could see only the shapes of furniture and a fire glowing on one side of the room. There was a delicious smell of something savory cooking.

"Wak, wak, wak," chuckled a harsh, horribly familiar voice.

Leo, Mimi, and Bertha stopped dead.

"What was that?" Bertha gasped, looking around blindly.

The door slammed shut behind them. They heard the sound of the key turning in the lock.

"Oh, no," Mimi muttered.

Leo blinked frantically, trying to see. Dimly he made out Freda the duck staring at him belligerently from the hearth rug. And right beside her, slowly rising from an armchair, was Conker.

Leo spun around, but there was no escape. The door was shut and locked, and the man with the gong was standing against it, slipping the key into his pocket.

"Got them!" quacked the duck triumphantly.

This can't be happening, Leo thought, numb with shock. *After what Jim said . . . after all we've been through . . .*

Bertha shouldered past him and faced the man, her head lowered threateningly.

"Stand aside," she said, in a low, frightening voice that Leo barely recognized.

There was a swift movement in the shadows, and the next moment the man was no longer alone. Tye the Terlamaine stood beside him, her golden eyes gleaming, her dagger in her hand.

"Oh, my liver, lungs, and left big toe!" muttered Conker, snatching up a piece of firewood and scrambling to join them.

Leo's numbness vanished, swamped by a wave of anger. His only weapon was the stick Jim had given him. Well, it would have to do. He raised the stick and stepped forward to stand beside Bertha. Through the gloom, he saw Mimi's pale face appear on Bertha's other side. Mimi's mouth was a straight, hard line. She was also brandishing her stick.

"Stand aside," Bertha said again.

"Shut your mouth, pig," hissed the Terlamaine. "Do you know who you are speaking to?"

"Do you know who *you* are speaking to, tiger-woman?" shrieked Bertha, bristling. "Shut your own mouth!"

The man sighed. "There's no need for this," he said. "There's been a mistake. Mimi and Leo misunderstood —"

"Conker's fault," quacked the duck. Conker glared at her.

The man looked from Leo to Mimi and back to Leo again. "Conker meant you no harm," he said. "If all had gone well, he, Tye, and Freda would have brought you safely to me. Unfortunately —"

"How did I know they'd run off?" Conker interrupted in injured tones. "I thought they trusted me. After all I'd done for them . . ."

Bertha looked at Leo inquiringly. He shook his head in confusion.

"It is not surprising that the Langlanders lost their faith in you, Conker," said Tye in her deep, husky voice. "You pushed them into the Gap without telling them what it was, and there are no Gaps where they come from, you *know* that."

"Yes, well," grumbled Conker, "I forgot, didn't I? A person can't remember everything."

"There are no Gaps on the coast?" Bertha exclaimed. "Why, I had no idea! What a very amazing place the coast must be! No Gaps, no witches, moovlies . . ."

The man, Tye, and Conker all looked quickly at Mimi and Leo.

"What?" demanded Bertha, glancing around. "What did I say?"

"Oh, nothing, nothing!" Conker babbled. "Just — well, yes, the coast is a very amazing place. Parts of the coast, anyway — the part where our young friends come from, obviously, and —"

"Quite!" the man cut in loudly.

Conker shut his mouth with a snap. "Well, I'm sorry I gave you a fright, but what else was I to do?" he said to Leo and Mimi rather sulkily. "I had to get you out of there before any more folk saw you, and I was under orders not to tell anyone about that Gap. So when old Pop suddenly turned up, just as I'd got the door open, I —"

"You panicked," Tye said curtly. "You pushed them in without a word. They found themselves alone in Flitter Wood — and look what that led to!"

"The Flitters told us you were dangerous," Mimi said, lifting her chin. "They were terrified!"

"The Flitters are only afraid of one of us," Tye said coldly. "And they have very good reason for that."

She, the man, and Conker all turned to frown at Freda.

The duck fluffed her feathers irritably. "All that happened ages ago," she said. "And I don't know what all the fuss was about anyway. I only ate a few of them."

"It was unforgivable!" hissed Tye. "Are you blind, that you cannot tell the difference between a Flitter and a dot? And then yesterday you chose to threaten them, as a way of catching the Langlanders! Oh, you and Conker are a pretty pair!"

"We've been through all this before, many times," the man broke in quickly, as Conker scowled furiously and opened his mouth to reply. "The important thing now is to convince Leo, Mimi, and Bertha that we're not their enemies."

"You could start by telling *her* to drop that knife," said Mimi, pointing at Tye.

"I will do no such thing, until you call off your pig," snapped Tye, before the man could speak.

"I *beg* your pardon!" said Bertha, baring her teeth in outrage. "I am no one's pig but my own, thank you *very* much!"

"Tye, sheath your dagger," said the man.

Tye hesitated, then, expressionless, did as she was asked.

Leo lowered his stick, and after a long moment, Mimi did the same.

"Good," the man said. "That's something, at least."

He threw down the gong and strode to the fire. He put Bertha's hat carefully on the hearth rug to dry, then lit a lantern that was standing on the mantelpiece. As the lantern flame gathered strength, Leo saw that a black pot hung over the fire. Some sort of stew was bubbling inside the pot. It smelled very good and, despite himself, Leo's mouth watered.

"Now," the man said, carrying the lantern across the room and setting it down in the middle of a long table where a round loaf of bread, a wedge of cheese, and a bowl of apples stood waiting. "It is a little early for dinner, but I suggest we sit down, eat, and talk together, like civilized folk. Conker, will you ladle out the stew?"

Conker nodded abruptly and went to a cupboard near the table. He started collecting bowls and spoons, counting under his breath.

"We won't sit down, or eat, or talk, until you unlock that door," Leo said in a level voice.

"That's telling him, Leo!" whispered Bertha approvingly.

The man gazed steadily at Leo. There was a strange look in his eyes. "I can't risk your running away again, Leo," he said slowly.

Leo shook his head. "We won't talk while we're prisoners," he said. "Why should we?"

The man smiled ruefully. "Why indeed?" he murmured.

He pulled the key from his pocket, went to the door, and unlocked it.

"Very well," he said. "Now will you sit down? Or is there something else you require?"

"Well, *I* would like to know your name," Mimi said challengingly. "You seem to know ours."

Tye made a small, outraged sound. Briefly Leo wondered who this man was, so shabbily dressed, so mildly spoken, yet obviously so highly respected.

The corner of the man's mouth tweaked. "You can call me Hal," he said.

Leo heard Bertha gasp, and looked around. Bertha's mouth was hanging open. Obviously the name Hal meant something to her — something important. Jim's voice suddenly echoed in his mind: *We've organized a hero for you. The best there is . . .*

Hal moved to the table, sat down at its head, and began cutting bread into chunks. Conker dumped a bundle of spoons onto the table, stomped over to the fire, and began splashing stew into bowls with more energy than neatness. Tye moved silently to his side and began carrying filled bowls to the table.

"Don't tell me you're *the* Hal — I mean, Hal, the great wizard who ended the Dark Time?" Bertha asked breathlessly.

"The very same," Freda quacked.

The man kept silent, and went on sawing bread.

As Leo and Mimi exchanged startled glances, Bertha gasped. "I can't believe this!" she squeaked. "Hal! *The* Hal! And you saved my hat! You knew my name! You invited me into your home! I — I threatened to knock you down! Oh!"

Clearly bursting with excitement, she moved a little closer to the table.

"Macdonald said that you were the bravest man he had ever heard of," she told Hal. "He said that while the heroes were fighting the monsters on the plain in the Final Battle, you went into the Blue Queen's castle all alone."

"There he's wrong, though I know that's how the story is often told," Hal said quietly, nodding his thanks as Tye placed a bowl of stew in front of him. "I wasn't particularly brave, and I wasn't alone."

"He certainly was not!" Freda sniffed, glaring at Bertha. "Alone, that is. *We* were with him."

"Oh, *really*," Bertha drawled. "Well, I'm sure you were a *great* help."

"Conker and Freda got me through the battle, and into the

castle," Hal said. "Without their protection I would never have survived. My life before that had been a placid one. It hadn't prepared me for fighting four-headed beasts."

He grinned, and again ten years at least were wiped from his face. "Or any beasts at all, in fact," he added.

"You were hopeless in those days, that's true," Freda agreed. "But you're a lot better now."

"You are indeed," Conker said, plumping the last heaped bowl onto the table and sitting down in front of it. "You showed that swamp lurgie a thing or two on our last gig. It was out of that village quick smart. I wouldn't be surprised if it's still running."

Hal slapped him on the back affectionately. "Swamp lurgies aren't much of a problem, and you know it, old friend," he said. "But, yes, I've improved since the day when you fought your way into the Blue Queen's castle with me clinging to your coattails, no doubt about that."

"When we finally got to the castle it was practically empty," Conker told Bertha, his good humor completely restored by this chance to relive a great adventure. "All the queen's monsters were fighting in the battle. There were just a few guards, that's all, and Freda, Tye, and I — Tye had joined us by then — soon disposed of *them*, didn't we, Freda?"

"No problem," said the duck.

"After that it was easy," Hal said. "Just a matter of finding the right room. None of the doors were locked. Spoiler and the queen thought they had nothing to fear, you see. So I was able to — do what I had to do."

He frowned slightly and pushed the board of cut-up bread into the middle of the table.

"Oh, you're so *modest!*" Bertha breathed admiringly. "And you saved the world!"

Hal hunched his shoulders as if the praise embarrassed him. "I broke the queen's power, that was all," he said.

"*All?*" Bertha cried, her voice rising to a squeak. "What do you mean, *all!* Why, you're a hero! You should be living in the best house in the land! What are you doing *here?*"

Hal raised an eyebrow quizzically, and she blushed.

"Not that this isn't a very pleasant little place," she added hastily. "Very pleasant! With a water view, too."

"I live here because here I can be private," Hal said. "No one else will live on this side of the bridge, and very few folk know this house exists. I'm often away — traveling with Conker, Freda, and Tye — but it's good to come back to peace and quiet."

"Oh, I *do* understand," Bertha said, nodding vigorously. "Being famous can be quite *exhausting*, can't it? Sometimes I long for peace and quiet myself."

Freda laughed maliciously. Bertha turned to stare at her.

"This place has another advantage," Hal continued. "The Blue Queen has by no means accepted her defeat, you know. She's still dangerous. It does no harm for someone to keep a watchful eye on her."

He didn't look at Leo and Mimi as he spoke, but Leo was sure he intended them to hear. Hal wanted them to know that it was he who had sent word to Conker that the Blue Queen was on the move. It was Hal who had tried to protect them.

Bertha abruptly became serious. "I think the queen's power might be growing again," she said in a low voice. "There were lots of bears in the forest. Many more than usual, Jim said. And that new troll . . ."

"It wasn't there when Tye and Freda and I crossed the bridge this morning," Conker put in. "It's appeared since."

Hal didn't comment, merely pulling Bertha's bowl of stew a little closer to the table edge, and beckoning her to join him. Tye and Freda had already taken their seats. Only Leo and Mimi were still standing.

"What do you think?" Leo whispered to Mimi out of the corner of his mouth.

"I think we should be very careful," Mimi whispered back. "How do we know that this man's really Hal? We've only got his word for it — his and Tye's and Conker's. For all we know the real Hal is buried under the floorboards, or floating in the river."

"Don't be ridiculous!" Leo muttered. "Of course he's the real Hal. Jim waved to him. Jim recognized him!"

"Well, okay, so he's the real Hal," Mimi hissed impatiently. "I still don't trust him. There's something shifty about him. He says all the right things, but he won't look us in the eye while he says them. He's keeping something to himself, and I'm not going to relax for a second till we find out what it is."

She stalked over to the table and sat down. As Leo followed and took his place beside her, he stole a look at Hal. All his instincts were telling him that the man deserved his trust.

But why do I feel like that? Leo thought suddenly. *I've just met him. Could it be an enchantment, like the one in Deep Wood? Hal's a wizard. He's supposed to have lost his powers, but maybe he's still strong enough to bewitch people like us.*

The thought was very unpleasant. Leo pushed it aside, telling himself not to be stupid. He had good, sensible reasons for trusting Hal. Hal had driven back the troll. Hal was the hero of the Dark Time. And Jim and Polly wouldn't have sent Leo, Mimi, and Bertha to anyone who wasn't completely reliable.

But as Leo picked up his spoon and began to eat, he knew that, however he felt, Mimi was right to be a little wary. They couldn't afford to make any more mistakes.

CHAPTER 26

While they were eating, there was no talk about the quest to save Mutt. When Mimi tried to raise the subject, Hal calmly said it must wait until dinner was over. So while Mimi simmered in frustration, Bertha seized her chance to ask question after question about the Dark Time's great final battle.

Conker regaled them with spirited accounts of the battle and its heroes, pushing apple cores and crumbs of bread around the table to illustrate his descriptions.

Hal said much less, and when Bertha questioned him about his famous single-handed combat with the Blue Queen, he shook his head, refusing to speak.

This impressed Leo more than any thrilling tale would have done. He knew that if something very frightening or very heart-wrenching had happened to him, he would find it difficult to talk about it — especially to strangers.

All the same, he found himself wishing that Hal would unbend a little — treat them a little *less* like strangers. Hal was polite, but he kept his distance, and as the meal went on he seemed to become more and more withdrawn.

When all the plates were empty, Conker, Tye, and Hal began clearing the table. Mechanically, Leo got up to help.

Bertha yawned. "I might go and see if my hat is dry," she said, looking longingly at the hearth rug.

"Good idea," Hal said, his eyes warming as he smiled at her.

Hal doesn't hold himself apart from all of us, Leo thought. *He's fond of Bertha. It's Mimi and me he doesn't like.*

Fighting down disappointment, he picked up a pile of dirty dishes and followed Conker out to the long, narrow room that served as Hal's kitchen.

As he expected, the kitchen was as tidy and well organized as the main room of the house. It was furnished simply with a long, scrubbed wooden bench facing two large storage cupboards.

Pots and pans stood on a shelf above the bench. A net of onions and bunches of herbs hung from hooks fastened to the ceiling. A green dish towel hung over the sill of the window beside the back door.

Why should Hal like us? Leo thought dismally, as Hal brought the kettle from the fire and poured hot water into the dish-washing bowl. *Hal knows we broke the music box rules. He knows we caused the quake. He knows that, because of us, the Blue Queen's put more bears in the wood, and a new troll on the bridge. For Hal, we're just trouble.*

Hal said something about fetching more water, picked up the empty kettle, and disappeared through the back door into the night.

Conker began washing up, clattering dishes and spoons noisily, as if to discourage conversation. Leo went to the window to get the dish towel.

The window had swung shut, jamming the towel in place. Leo pushed at the wooden frame, the window opened with a little jerk, and fresh, river-smelling air streamed in, cooling his face.

As he pulled the towel free, he heard a voice drifting from outside — Hal's voice, very quiet and low.

"Stop arguing," Hal muttered. "Just do what you're paid for, and deliver the message."

"It's all very well for you to say," squeaked a tiny voice in reply. "It's dangerous, I tell you!"

"What happened to your motto — 'The mail must go through,' or whatever it is?" Hal whispered furiously.

"That's been changed," the squeaky voice said. "Now it's 'The mail must go through *if possible.*'"

"Leo! Are you going to dry up, or not?" called Conker from the other end of the room.

Guiltily, Leo spun around. He hurried to the bench and began wiping dishes, wondering uneasily about what he'd heard.

Tye had gone back into the living room. Hal didn't return. Conker obviously didn't feel like talking. Leo stolidly dried dishes, feeling like an unwelcome intruder and trying not to mind.

When at last the job was done, he trailed back into the living room to find Mimi still sitting at the table, staring down at her folded hands, Freda and Tye keeping silent watch on her, and Bertha stretched out on the hearth rug beside her hat, snoring gently.

He wanted to tell Mimi about hearing Hal arguing with the messenger mouse, but he couldn't. Not with Freda and Tye listening to every word he said, and Conker stacking clean bowls into the closet close by.

Hal came in with the filled kettle and put it back on the fire.

"Good," he said in a low voice, glancing at the sleeping Bertha. "Now we can talk freely."

He sat down heavily at the head of the table again. Leo sank down beside Mimi. Suddenly there was a strong feeling of tension in the room.

"For generations Langlanders used this world as their personal playground," Hal said abruptly. "I thought those days had ended."

Leo thought instantly of Spoiler, and was filled with shame. Did Hal know who Spoiler really was? It sounded as if he did. He must have discovered Spoiler's secret when was battling the Blue Queen. No wonder he hated Langlanders — hated the very name.

"We're not here for fun," Mimi said in a flat voice. "We're here to get my dog back. When we've done that we'll go straight home and be no more trouble to anyone."

Hal closed his eyes as if Mimi's sharpness pained him.

"I assume it was you, Leo, who inherited the music box from Bethany Langlander?" he asked.

Leo's stomach lurched. "Yes," he managed to say.

Hal nodded. "But if my instincts are correct, it was Mimi who —?"

"Yes," snapped Mimi. "I was the one who wound the music box more than three times. I'm the one who opened the Rondo gate."

"Keep your voice down," Hal warned, opening his eyes and glancing over his shoulder at Bertha.

"I do not know why you insist on this secrecy, Hal," Tye complained, moving restlessly. "If *we* can live with the knowledge that the Langlander world exists outside our own, why should others in Rondo not live with it, too?"

"Most folk wouldn't believe it!" Conker snorted. "They'd think we'd gone crazy if we told them."

"And what good would it do for those few who *did* believe?" Hal muttered. "They'd learn that their world is just a small painted box inside another, far larger, far more unfriendly world. They'd learn that it's at the mercy of any stranger who chooses to treat it carelessly. They'd learn to fear."

"At least they'd know the truth," Leo exclaimed, before he could stop himself. "Haven't they got a right to that? Even if it makes them unhappy?"

Tye gave a short, triumphant laugh. Hal took a breath, then pressed his lips together as if thinking better of what he'd been about to say.

It was Mimi who broke the silence. "Will you help us rescue my dog, Hal?" she asked bluntly. "I'm not asking you to fight the Blue Queen. I know you've lost your magic, and I know we could never defeat her on her own ground. If we're going to get Mutt back, we'll have to *steal* him back. We'll have to sneak into the castle and find where she's keeping him. And you know your way around the castle better than anyone. You can help us trick the Blue Queen — if you want to risk it."

"Shut your mouth, girl," Tye hissed. "Hal is not afraid. Not for himself."

"But is he afraid —?" Leo felt his face grow hot as everyone looked at him. "Is he — are you — afraid the Blue Queen will capture Mimi and me and — use us to make herself more powerful?"

Hal looked up. "What gave you that idea?" he asked sharply.

Because we think the Blue Queen used Spoiler that way.

The words were trembling on Leo's tongue, but he couldn't bring himself to say them. He couldn't bear to admit that he knew Spoiler was a Langlander.

"Well, we wondered —" he stumbled on, his blush deepening, "if maybe the queen can use living things from our world to make herself stronger."

"She's not a vampire, if that's what you mean," Conker said with assurance. "She walks around in the sun, and they say she's got a big mirror in her room that reflects her perfectly. Vampires can't bear the sun, and they have no reflections."

Leo stared at him, and he shrugged. "Freda and I know a lot about vampires," he said, with a touch of pride. "Vampire dens are always crawling with dots. We've cleaned up quite a few of them — for good money, too. Right, Freda?"

"Right," the duck agreed.

"We go to the dens during the day, while the vampires are

asleep," Conker went on chattily. "Safety first, I always say. They usually leave our pay in envelopes stuck to the tops of their coffins."

"I doubt Leo and Mimi believe that the queen is the ordinary sort of vampire," Hal murmured. "But, whatever they were thinking, they were wrong. She won't gain any new power by capturing them. That's one thing we don't have to worry about."

Leo caught his breath. Hal sounded so confident. It was impossible to disbelieve him. So — George Langlander hadn't helped the Blue Queen create the Dark Time. He'd just battened on to her, encouraged her, flattered her, and enjoyed the power and the wealth her wicked deeds brought him. In a way, that made Leo despise him more than ever.

"Then why did the queen try to make us go with her?" Mimi demanded. "And why did she take Mutt?"

"Perhaps she found you and your dog . . . interesting," Tye said, very softly. "The Blue Queen likes curiosities. I myself was once part of her collection. I was kept chained in a cage, with a leather collar around my neck. Oh, I was a curiosity indeed! The only one of my tribe the Blue Queen had not murdered. The last Terlamaine."

As Mimi and Leo stared at her in horror, she lifted her head proudly.

"Hal freed me," she said. "He found me in the castle, and he freed me. He is my tribe, now."

So you defy Hal at your peril. The unspoken words were as clear as if they had been scrawled on the walls in blood.

Mimi refused to be cowed. "Listen," she said, leaning forward and speaking directly to Hal. "You don't like Langlanders. You don't want Langlanders coming into your world anymore. And *we* want to save Mutt. So . . . what about if you help us, and in return we promise never to come here again, and to make sure no one else does, either?"

Hal's face went blank. Freda burst out laughing, her masked eyes sparkling with malicious humor.

Mimi scowled. "Don't you believe we'll do it?" she demanded.

She thrust out her hand and tapped the black and gold ring gleaming on her finger. "We know all about this," she said. "The Blue Queen told us. We know it's the Key that's let Langlanders move in and out of Rondo for generations. And if you help us save Mutt, I swear that the moment we get home I'll destroy it — smash it with a hammer or something — so no one will ever be able to use it again."

There was a stunned silence. Even Leo was tongue-tied.

Leo's mind was whirling with a powerful mixture of emotions. He was full of admiration for Mimi's bold plan. At the same time he was irritated because Mimi had offered to destroy the ring without consulting him. And most of all he was deeply satisfied, because he'd suddenly thought of the perfect way to deal with Spoiler.

Abruptly Hal pushed back his chair and stood up. His eyes were deeply shadowed. Suddenly he looked like a man who carried the weight of the world on his shoulders.

"That is enough for tonight," he said. "Early as it is, we all need sleep."

"Hal, you must —" Tye began.

"But —" Mimi began at the same moment.

"We will talk again in the morning," Hal said. And his voice was so firm, and his face so haggard, that Tye fell silent and even Mimi seemed to realize that there was no point arguing.

Conker lit a candle and took Mimi and Leo to a small white room that opened off the kitchen. In the room were two narrow beds with green spreads, separated by a simple but beautifully made cabinet. Above the cabinet was a window covered by a green-and-white-striped curtain that stirred in the soft night breeze.

Leo went to the cabinet and ran his fingers appreciatively over the smooth golden-brown wood.

"You'll find blankets in there," Conker said gruffly. "Nice piece, isn't it? Hal made it. He made every stick of furniture in this house, as a matter of fact."

"Really?" Leo asked eagerly.

But Conker seemed to regret having started a conversation. He thrust the candle into Leo's hand, muttered a hurried good night, and left the room.

"He's not very friendly anymore, is he?" Leo said. "And Hal's just . . . cold."

"So? What do you care?" Mimi pulled the cabinet doors open to reveal a pile of thin, neatly folded gray blankets and two extra pillows. She threw some blankets onto her bed, then turned and regarded Leo with her head to one side.

"You know, Leo," she said. "Your trouble is, you're not *used* to people not liking you. You should try being me some time."

Leo didn't know how to answer that. Suddenly the room felt stifling. Suddenly all he wanted was to open the window wide, and breathe fresh air. He pulled the curtain aside, and stepped back in shock.

The window was open, but rough boards had been nailed across the frame on the outside, leaving only narrow gaps through which air could flow.

Leo remembered the hammering he'd heard when they'd first arrived at the house. *Conker preparing this room for us*, he thought numbly.

"Right!" Mimi snapped, glaring at the boards. "That's it. Whatever game Hal's playing, he's not going to help us, that's obvious. In fact, it looks like he's going to try to stop us getting to the Blue Queen at all. I'm getting out of here. Are you coming?"

Leo nodded. Despite the open door, the bare little room felt like a prison.

Quickly he and Mimi arranged blankets on the beds, padding them with pillows so that they looked as if someone was asleep beneath them. Then Leo blew out the candle and they slipped out of the room into the dark kitchen.

Hearing that Conker and Freda were still awake, murmuring to each other before the fire, they crept to the back door, pressed themselves into the deep shadows, and waited.

Minutes ticked by. Mumbling snores began drifting through the house.

Soon we can go, Leo thought. He was longing to move. His body seemed a mass of aches and itches. He'd stopped even trying to make sense of all this.

First you trust them, then you don't. Then you trust them, then you don't . . .

He heard the tiny sound of a board creaking and abruptly he was fully alert. Someone was moving through the house.

A slender figure glided silently into the kitchen. It was too dark for Leo to see the prowler's face, but he knew it was Tye. *She can see in the dark,* he thought with a shiver.

Tye stopped at the doorway of the small bedroom, and cautiously peered in. She stared into the darkness for a long moment. Then she pulled the door shut, locked it noiselessly with a key she had ready in her hand, and prowled back the way she had come.

Suddenly Leo was furiously angry. He hadn't a moment's doubt that Hal had given Tye the order to lock Mimi and him in. What game *was* Hal playing? Shaking off Mimi's hand as she tried to hold him back, he edged out of hiding.

He felt his way to the other end of the kitchen, and peeped into the living room. Bertha was still stretched out by the fireside. Conker was slumped in the armchair, snoring, twitching, and mumbling in his sleep. Freda was on the wooden stool, her head tucked under her wing.

But Tye was standing at the door of another room that lay right beside the kitchen. Hal's bedroom, Leo guessed.

Leo heard soft, rapid breathing behind him. Mimi hadn't been able to resist following him. He hoped Tye's ears weren't as sharp as her eyes.

"They are asleep, and the door is locked," he heard Tye say in a low voice. "But I cannot understand why you insisted on this delay, Hal. The task is distasteful to you, I know, but time will not make it any easier. You should have let me do it. It would not have worried me in the least."

Mimi drew a sharp breath. Leo's heart felt as if it had stopped.

"No!" Hal said grimly from inside the room. "This is my responsibility."

"Oh, *everything* is your responsibility, Hal!" spat the Terlamaine. "Why should these reckless Langlanders weigh on your conscience?"

"They're so young, Tye!" came Hal's low, agonized whisper.

Tye growled. "They were old enough to come here," she replied remorselessly. "They are old enough to face the consequences."

CHAPTER 27

ESCAPE

Horrified, Leo and Mimi crept back into the kitchen, praying that Conker's snores and mumbles, which had grown louder, would mask the sound of any creaking boards.

"We've got to get out of here, right now!" Mimi whispered frantically. "What about Bertha?" She was shivering as if she were freezing.

Leo fought down his confusion and fear. "She'll be okay," he whispered back. "Hal's got no reason to hurt her."

Hoping with all his heart that what he'd said was true, he felt his way to the back door. He ran his fingers over the heavy bolt and gave it a small, experimental tug. The bolt didn't budge.

He resisted the urge to tug harder. The bolt was too stiff to open silently, and he knew that even Conker's snores wouldn't mask the squeal of grating metal.

He turned his attention to the window.

"Hurry, Leo!" gasped Mimi through chattering teeth. "Tye might come back. She might decide to kill us herself, whatever Hal says. And if she finds us gone . . ."

"She won't come back," Leo muttered, and wished he felt as sure as he sounded. He found the window catch and cautiously slid it open. It was loose, and didn't make a sound.

Holding his breath, he pushed the window gently. There was the faintest sigh of wood sliding against wood, then the window swung smoothly open.

Leo let out his breath in relief. He caught the window as it began to swing shut again. He helped Mimi climb through the gap and heard the soft thump as she landed on the grass outside. He was halfway through the window himself when, over the buzz of Conker's snores, he heard sounds he'd been dreading.

Voices. Footsteps. Coming closer.

Recklessly, Leo leaped for the ground. He caught his foot on the windowsill, twisted awkwardly in the air and fell, sprawling. He lay stunned, gasping for breath. Trailing willow tips tickled his nose. *That's not how it works in the moovlies*, he thought, and had an absurd urge to laugh.

"Leo!" he heard Mimi whisper urgently. He felt her tugging at his shoulders. Dazed, he looked up and saw light glowing behind the kitchen window, which had swung shut again. He could hear the dull murmuring of voices. Then his heart jumped into his throat as he heard the rasping sound of the bolt on the back door being drawn back.

The door was opening. Soft, flickering light was spilling out onto the grass. There was no time get up, no time to run. Leo rolled desperately beneath the shelter of the trailing branches of the willow tree, pulling Mimi with him.

"Thank you very kindly," they heard a voice say in a piercing whisper.

Leo parted the leafy curtain and peered through the gap.

Bertha, her hat balanced crookedly on her head, appeared in the lighted doorway. Tye, candle in hand, was close behind her.

"I'm *so* sorry to be a trouble," Bertha whispered, stepping out onto the grass. "And I *do* hope we haven't woken Leo and Mimi. But I just *had* to get out of there. If I'd stayed I wouldn't have got a wink of sleep. I must have dozed off for a minute, and the next thing I knew the house was dark and Conker was making that terrible noise!"

Tye murmured something Leo couldn't hear.

"It's not just the snoring," Bertha went on, blowing a trailing ribbon out of her eyes. "He seems to be fighting something in his sleep as well! Mumbling and groaning and thrashing around. He gets nightmares, I suppose, poor thing . . . monsters, and the Blue Queen, and so on."

"Dots, actually," Tye said somberly. "He hates them."

She pointed to her left. "The work shed is that way, beside the house. There is plenty of sawdust on the floor. You should be quite comfortable."

She turned to go back inside.

"Ah — you *will* call me in time for breakfast, won't you?" Bertha whispered anxiously after her. "I wouldn't want to miss it. Not that I usually eat very much breakfast, of course, but I have to keep up my strength."

Tye hesitated. She glanced at the dark, barred window of Mimi and Leo's bedroom, and quickly looked away again.

"Breakfast will be . . . quite late," she said in a low voice. "Hal has something to do before he will eat. Sleep as long as you wish."

"How kind!" Bertha said graciously. "Good night, then."

"Good night," said the Terlamaine. With another glance at the barred window she slipped back into the kitchen, and closed the door. The bolt rasped as she secured it again. The flickering light shining through the kitchen window went out.

Humming softly to herself, and keeping her head very steady so her hat wouldn't fall off, Bertha ambled toward the side of the house. She rounded the corner and disappeared from view. After a few moments, Leo and Mimi heard a door creak. Bertha had found the work shed.

"What luck!" Leo whispered. "Now we can tell Bertha what's happened, and she can come with us."

Mimi moved uneasily. "I don't know," she muttered. "She thinks Hal's so wonderful. She might not believe us. She might even try to stop us leaving — or raise the alarm, or something."

"Mimi, don't you trust *anyone*?" Leo sighed.

Mimi considered this. "I trust you," she said seriously.

Leo was dumbfounded, pleased, moved, and terribly embarrassed, all at the same time.

"For the moment, anyway," Mimi added, spoiling the whole thing. "I've got no choice, really."

They crawled out from the shelter of the willow tree, and stood up. It was very dark. The sky was like black velvet, sprinkled with stars. There was no moon, but it seemed to Leo that a faint glow was visible above the willow trees that sheltered the front of the house. He wondered what it was.

As silently as they could, he and Mimi felt their way around to the side of the house. The dark bulk of the work shed loomed to their right, not far away.

"Be careful," Leo whispered as Mimi crept to the door and raised her hand to knock. "If we scare her, she might —"

"Who's there?" squeaked Bertha's voice from the other side of the door.

Mimi jumped back in fright.

"*Shh!*" Leo hissed. "Bertha! It's only us."

The door swung open. Bertha's startled face peered out from the gloom within. Her head looked as if it were floating in darkness, all by itself.

"What are you doing here?" she whispered. "Did Tye and I wake you? I'm *terribly* sorry, but I just had to have some privacy. What with Conker snoring and having nightmares about dots, and that creepy, bad-mannered duck who wears her mask even to *sleep* —"

"Bertha, let us in!" Leo broke in desperately. "We have to talk to you. It's urgent!"

"*Urgent?*" Bertha's eyes brightened. "Ooh, how exciting!"

She backed away from the doorway. Mimi and Leo slipped into the shed, closing the door after them.

They sat down in the darkness, which was filled with the tangy smell of wood shavings, and Mimi started telling Bertha about what had happened, and why they wanted to run away.

This must be where Hal makes his furniture, Leo thought, breathing in the wood smell. He wished the shed weren't so dark, so he could see Hal's workbench.

"*Well!*" Bertha's gasp broke into his thoughts. He realized that Mimi must have reached the end of her story.

"I never would have believed it!" Bertha went on, sounding very upset. "Barred windows! Locked doors! And a death plot! It's — it's incredible! Mind you, I never did trust that Conker person . . ."

"I don't think Conker even knows about it," Mimi said. "It was Tye who —"

"Well, of course!" hissed Bertha. "Everyone knows Terlamaines are cunning. And I'd believe *anything* about that duck! But are you quite, *quite* sure that *Hal* —?"

"Yes," Mimi said firmly. "We both heard it."

"And I heard something else," Leo added, suddenly remembering Hal's conversation with the messenger mouse. Quickly he repeated everything he'd heard through the kitchen window while Conker was washing dishes.

When he'd finished, there was a short, stunned silence.

"Leo, why didn't you tell me this before?" Mimi exclaimed at last.

"First I couldn't get you alone, then I forgot," Leo said, his face growing hot.

"*Forgot?*" Mimi snapped. "How could you forget something like *that?*"

"At the time it just seemed strange," Leo said, defending himself as best he could. "It didn't seem so — ominous."

"I can't see why," Mimi said coldly. "Obviously the message was for the Blue Queen. I suppose Hal was telling her we'd escaped the troll, but that he'd deal with us himself."

"This is terrible, just terrible," said Bertha, shaking her head. "Hal! In league with the Blue Queen! But Hal was the one who broke her power!"

"He wouldn't talk about that, though, would he?" Mimi said slowly. "How do we know what happened when their magic clashed? The clash took most of the Blue Queen's power, sure, but it burned away *all* of Hal's. For all we know it left the Blue Queen with some sort of hold over him that he can't break. He mightn't like doing what she wants, but he mightn't be able to help it. I've read about things like that."

"Oh, it can't be!" Bertha wailed softly.

But Leo said nothing, because Mimi's explanation, which once would have seemed to him the wildest of wild guesses, made a horrible sort of sense.

How would a good man look if he'd fallen under the power of someone wicked? If he had to watch an evil he'd tried to destroy growing in power all over again, without being able to lift a finger to stop it? If he was forced, against his will, to play the role of spy and killer?

He'd look as if the weight of the world were on his shoulders. Like Hal did.

"We'd better get you away from here at *once*," said Bertha, clambering to her feet. "How *fortunate* that I brought my hat with me when I left the house. I thought that if I left it where it was, Conker might kick it or fall on it or something."

She poked her head in Leo's general direction. "Just tie the ribbons for me, will you, Leo?"

She was trying to make Leo feel better, and he knew it. He did his best to straighten the hat, and tie the ribbons into a bow under Bertha's chin. It was difficult in the darkness, and he wasn't sure he'd done a very good job, but Bertha seemed satisfied.

"Thank you," she said. "I couldn't manage the bow myself, and I didn't like to ask that tiger-woman, somehow. Well, now I realize why, of course! I just had an *instinct* not to trust her. I'm very sensitive about these things."

They crept out of the shed, and stopped dead. Now that they were directly facing the river, all of them could see, through a gap in the willow trees, seven white, humped shapes grouped together on the darkness of the bank.

"The swans!" Mimi hissed fearfully.

"It's all right," Bertha whispered, peering at the shapes. "They've got their heads under their wings. They're asleep. Come on!"

They turned their backs on the river and stole away from the house as quietly and quickly as they could. No one called after them. There was no sound from the riverbank. Breathing sighs of relief, they pushed through the last of the willow trees and stepped out into the open. And there they stopped, staring.

Before them lay a vast stretch of open grassland which swept on and up to the castle on the hill. The land was dark, but the castle was ablaze with light. Light streamed from every window and spilled through the huge front doors, so that the moat shone like a broken ring of gold. The whole place glowed like a vision, a dream, a castle in a fairy tale.

"Do you suppose it's like this every night?" Bertha murmured, gaping at the light. "All those candles! Think of the expense!"

"The Blue Queen must have got Hal's message," Mimi said in a flat voice. "She's celebrating. There's some sort of party going on up there. I can hear music."

And when Leo concentrated, he found that he, too, could hear music. Familiar music.

"Lawks-a-daisy!" breathed Bertha. "It's 'The Pom-Pom Polka!'" And she actually began moving gently to the rhythm of the faraway sound.

Leo felt a shiver run down his spine. Could this be just a coincidence? Or had the Blue Queen chosen the tune as some sort of cruel, gloating joke? His thoughts flew to Jim, to Polly, to Grandma, and to little Rosebud.

"There's no point in just standing here," Mimi snapped. "Let's go."

"*Psst!*" The loud hissing sound made them all jump.

"Who's that?" Bertha squeaked, spinning around to look behind her.

"*Psst!* Want a hidey-hole?" a harsh voice whispered.

And there on the ground, right beside their feet and almost invisible in the gloom, was an inky black splodge. As they stared at it, it widened invitingly.

"*Urk!*" squealed Bertha in disgust, edging away from it.

"Come on in!" the hole leered. "Comfort, security, and satisfaction guaranteed!"

Recovering from his shock, Leo looked carefully at the hole in the ground. "Are you the hidey-hole we met in town?" he asked it.

The hole pulsed with wheezing laughter. "Are you joking?" it chortled. "I'm a red-blooded country hidey-hole, I am."

"You *look* like the hidey-hole we met in town," Mimi said suspiciously.

The hole's laughter stopped abruptly. "Don't give me that, girlie!" it snapped. "Those townie holes couldn't look like a proper hidey-hole if they tried. Bunch of puny, smart-talking softies! Why, in my time I've had three goats, four geese, and a couple of squirrels in my gullet, and *still* had room for a parrot. Don't you tell me that your namby-pamby townie so-called hidey-hole could have done that!"

"It could have," said Leo. He didn't really think so, but he was finding this hidey-hole very irritating.

"Yah!" jeered the hole. "Sez you!"

"If you don't know us, why are you here?" Mimi asked bluntly.

"You called me!" said the hidey-hole. "I heard you, clear as day!" It pinched in its edges to make itself small. "*Oh, I'm so scar-ed!*" it whined in a weak, babyish voice. *"Oh, what's going to happen to us! Oh, look at this huge space we've got to cross to get to the castle. And there's nowhere to hide. Oh, if only there was somewhere to hide!"*

"Well, I *certainly* didn't think *anything* like that!" huffed Bertha indignantly.

Leo was just about to say that he hadn't said anything like that either, when he realized two things: Bertha had said *think*, not *say*. And Mimi had suddenly become very quiet.

"You hear our thoughts!" he exclaimed.

"Of course I do, dummy," the hole said rudely. "What else? Or have those town hidey-holes got so soft they don't pick up mind messages anymore? Maybe in town you have to fill in a form, do you? I heard some fool was trying to bring that in. A signed request-for-help form, plus two copies, stamped by the president of the Hidey-Holes' League and —"

"No!" Leo broke in, determined to get back in control of the situation. "The hidey-holes in town still read minds. It's just that we didn't realize it till we met you. We're —" he hesitated.

"They're from the coast," Bertha finished for him apologetically.

"The coast!" exclaimed the hidey-hole. "Oh, I *see. Right!*"

It curled itself into a grotesque grin, and spoke to Leo very slowly and clearly. "If . . . you . . . want . . . a . . . place . . . to . . . hide . . . I . . . can . . . help . . . you."

This hidey-hole was truly annoying, but Leo knew he had to seize the amazing opportunity it offered at all costs. Obviously hidey-holes could move around. Was it possible . . . ?

"We're on our way to the castle," he said to the hole. "Could you take us there? I mean, could we all hide inside you while you —"

The hidey-hole's grin changed to a sneer of disdain. "What do you think I am, a covered wagon?" it snorted. "Of course you can't —"

"They're from the coast. They don't understand," Bertha put in, clearly embarrassed by Leo's ignorance.

Leo thought rapidly. "Then could you come with us to the castle?" he asked the hidey-hole. "We're sure to need you once we're inside."

"I don't know," the hidey-hole grumbled. "That sort of job could take all night. The whole night on one job . . ."

"It's a very important job, though," Bertha said quickly. "We're on a quest to save a friend from the Blue Queen."

"Yeah?" murmured the hole with interest. "A quest, eh? Well, that puts a different complexion on it. I haven't been on a quest for ages. Still, the whole night on one job . . ."

"Well, we can't waste any more time," Bertha said briskly. "We're off. If you want to be a hero, come with us. If you'd rather hang around here in case another needy squirrel comes along, that's up to you."

She trotted off across the grass without looking back. Afraid of being left behind, Leo and Mimi ran after her.

"It won't be able to resist," Bertha muttered out of the corner of her mouth as they caught up with her. "Hidey-holes are terribly conceited. They love boasting to their friends about all the clever, dangerous things they've done. It'll follow us. You wait and see."

And, sure enough, when Leo glanced over his shoulder he saw an inky black patch sliding furtively behind them. His heart lightened. If he, Mimi, and Bertha had a hidey-hole with them when they entered the castle, they'd be much safer.

Safer! a voice whispered in his mind. *Are you crazy? Nothing can make you safe in the Blue Queen's castle! You haven't got a chance.*

Leo's steps faltered. He glanced at Mimi. She was trudging along, her eyes fixed on the castle, her face absolutely expressionless. She hadn't said a word since they first began talking to the hidey-hole.

Leo knew why. Wincing, he remembered the hidey-hole's offensive mimicking of the call for help it claimed to have heard.

Oh, I'm so scared! Oh, what's going to happen to us? . . .

Those panicky, terrified thoughts hadn't been Leo's. And they hadn't been Bertha's.

They'd been Mimi's. It was Mimi the hidey-hole had heard — Mimi, wailing in her mind like a frightened child. Far from being as cold and unemotional as she had seemed when they first saw the castle, Mimi was terrified.

And thanks to the hidey-hole, I know it, Leo thought. *And Mimi knows I do. That's why she's drawn back into her shell like a snail.*

He wondered if he should say something to her, and decided it was better not to. He might make everything worse.

So he said nothing. Mimi didn't open her lips either, and even Bertha didn't seem to feel like talking. With the hidey-hole trailing behind them, they moved on through the darkness in silence, till at last they reached the bottom of the hill on which the castle stood.

There they stopped, looking up in fear and awe.

The castle blazed above them like a giant beacon. Music swept down on them in waves — the merry, jigging tune of "The Pom-Pom Polka," repeated over and over again. There was no doubt now that the tune was no coincidence.

"The Blue Queen knows we were at Jim and Polly's cottage," Leo whispered. "She knows Jim and Polly hid us."

"Of course she does," Mimi said bitterly. "Jim wrote to Hal asking him to help us, didn't he? And Tye and Conker saw Bertha at the cottage. They just put two and two together, didn't they? It was probably all in that message Hal sent."

Leo felt sick. He wondered what hideous revenge the Blue Queen was planning for the little family in the woods.

Because of us, he thought. *Because we used their cottage as a hiding place, without giving a thought to what it might mean for them until it was too late.* And suddenly, with a sinking feeling, he remembered what Hal had said about Langlanders using this world as a playground.

"Oh!" moaned Bertha. "If only we could send Jim and Polly a warning! Are you *sure* that neither of you has a pen?"

Leo and Mimi searched their pockets, just in case the previous owners of their clothes had, by some miracle, left a pen or pencil behind. All Leo found were butter cake crumbs, and all Mimi had was Conker's lemon drop, now even grubbier than it had been before.

"Keep it," advised Bertha, as Mimi moved to throw the lemon drop away. "You might need it."

"I'd never eat this!" Mimi snorted.

"You'd be surprised what you'll eat when you're starving," Bertha said darkly.

Starving in the Blue Queen's dungeons. Bertha's unspoken words sent shivers down Leo's spine. Mimi took a deep breath, and pushed the lemon drop back into her pocket.

"Why don't we just call a mouse and ask it to *tell* Jim and Polly to escape?" Leo suggested in desperation.

"Will mice still do that sort of thing on the coast?" Bertha asked in surprise. "How marvelous! I'm afraid they won't do it here. They *insist* on messages in writing."

"Are you going to stay here blabbing all night?" grumbled the hidey-hole behind them.

"We'd better keep moving," Bertha muttered. "We don't want to lose it."

She sighed and began toiling rapidly up the hill with Mimi close behind her. Leo followed more slowly, feeling very close to despair. Mimi's determination to save Mutt, and his own mad urge to somehow make Spoiler pay for the misery he'd caused in Rondo, had brought disaster on four perfectly innocent people. Suddenly it seemed not only foolhardy, but wrong.

We should just turn back, right now, he thought miserably. Then he realized if they did that, the whole awful mess would have been for nothing. The Blue Queen would have snatched Mutt, used Spoiler to try to kidnap Mimi, ordered Hal to kill both Langlanders against his will, and planned some ghastly punishment for Polly and Jim, without anyone lifting a finger against her.

And that can't happen, Leo thought, hurrying after the others. *We mightn't be able to do anything to help Polly and Jim, but at least we can finish what we started. We can show the queen that she can't steal people's friends and get away with it. And we can fix Spoiler once and for all!*

"Our mice *used* to carry spoken messages," Bertha was saying to Mimi as he caught up with them. "When I was a piglet, that was. But then there were a few awkward incidents. An old man was told to go home because his wife was dead, for example, when the message should have been that his wife wanted him to bring home some *bread*."

She blew back a troublesome poppy that had flopped from its place on her hat to dangle over her left eye. "Well, the old man was cross, naturally, when he got home and found his wife still alive," she went on. "And his wife, who was a cranky old thing anyway, was furious because there was no bread to go with the broth for dinner. So they complained to the authorities, and the mouse concerned was fined a week's pay. *It* complained to the Messenger Mouse Union, and the whole fleet went out on strike."

She's trying to take our minds off Jim and Polly, Leo thought. *Maybe she's trying to take her own mind off them, too. She really liked them. She doesn't want to think about what might happen to them.*

"What then?" he made himself ask, as if he were really interested in the story.

"The mice claimed the mistake was the old woman's fault, because she'd mumbled her message — she wasn't wearing her false teeth, apparently, when she spoke to the mouse," Bertha said. "The woman said that the mouse should have realized just by looking at her that she wasn't dead. And the *mouse* said —"

"Watch it!" growled the hidey-hole behind them.

Bertha, Mimi, and Leo stopped dead and looked up. Without realizing it, they had almost reached the top of the hill. The castle loomed above them. The ground ahead of them was flooded with light. A few more steps and they would have been clearly visible.

Keeping low, Leo peered up at the castle. His eyes watered in the glare. The drawbridge was down. Guards wearing fancy blue-and-gold uniforms were slumped against the walls on either side of the huge front doors, which were gaping wide.

"They look as if they're asleep," Mimi whispered hopefully.

"Can't depend on that," said the hidey-hole. "It might be a trick. Hold on."

It moved past Mimi, Leo, and Bertha, right to the edge of the light, then pursed itself up into a small black spot and disappeared into the ground.

A few seconds later, Leo thought he saw one of the spaces between the boards of the drawbridge widen very slightly. He rubbed his eyes, and when he looked again the space was back to normal.

"Drunk as skunks," the hidey-hole announced, reappearing just in front of his foot. "Snoring their heads off. You can't hear it from here, because of that infernal music. There's no one else in sight."

"Right," Bertha said briskly. "We'd better go straight on, then. We'll never get a better chance. Once we're inside, we'll decide what to do next."

"Okey-dokey!" said the hole enthusiastically. "See you in there!"

It shrank to a pinpoint and disappeared beneath a clump of grass. Bertha instantly moved into the light and began trotting boldly to the drawbridge.

"I can't believe we're doing this," Leo panted as he and Mimi ran after her.

"It's what we came for, isn't it?" Mimi snapped. But Leo wasn't fooled. Mimi was breathing hard and her eyes were huge and dark. She was as scared as he was.

For the dozenth time he wondered if he should take Mimi into his confidence about his plans for Spoiler, and for the dozenth time he decided against it. Mimi's mind was fixed on Mutt. She'd automatically argue against anything that she felt was a distraction.

Once she has Mutt, it will be different, Leo thought. *So finding Mutt has to come first.*

When Leo and Mimi reached the drawbridge, Bertha had already begun tiptoeing cautiously across, her trotters making tiny clicking sounds on the planks. At the other end of the drawbridge, the great doorway gaped like a hungry mouth waiting to swallow her up.

Well, it's too late to turn back now, Leo thought grimly. And suddenly his fear disappeared, and a reckless excitement took its place.

"Come on," he breathed to Mimi. "As fast as we can."

They ran lightly after Bertha. Just as they reached the sleeping guards, Leo thought he caught a gleam of white out of the corner of his eye. He turned his head quickly, but all he could see was the castle wall, and the rippling water of the moat.

The sight made him uneasy, but he had no time to think about why this should be. The next moment, he and Mimi were past the guards, through the doorway, and standing beside Bertha in a grand, deserted entrance hall that echoed with the sound of "The Pom-Pom Polka."

"If we ever get out of this, I never want to hear that tune again as long as I live," said Bertha.

"*Psst!* Ready to hide yet?" a voice hissed hopefully from the wall of a broad staircase that led from the hall to the upper floors of the castle.

"Not yet," Leo whispered. He was looking around, trying to decide what was best to do next.

The music seemed to be coming from behind a blue velvet curtain on one side of the entrance hall. The Blue Queen was probably in there, entertaining her guests, though Leo couldn't hear the sound of any voices.

He had to be sure. Beckoning to Mimi and Bertha, he crept to one edge of the curtain, tweaked it cautiously aside, and peered through the narrow gap into the room beyond.

CHAPTER 29

The room behind the curtain was a vast ballroom, paneled with mirrors and ablaze with light. Huge crystal chandeliers hung from the mirrored ceiling. The floor was smooth, glossy black, and it was crowded with silent dancers — weird, monstrous beings wearing fantastical, vividly colored clothes.

"Oh!" Bertha whispered in horror. "Oh, lawks-a-daisy, this is — frightful! The Blue Queen's power *is* coming back! She's creating monsters all over again. And no one knows! No one has the faintest idea!"

Leo stared at the dancing throng, repelled yet unable to tear his eyes away.

None of the creatures were alike, but all danced with the same frenzied, unsmiling determination. None of them made a sound. They were all as silent as their own reflections, endlessly repeated in the mirrored walls. Even their feet skimmed noiselessly over the shining floor.

The only sound was the rollicking music, which was pouring from a vast golden organ suspended on a platform over the dance floor. The organ was being played eight-handed by a repulsive, spiderlike beast wearing a glittering purple vest and four pairs of sequined purple gloves.

Leo gaped, unable to take in what he was seeing. Feathers, fur, spines, horns, scales, jerking limbs, bobbing heads, clashing colors, and glittering jewels mixed and mingled in front of his eyes like a vision in a feverish nightmare.

A bulky figure with silver plumes of hair and a cluster of three bulging eyes, one purple, one red, and one blue, whirled out of the throng, its arms around what looked like a giant snail standing upright. A bald man with leathery bat's wings dragging behind him capered alongside a pencil-thin creature whose round, vacantly smiling face was framed by a stiff fringe of yellow daisy petals.

Leo realized that Mimi was tugging at his arm. He turned to look at her. She was staring fixedly at one end of the room.

He followed her gaze, and caught his breath. The Blue Queen was sitting apart from the dancers on a raised golden throne. She was wearing a magnificent dress of midnight blue velvet studded with tiny, glittering jewels, and her hair flowed from beneath her tall crown like a veil of white gold.

Beside her, on a slightly lower chair, and in a rather dingy sequined evening jacket, sat Spoiler, looking anxious, his foot tapping restlessly to the music. On her other side was an elegant marble stand on which stood a golden cage filled with dancing blue butterflies.

And crouched miserably at the Blue Queen's feet, wearing a

gold collar that was linked to her wrist by a heavy golden chain, was Mutt.

Leo gripped Mimi's arm and tried to draw her back. She resisted him, holding on to the edge of the curtain and shaking her head. Her eyes were bright with tears.

Suddenly Leo was thinking very clearly.

"We can't do anything for Mutt now," he breathed in Mimi's ear. "You know it. You said it yourself. We'll have to steal him back — it's the only way. Come on."

She frowned, but at last let him pull her away from the curtain. He led her quickly to the foot of the great stairs. Bertha followed, for once shocked into silence.

"So?" whispered the hidey-hole from the stairway wall. "What's the plan?"

"We find the Blue Queen's bedroom," Leo said softly. "It looks as if the queen keeps Mutt very close to her. There's a good chance she takes him to her room at night. So we'll hide in there, and when she goes to sleep we'll creep out and get Mutt."

And after that, he promised himself silently, *it will be Spoiler's turn. He'll be asleep. We'll find him and we'll take him home with us. See how he likes it in the modern world with no money, no home, and no one to believe him when he tells them who he is. Mimi will break the Key. I'll hide the music box. And Rondo will be free of Spoiler forever.*

"The queen's bedroom will be upstairs," the hidey-hole said knowledgeably. "That's how it is with rich people. They like views, and also they seem to think that the higher up they are, the safer they and their jewels will be. I know these things. I've got a friend who specializes in hiding burglars."

As Bertha, Leo, and Mimi looked at it, rather startled, its edges pinched slightly inward.

"Not a *good* friend, of course," it added hastily. "A fairly distant friend, really. Actually, just a friend of a friend. You know how it is. Some holes will mix with anyone, and you have to be polite, right?"

"Right," Leo said quickly. His plan depended on the hidey-hole, and he wasn't about to have an argument with it.

"Well, I'll go on up and have a look around," the hole said, and disappeared abruptly into the wall.

This hadn't been part of Leo's plan at all. He'd expected the hole to be with them, providing security as they searched the castle. Glancing nervously over his shoulder at the blue curtain, he urged Mimi and Bertha up the stairs.

They reached the first floor and hesitated. They were standing in a huge space thickly carpeted in blue. A crystal chandelier blazing with candles flooded the area with light. Broad, blue-carpeted hallways stretched away on every side. The hallways were studded with gold-and-white doors, all firmly shut.

Leo realized that the plan he'd outlined so confidently downstairs wasn't going to be as easy to carry out as he'd thought. The castle was huge. It might take them all night to find the Blue Queen's bedroom.

There was no sign of the hidey-hole. Leo hoped desperately that it hadn't decided to abandon them because it regretted mentioning its ties with the world of crime.

"Will we start searching here, or go up to the next floor?" Bertha whispered.

"I think we should go to the next floor," Leo said, very aware of Mimi's tense silence, and trying to sound as if he knew what he was doing.

They climbed the second flight of stairs. When they reached the top, panting, they found themselves in a blue-carpeted space exactly like the one on the floor below. The music from the ball-room was noticeably fainter, otherwise Leo would have thought that they hadn't moved at all.

"This castle certainly has a lot of rooms!" puffed Bertha, peering dismally along the deserted hallways, with their rows of gold-and-white doors. "I suppose the queen needs them to keep all her monsters in. They probably don't like sharing."

"*Psst!*" hissed the hidey-hole, appearing in the wall just behind her shoulder.

Bertha jumped violently. "Don't *do* that!" she whispered angrily, turning and glaring at the hole.

It pulsed with silent laughter. It seemed very pleased with itself.

"I've found the room you're after," it wheezed. "It's right at the top of this dump. In the tallest tower."

It sank back into the wall and came into view again at the foot of the next flight of stairs. "Coming?" it asked, and began gliding rapidly up the stairs like a large blot of black ink, not troubling to hide itself at all.

"How do you know it's the Blue Queen's bedroom?" Leo panted, as he, Mimi, and Bertha hurried after it.

"Oh, just a few little clues," smirked the hidey-hole, pausing in the middle of a stair. "One, it's stuffed with jewels and magic books. Two, it's got the best view in the place. And three, it's got a crown on the door with THE BLUE QUEEN written underneath it."

Exploding into wheezing guffaws once more, it slid up to the next stair and raced on.

Leo, Mimi, and Bertha followed as fast as they could, climbing higher and higher through the castle, the music from the ballroom growing fainter with every step.

The last flight of stairs twisted upward in a lacy gold spiral. When they reached the top, they found themselves on a small landing, facing a single, very grand door painted midnight blue. As the hidey-hole had said, the door bore a large golden crown, with the words THE BLUE QUEEN written below it in fancy script.

"As if everyone in the castle wouldn't know whose room it is!" snorted Bertha. "Some people just *love* seeing their names in print."

The hidey-hole slid casually under the door. "All clear!" they heard it whisper from the other side. "Try the door. If you can't open it, I can probably help you pick the lock. I've learned a few tricks from . . . ah . . . from a very distant friend of a friend of a friend of mine — who I hardly know at all."

Cautiously Leo twisted the shining gold doorknob. To his surprise it turned easily. He pushed, and the door swung smoothly open, revealing a large room filled with dancing shadows and strange, flickering blue light.

Leo took a step back. Mimi darted past him into the room, but still he hesitated.

"Come on!" the hidey-hole called impatiently from the flickering blue dimness. "First rule of successful hiding: Don't dillydally!"

"It's strange that the door wasn't locked," Leo murmured to Bertha, who was standing back politely, but craning her neck to see past him into the room.

"The queen probably thinks everyone's too scared of her to try to steal anything or pry into her secrets," Bertha said. "And she'd be right, wouldn't she? No one with any sense would come here — except for us."

Unable to restrain her curiosity any longer, she edged past Leo and squeezed through the open doorway.

Except for us, Leo repeated grimly to himself, following her into the room and closing the door behind him. *And of course we've got tons of sense, haven't we?*

As his eyes adjusted to the dim light, he looked uneasily for the source of the blue light. He found it in the black marble fireplace, where tongues of blue flame flickered lazily over the coals. Before the fire stood a thronelike blue velvet armchair.

Shuddering, Leo turned to survey the rest of the room. He saw walls festooned with drapes of midnight blue silk. He saw carved golden chairs, glass tables, cabinets filled with old books of magic, chests cluttered with jewels, silver-backed hairbrushes, and bottles and jars of every shape, color, and size. He saw a long mirror in a golden frame fixed to a wall. He saw a huge bed covered by a white fur throw, in the middle of which the hidey-hole was sprawled luxuriously.

"Lawks-a-daisy, what a room!" gasped Bertha, wandering around and gazing at everything in fascination. "I've never seen anything like it!"

"Told you," said the hidey-hole smugly.

Mimi was standing motionless at the end of the bed. She was staring down at an empty golden cage that stood there on the floor, chained to one of the bed's legs.

I was right! Leo thought with a rush of relief. *That cage must be where poor Mutt has to sleep.*

He moved to Mimi's side. Mimi shivered and opened her lips for the first time since seeing Mutt in the ballroom.

"This is horrible," she said. "It's the most horrible room I've ever been in."

Leo nodded. The room was lavishly furnished and smelled of exotic perfume, but it had an evil atmosphere that no luxury could disguise. It was as if the terrible plans that had been hatched there, and the wicked deeds that had been done, had left their mark. Its thick, blue-tinged air was heavy with menace.

"Ooh, look!" Bertha squeaked, stopping at a pair of tall, narrow glass doors that faced out toward the front of the castle. "There's a little balcony out here! I love balconies! They're so romantic. I always wanted one in my sty, but mean old Macdonald wouldn't build it for me."

She nosed the balcony doors open and stepped out eagerly, but almost immediately she backed halfway in again.

"The dancers are leaving!" she hissed. "They don't live here after all!"

Leo and Mimi rushed to join her. Keeping low, they peered down through the balcony rails.

Far below, the Blue Queen's guests were gliding across the draw-bridge in sedate rows of three. The silver-haired, three-eyed dancer Leo had noticed in the ballroom was leading the silent procession, with the bald, bat-winged man and a tiny, gnomelike creature whose narrow, knobbly chin reached to its knees.

There was no sound at all except the lapping of the water in the moat.

"The music's stopped," Leo murmured. "The party's definitely over. "We'd better —"

He broke off with a gasp. The first three guests had reached the end of the drawbridge, stepped off onto the grass and vanished in a cloud of glittering dust.

"They aren't real!" breathed Bertha, as the next three dancers followed the first set into sparkling oblivion. "They're all illusions that can't exist outside the castle! Oh, thank goodness! I was so *worried*!"

Leo's scalp was prickling. The Blue Queen had been presiding over a lavish party at which she, Spoiler, and Mutt were the only guests who were real. What kind of maniac would do that? No wonder Spoiler had looked edgy.

Whispering to Bertha and Mimi to follow him quickly, he backed off the balcony. The hidey-hole was still spread out on the white fur bedcover, looking very relaxed.

"Get up!" Leo urged, running over to it with Bertha and Mimi close behind him. "We've got to hide! The Blue Queen will be here any minute!"

"Oh, so *now* it's urgent!" groaned the hidey-hole, yawning horribly. "Just when I've got comfortable. Isn't it always the way?"

It slid from the bed, yawned again, and sank sulkily into the dark blue rug.

Seconds passed, and nothing happened.

"Where are you?" Leo whispered, looking around frantically.

"Keep your shirt on, worryguts," said a sleepy voice. And an inky black patch appeared right in the center of the long, gold-framed mirror that was fastened to the wall beside the bed.

"You can't stay there!" Mimi hissed, horrified. "That's a magic mirror — at least, I think it is."

"Who cares?" yawned the hidey-hole. "I'd like to see some spook try to interfere with *me*. Anyway, I'm not moving. Mirrors give you the best view. Second rule of successful hiding: If there's a mirror, use it."

It stretched itself till it covered the whole bottom half of the mirror.

"Well, are you getting in or not?" it said rather indistinctly. "Take it or leave it."

And at that moment, the muffled sounds of footsteps and arguing voices seeped through the bedroom door.

Bertha, Mimi, and Leo leaped for the hidey-hole and tumbled inside it.

"Well, that's more like it," said the hole, and sank beneath the mirror's surface just as the door flew open, and the Blue Queen, carrying Mutt and the cage of blue butterflies, swept into the room.

CHAPTER 30

THE MIRROR

Leo was astounded to find that despite being in the hidey-hole he could see the queen's bedroom as clearly as if the mirror were a blue-tinted window. So this was what the hidey-hole had meant when it had said that mirrors gave you the best view.

"I am sick to death of your whining, George," the Blue Queen shouted over her shoulder. "Go to bed and leave me alone."

"But you don't understand," moaned a voice that Leo recognized as Spoiler's. "You blame me for failing you, but I couldn't help it. I had the girl in the palm of my hand, but then the boy —"

"That is enough!" the queen snapped. "I have heard it a hundred times! Leave me in peace!" She nodded at the door and it slammed shut. Dismayed, Leo heard a lock clicking into place.

With a deep sigh, the queen put down the butterfly cage and went to the end of her bed, taking off the gold bracelet that fastened Mutt's chain to her wrist.

She bent, and the chain rattled. They heard the cage door opening, then closing again with a clang. Mutt whined piteously. Leo felt Mimi stir beside him, and touched her arm warningly.

"You hate me, tiny dog, do you not?" the Blue Queen said in a hard voice, straightening up and staring down into Mutt's cage. "You wish to leave me, and return to Mimi Langlander?"

She kicked the cage contemptuously and turned away. "Well, too bad for you," she spat over her shoulder. "You will never see that ugly little fiddle player again. I am your mistress now!"

Inside the mirror, Leo could feel Mimi trembling like a leaf buffeted by a gale. He understood how she felt. He was hot with rage himself. It was all he could do to prevent himself from bursting out of the hidey-hole and throwing himself at the sneering woman who was now walking toward him.

The Blue Queen smoothed her eyebrows and bent closer to the mirror.

"Look out," breathed the hidey-hole. "She'll see you if you're too close to the surface."

Leo, Mimi, and Bertha shrank back. The Blue Queen thrust her face forward, inspecting it carefully. Leo could see every pore of her skin, every fine line of discontent that marked her brow and dragged down the corners of her mouth. He held his breath as the queen's white hand moved to stroke the silken strands of her pale blond hair.

"Magic mirror, tonight I do not need to ask you if I am still the most beautiful woman in the land," the queen purred. "Tonight, a hundred beings have told me so already."

A hundred phantoms you created to flatter you, thought Leo in disgust.

But he stayed absolutely still and didn't stir until the queen, apparently satisfied with her reflection, had moved away, kicked off her shoes, and lain down on her bed.

"Oh, why is everything left to me?" the queen sighed, yawning. "There is so much to do — so much to think about. And I am tired. So tired . . ."

Her eyelids fluttered closed. She began to breathe evenly.

Mimi moved forward. Leo's heart lurched.

"Wait!" breathed the hidey-hole. "Third rule of successful hiding: Don't make your move too soon."

Mimi drew back, but she didn't relax. Leo could feel her crouched beside him, tense as a stretched rubber band.

The minutes ticked by. The only movement in the room was the slow rising and falling of the Blue Queen's chest, and the only sound was the sound of her breathing.

It was warm inside the mirror, and as roomy and comfortable as the hidey-hole had promised. The dim blue light was restful. All there was to see was the quiet room and the sleeping queen. Even the blue butterflies were still.

Bertha's head nodded. Her eyes closed. She was falling asleep herself. Leo hoped fervently that she wouldn't snore.

"I'm not waiting any longer," Mimi whispered. "I'm going to get Mutt. I'll bring him back here. Then tomorrow morning, when the queen's gone, we can all sneak out."

Leo could feel his plan to capture Spoiler unraveling. Desperately he tried to pull the threads together. Could they somehow trick the queen into unlocking the door before morning?

"I knew this job would take all night," grumbled the hidey-hole. "Oh, well. Off you go, then."

"I'll come with you," Leo whispered, but Mimi shook her head.

"Mutt might bark at you if you take him by surprise," she hissed.

Bark at me and bite me, too, for all I know, Leo thought, remembering Mutt's rather snappy nature, and he nodded reluctantly.

Mimi moved forward again. Bertha sighed, smacked her lips, and slept peacefully on.

"Softly, softly," murmured the hidey-hole. Mimi moved in front of Leo, blocking his view. The darkness at his back gave a tiny shudder, and the next minute he was seeing Mimi through blue-tinted glass. She was outside the mirror.

His heart in his mouth, he watched her creep past the sleeping queen, down to the foot of the bed. She bent, and he heard the tiny rattle of the cage door opening. Mutt gave a frantic whine of joy.

No, Mutt! Leo thought in terror. He glanced at the Blue Queen, but she hadn't stirred and there was no change in her slow, even breathing.

He looked again at the foot of the bed and held his breath, waiting for Mimi to straighten up and hurry back to the mirror with Mutt in her arms.

But long moments passed and nothing happened. Straining his ears, wondering what had gone wrong, Leo heard another muffled whine and a small jingling noise. He frowned, trying to work out what the jingling noise was. It was a metallic sound, like nails being shaken up in a plastic packet. Like a length of chain . . .

Chain! Leo went cold all over. Suddenly he knew what had

happened. Mutt wasn't just locked in the cage. He was chained to it, too. Mimi was trying to free him and she couldn't.

But she'd never give up. Leo knew that. She'd keep trying to break that chain all night if she had to.

At that moment he saw movement in the shadows at the end of the bed. He saw the small, tousled figure of Mutt straining fruitlessly against the chain that stretched taut between his gold collar and the cage.

Then Mimi moved into view. She'd given up trying to free the chain from the cage. She crawled to Mutt and started fumbling with his collar, looking for a way to get it off. The little dog whimpered, rubbing his head against her and frantically licking her hands.

Leo couldn't bear to watch anymore. Whatever Mimi said, he had to help — to try to help. Maybe he'd be strong enough to break the chain, or pry open one of the links. Gold was a soft metal, he'd been told — much softer than steel or silver, anyway.

"I'm going out there," he whispered, edging forward.

"I wish you people would make up your minds," the hidey-hole grumbled. "Fourth rule of successful hiding: Make a plan and stick to it."

Leo leaned toward the surface of the mirror. He took a deep breath . . .

And suddenly, shockingly, the room was filled with cackling laughter.

Leo jerked back, his eyes bulging in horror. The Blue Queen was sitting up, swinging her feet to the ground and standing. Her eyes were sparkling triumphantly as she looked down at Mimi crouched, frozen, at the foot of the bed.

She wasn't asleep, Leo thought numbly. *She was never asleep. She was just pretending. She knew . . .*

"So, you fell into my trap, girl," the Blue Queen sneered. "You followed the light and the music. You crept past the guards I had put to sleep. You saw me in the ballroom, presiding over a gathering created to make you think I was well occupied and unsuspecting. You took the chance I gave you. You found my room and hid inside it — thinking yourself very clever, no doubt."

Her lips curved in a malicious smile. "I felt your presence the moment I entered. Where were you hiding? Out on the balcony, perhaps? Or simply under the bed? It did not matter. I knew you would reveal yourself soon enough. Now you are my prisoner, just as I had planned. My only regret is that I went to so much trouble to deceive you. That was because I thought your cautious cousin would be with you."

"He stayed behind at the bridge," Mimi said sullenly. "He wouldn't come to the castle. He said we'd be caught. He said Mutt wasn't worth it."

She looked and sounded so utterly convincing that Leo felt a stab of confused anger. It only lasted an instant before he realized that she was acting — acting superbly — to prevent the Blue Queen from realizing that he was close by.

The Blue Queen shrugged. "As it happens, he was quite correct," she drawled, her lip curling. "But his restraint surprises me, I confess. I had thought he would not be able to resist playing the hero. His type usually cannot. I was looking forward to meeting him again."

Her words sounded venomous. Leo shivered, despite the warmth of the room. Why did the queen hate him so much — him in particular? Certainly he'd defied her, the first time they met in his bedroom. But Mimi had defied her, too.

"I'm *glad* my cousin isn't here," Mimi said, every word dripping with scorn. "He'd probably try to fight you, and I know that won't work. You're a sorceress, and this castle is your territory, controlled by your magic. No one can save me, or Mutt, by fighting."

She was looking at the Blue Queen, but her words, disguised by their scornful tone, were a message for Leo, and he knew it.

Stay where you are, Mimi was telling him. *You can't fight her. Bertha can't fight her. We have to try to trick her somehow. If we bide our time, there's still a chance.*

"I am glad you understand your position," the Blue Queen said softly.

"It's getting a bit interesting, now," the hidey-hole muttered in Leo's ear. "Do you want out? Should we wake the pig?"

Leo gritted his teeth and shook his head.

He knew Mimi was right. He knew he had to stay where he was, for now at least, and on no account should he wake Bertha. If Bertha saw the Blue Queen menacing Mimi, she wouldn't be able to restrain herself. She'd burst out of the mirror and attack. And, without question, the results of that would be disastrous.

"So — what am I to do with you now, Mimi Langlander?" the Blue Queen purred.

Mimi lifted her chin. "You can give my dog back and let us go home."

The Blue Queen smiled and shook her head. "Oh, but I cannot do that," she said, in a gentle, reasonable tone. "I gave you the ring you wear on your finger, and I took your dog in return. It was a fair bargain."

"It wasn't a bargain!" Mimi burst out, looking in horror at the black-and-gold ring winking on her hand. "I didn't agree to it. You took Mutt without asking. And I only found the ring afterward, lying on the rug where you'd dropped it!"

"But you picked up the ring, did you not?" the queen said, her voice hardening. "You put it on. You used it to come to Rondo. You accepted my bargain, in other words, and now you cannot break it."

Mimi stared at her, speechless.

The Blue Queen held her gaze for a long moment. Then, abruptly, she shrugged and turned away. "Ah, I am tired of this game," she said carelessly. "Take your dog back then, if you care so much. He no longer amuses me."

Leo's heart gave a great leap.

Mimi's eyes widened incredulously.

"I — I can have him?" she breathed, clutching Mutt to her chest. "You'll release him — just like that — and let us go?"

"Oh yes," the queen said absentmindedly, moving to the mirror and stroking her smooth cheek with long, white fingers. "Our bargain will be dissolved the moment you return the ring to me. To tell the truth, I will be glad to have it back. I miss it more than I had thought I would. It is a pretty thing."

"The — the ring?" Mimi stammered. "But — the ring is our way home!"

Sensing her dismay, Mutt whined and rubbed his head against her neck. Her arms tightened around him.

"Ah, yes," the Blue Queen said lazily, gazing at her reflection in the mirror. "Well, that is a pity, in some ways. I daresay you have parents who will miss you, for a time. But surely this world with Mutt is better than the other world without him? He is your dearest friend. Your *only* friend, in fact, if I am not mistaken."

Behind the mirror, Leo sat frozen, watching her beautiful lips curve in a malicious smile.

Mimi, don't do it! he wanted to shout. *Mimi, don't give her the ring. We must go home. We need to go home. Our parents are there. Our friends! All the people who love us!*

But who loves Mimi, really? a cold voice said in his mind. *Who loves the ugly duckling?*

And he looked past the preening figure of the queen and saw Mimi crouched on the floor with Mutt in her arms.

Mimi's face was tearstained and pale in the sickly blue light. Her hair was tousled. Her eyes were huge and dark with fear.

But she didn't look like an ugly duckling anymore. Not at all. In fact, she looked just like a frightened heroine in a picture book. She looked beautiful.

When did that happen? Leo thought, confused. But in his heart he knew. It had happened so gradually that he hadn't noticed.

He remembered the first time he'd seen Mimi in the clothes that had chosen her in the tavern. He remembered her flying with the Flitters. He remembered her glowing face as she played the violin in Jim and Polly's cottage. He remembered her laughing with Bertha, and bravely facing the troll.

Mimi isn't an ugly duckling here, Leo thought. *Here, she's no more a misfit than anyone else.*

As he watched, Mimi looked down at the ring gleaming on her finger. He knew what she must be thinking: *In this world, no one thinks I'm a nuisance, or a weirdo, or too young to do things that matter. In this world, people accept me, just as I am. In this world there's magic. In this world I'm beautiful. In this world, I can fly. And if I stay, I'll have Mutt . . .*

But what about me, Mimi? Leo thought, in an agony of fear. *I want to go home! I want to go back to Mom and Dad, and Einstein, and my friends. I want to go to school, play soccer, sit in my own room, sleep in my own bed, work on my computer. I want to live in my own world. You can't give away our only chance to get back! You can't!*

CHAPTER 31

"Well, Mimi Langlander?" drawled the Blue Queen, without turning from the mirror. "What is your decision?"

Mimi raised her head. Mutt whimpered as she put him down and slowly got to her feet.

Leo held his breath.

"I can't give the ring back," Mimi said in a dead-sounding voice. "I have to use it to take my cousin home."

Leo sank back. The relief was so tremendous that he felt weak.

"But surely you owe your precious cousin nothing!" the queen said, raising her perfect eyebrows. "He forced you to face me alone, did he not?"

"He came to Rondo because of me," Mimi muttered. "He didn't want to do it. I can't make him stay here."

The queen's lips curved in a tiny, satisfied smile.

She knew Mimi would say that, Leo thought suddenly. *She was just tempting her — torturing her!*

A wave of helpless anger rushed through him. His whole body tingled with the urge to leap from the mirror, wipe that smug smile off the queen's haughty, beautiful face.

"Easy!" the hidey-hole breathed in his ear. "Fifth rule of successful hiding: Don't lose your temper."

Leo took a deep breath, and remained still.

"Please," Mimi whispered, clasping her hands. "Let me take Mutt. You have so much . . . but I only have him. Please!"

The queen paused. She put her head to one side, then to the other, as if admiring the effect. Then she sighed, and turned away from the mirror at last.

"Oh, very well," she said carelessly. "Since you beg. Keep the ring, then, and give me something else in exchange for your wretched dog. I cannot let you have him and receive nothing in return — even *I* am bound by some rules. But surely you have some other trinket that will do?"

The expression of wild hope that had flamed on Mimi's face slowly died.

"Well?" the queen snapped, tapping her foot impatiently.

"I don't have anything to give you," Mimi said helplessly. "Unless — would my clothes do?" Her fingers flew to the high collar of her jacket, and she began rapidly undoing the first of the tiny buttons.

The queen's lip curled. "Do you insult me by offering me old clothes?" she sneered. "Ah, this is hopeless! If your hair was fine and long, you could offer me that, I suppose. But as it is . . ."

Mimi's fingers froze on the buttons of her jacket.

"Hair!" she burst out, her face lighting up. "Oh, I forgot! I *do* have something. Here!"

She plunged her hand inside the neck of the jacket, and pulled out Aunt Bethany's silver chain with the ugly pendant swinging from it, dull as a pebble in the soft blue light.

"I don't see how anyone could forget *that*," the hidey-hole rasped in Leo's ear.

But Leo was speechless with relief, and couldn't answer. He'd forgotten about the pendant, too. For a long time it had been hidden under Mimi's new jacket. Even before that, he remembered, she'd been wearing that awful pink thing zipped right up to the neck.

And all the time the pendant was there, Leo thought. *Mimi's lucky charm, just waiting till it was needed.*

Instantly he felt embarrassed at the thought. *This world has really got to you*, he told himself severely. *That's exactly the sort of soft thing that Mimi might say. It's just a lucky coincidence she was wearing the pendant, and that's all there is to it.*

"That will do," the queen said. Lazily she stretched out her hand.

Eagerly Mimi began to pull the chain over her head. The catch snagged in her hair at the back, and she struggled to free it.

"Make haste!" the queen snapped. Mimi glanced up quickly, her hands behind her head, her fingers still working to free the chain. Her forehead creased in a puzzled frown.

"What —?" the Blue Queen began. She broke off and looked sharply around at the door.

"What's happened?" Leo whispered.

"Use your ears!" hissed the hidey-hole. "My word, this is getting quite exciting!"

And then Leo heard it — the distant sound of shouting and the much louder pounding of running feet. He jumped violently as the bedroom door flew open with a crash.

Spoiler burst into the room, panting and wild-eyed, with his hair standing on end. He was wearing faded pajamas printed with pale pink crowns.

Mutt began yapping ferociously. The butterflies fluttered, panic-stricken, against the bars of their cage.

"What is the meaning of this?" shrieked the Blue Queen. "How *dare* you —"

"We're invaded!" Spoiler yelled. "They're fighting the guards! Your precious butterfly spies didn't warn you about *that*, did they? I *told* you they were no use at night! What —"

His voice broke off in a strangled gasp. His eyes bulged. His mouth fell open. He pointed with a shaking finger at Mimi, standing motionless with her hands behind her head and the pendant, suspended on its chain, dangling just below her chin.

Mutt snarled, showing all his tiny teeth.

"Leave us, George," the Blue Queen ordered, swiftly moving to stand between Mimi and the gaping man. "We are discussing business that is no concern of yours."

Spoiler's weak, heavy face flushed scarlet. "No concern of *mine*?" he spluttered. "You cheat — you filthy cheat! She's here! *It's* here! You were going to take it for yourself and shut me out, weren't you? *Weren't* you?"

It? Leo thought, confused. What does he mean, *it*? Is he talking about the ring?

"Be *quiet*, you fool," barked the Blue Queen, glancing quickly at Mimi. "Be quiet or I will —"

"You'll what?" bellowed Spoiler, flecks of white foam gathering at the corners of his mouth. "Tie up my tongue? Bring me out in boils? Try your best, witch! I'm immune to your spells, and don't you forget it! Oh, how often I've thanked my lucky stars that I made *that* part of the bargain."

"And how often have I regretted agreeing to it!" spat the Blue Queen. "You have the brains of a newt, bursting in here, breaking through my shutting spell with invaders at our gates! Go and see to them. Trust me to handle this."

"Trust *you*?" panted Spoiler. "I'd rather trust a snake! You're not getting your hands on it, I tell you! It's mine! It was stolen from *me*! Now that it's back here, after all this time, do you think I'm going to stand by while *you* take control of it? What kind of fool do you think I am?"

"Every kind of fool!" shrieked the queen. "Stay, then! The invaders are on the stairs. There is no time to waste!" She raised her hand and the door of the bedroom slammed with a crash that shook the room. She whirled around to face Mimi again.

"Oh-ho!" chuckled the hidey-hole. "Listen to them! Going at it hammer and tongs! Oh, I love a good brawl. This is turning out to be a good night. Started out slowly, but . . ."

It rambled on, but Leo wasn't listening. He wasn't even aware of the sound of hurrying feet outside the room, or the rattling of the doorknob. He was gazing, transfixed, at the pendant swinging slowly on its chain just under Mimi's chin. He had suddenly understood that the pendant was the focus of Spoiler's rage.

But why does Spoiler want the pendant? Leo thought in confusion. *How does Spoiler even know about it? It came out of one of Aunt Bethany's jewelry boxes. It's got nothing to do with —*

And at that moment, as fists began to pound thunderously on the bedroom door, a bizarre idea occurred to him. He looked at the pendant with new eyes, noting its size, its shape . . .

His heart began to beat very fast. His hands began to sweat. He looked out of the mirror at Mimi, and saw that she had also guessed the truth.

She had managed to free the pendant's chain from her hair, but she wasn't lifting the chain the rest of the way over her head. Instead, she was letting it slide slowly back to hang around her neck again.

"What are you doing, dear?" the Blue Queen asked, with a ghastly, false sweetness that did nothing to disguise the sharpness in her voice. "Do not be disturbed by the noises outside. My guards will deal with the invaders, and until then my spell will hold the door against them. They cannot defy my magic as, unfortunately, my foolish friend, George, is able to do."

Mimi closed her fingers protectively over the pendant and said nothing.

The Blue Queen forced a smile. "Now, you were going to give that old thing to me, in exchange for your dog, remember?"

"That was before I realized what it was," Mimi said, tightening her grip on the pendant. "This is the Key, isn't it? *It's the Key to*

Rondo, and you've been after it ever since you first saw it hanging around my neck that afternoon in Leo's room."

There was a great thump, and then another, as a heavy boot kicked the door. Mimi didn't move her eyes from the Blue Queen's face.

"You didn't want me to realize the pendant was important, so you used one of your rings to trick me," she went on bitterly. "You said the *ring* was the Key, though I don't suppose it has any power at all. When we forced you to go, you stole Mutt and left the ring for me to find. You knew I'd come after Mutt, and the real Key would come with me."

Without releasing the pendant, she pulled the black-and-gold ring from her finger.

"This didn't bring us here, and it was never going to take us home," she said. "You can have it back."

She tossed the ring onto the floor. It rolled on the rug and hit the toe of the Blue Queen's shoe.

The Blue Queen didn't even look at it. Her face was tight with rage, but when she spoke, her voice was like honey.

"You are clever, Mimi Langlander," she murmured. "Now, be clever enough to give me the Key. Then you and your little dog can leave here in peace."

"Don't listen to her!" Spoiler screeched, dancing on the spot in rage and frustration. "She's trying to bewitch you! Cover your ears!"

Mimi lifted her chin. "You can't bewitch me, so you can stop trying," she said to the Blue Queen.

"That's it!" shouted Spoiler, punching the air with his fist. "You tell her! You show her what Langlanders are made of."

"Langlanders!" hissed the Blue Queen, her voice cold with contempt. "I warn you, girl —"

"Don't let her scare you," Spoiler panted. "She won't try hurting you while you've got the Key. The story goes that Rondo will end if the Key is harmed. And she can't take the thing from you, because she's a witch, and you've got to give it to her freely! But I can take it! *I* can."

He hurled himself forward, knocked the Blue Queen aside, and seized Mimi by the shoulders.

"Leo!" Mimi screamed.

"Whoops!" hissed the hidey-hole at the same moment. "This looks bad. Do you —? *Ow!*"

Leo had burst from the mirror without thought or hesitation. The fire had blazed up with a roar, spraying the room with blue sparks. The queen was staggering back, falling against the bed, shrieking in rage. People were shouting outside the door, which was shuddering as a strong shoulder smashed against it again and again.

Leo was aware of nothing but Spoiler throwing Mimi heavily to the ground and scrabbling for the pendant while she rolled and gasped, trying to fight him off.

And Leo wasn't the only one. Snarling, Mutt lunged forward, breaking his chain. He flew at Spoiler and sank his tiny teeth into the man's leg.

Spoiler howled. He kicked, trying to shake Mutt off, and howled again as the little dog hung on grimly. Then Leo was upon him, both arms wrapped around his neck, hauling him back.

Spoiler choked. His eyes bulged. His hands flew to his neck and tore at Leo's arms, trying to break the strangling grip.

Sobbing, Mimi struggled to her knees. Mutt released Spoiler's leg and sprang into her arms. Clutching him tightly, she began to get up. Spoiler made a last, frantic grab for her. One meaty hand clawed at the chain around her neck.

Mimi screamed and jumped to her feet. The chain snapped cleanly. The pendant fell to the floor, bouncing on the blue rug.

With a triumphant cry, the Blue Queen leaped for it. But Mimi was there before her. Snatching up the pendant, narrowly evading the queen's grasping hands, she dodged behind the thronelike velvet chair that stood before the fire. She shoved the pendant deep into her pocket and looked wildly around for a way to escape.

But there was none. She knew that as well as Leo did. The bedroom door was locked. The balcony doors led nowhere but to a terrible drop. There was nowhere to run.

The blue flames roared and spat. Sparks showered the room. Spoiler bellowed, rolled desperately, and broke Leo's grip. The next moment he was on his feet, kicking Leo viciously and limping after Mimi.

Groaning, Leo tried to get up to go after him, but fell back as a sharp pain shot through his ribs. He tried again, moving more carefully. This time he made it to his knees, then to his feet.

But he knew he'd never reach Spoiler in time to save Mimi, or the pendant. Spoiler had shouldered the Blue Queen out of his way. Only the chair stood between him and Mimi now. He and Mimi dodged around it, watching each other intently. Mutt growled in the crook of Mimi's arm, looking more than ever like a fluffy toy with teeth.

Spoiler's pajama leg was soaked with blood below the knee. His eyes were red. A swollen vein was throbbing in his forehead. His top lip twitched. His teeth were bared. He looked quite mad.

Then, suddenly, he snapped.

Snarling, he lifted the velvet chair and swung it violently aside. It crashed against the wall beside the fireplace.

Mimi screamed, turned on her heel and ran straight for the shuddering, spell-locked door.

And as she reached it, the door vanished.

A short, broad figure came hurtling through the gap. It was Conker, off balance and yelling in shock. Mimi ran into him, bounced back, and fell. Hal, very grim and drawn, stepped rapidly over her to catch Spoiler in a bearlike grip. Tye and Freda, both looking aghast, appeared in the empty doorway behind him.

"What are you doing here?" yelled Conker, staring wild-eyed at Leo and Mimi. "You're supposed to be home in bed! Oh, my heart and gizzards! We arrive at the castle to get your dog for you — and what do we hear but you screaming and yelling —"

"What happened to the door?" quacked Freda, looking very alarmed.

Spoiler was struggling and swearing in Hal's arms. Mimi was scrambling to her feet, backing away from them. His mind a whirling confusion of clamoring thoughts, Leo started toward her.

"Leo! Stop!" The Blue Queen's voice, high and thrilling, cut through the tumult.

Leo froze. Suddenly he couldn't move at all. *She heard Mimi call my name,* he thought dimly. *Mimi was frightened. She wasn't thinking. She called my name . . .*

"Turn to me!" the Blue Queen ordered. And, unwillingly, Leo turned. He couldn't help it. His body seemed to be acting by itself. It was as if he were a puppet, and the Blue Queen were holding his strings.

"Stop this, witch!" he heard Hal's deep voice say. "You have nothing to gain by it."

"I have a world to gain by it, as well you know," purred the Blue Queen. "You saw what happened to the door. Leo, walk out." She pointed to the balcony.

And Leo did as he was told. Sweat broke out on his forehead as with all his might he tried to resist the Blue Queen's will. But his legs moved, one after the other. His hands opened the balcony doors. Then his legs carried him on, out onto the balcony, right to the low stone ledge.

He looked down at the moat, far below. Seven white shapes were gliding on the dark water. The seven swans. Waiting.

"Climb onto the ledge, Leo," said the Blue Queen. "Stand quite still, facing me, and wait."

Leo felt the cold stone of the balcony ledge beneath his hands.

He felt himself following the order, and even in his terror he wondered at the fact that his injured ribs gave him no pain. He stood on the ledge, with his back to the terrible drop. The breeze blew around him, carrying with it the sour smell of the moat.

"Now, Mimi," he heard the Blue Queen say calmly. "Come forward and give the Key to me, or I will tell your friend to jump."

CHAPTER 32

DECISION

Hal, Conker, Tye, and Freda stood frozen to the spot. Even Spoiler had stopped struggling and was staring at Mimi with bloodshot eyes. But Mimi was looking at Leo standing on the balcony ledge. Her face was ghastly pale in the flickering blue light.

"Mimi, stay where you are," Hal said evenly. "The Blue Queen must *not* gain control of the Key to Rondo. Nothing is more important than that."

Mimi tore her eyes away from Leo and looked at Hal.

"We didn't know," she said dully. "We didn't know the pendant was important. We thought the ring brought us here. You must have known it didn't. Why didn't you tell us . . . ?"

Shadows deepened on Hal's grim face. The Blue Queen laughed. The fire spat. The blue butterflies fluttered in their golden cage.

"So all your plans have come to nothing, Hal," the Blue Queen sneered. "You could not prevent the opening of the Gate. You could not stop my pretty spies flying to me with word of it. You could not stop me from escaping Rondo, or making contact with the holder of the Key. And you cannot stop me now."

She turned to Mimi. "The Key!" she commanded, and held out her hand.

Slowly Mimi slid her hand into her pocket. "Tell Leo to get down, first," she said, her lips barely moving. "He might fall."

"He will not fall until I tell him to do so," the Blue Queen said, smiling slightly. "And that will be soon, believe me, if you continue to defy me."

Mimi drew her hand from her pocket. She frowned down at her clenched fingers for a long moment, then took a step toward the queen. The fire blazed up beside her, flooding her face with brilliant blue light.

Tye and Conker moved quickly forward.

"Do not touch her!" the Blue Queen snapped, holding up her hand. "Step back, or the boy will die instantly, and she will know it is all your doing."

Conker and Tye stopped and glanced at Hal as if waiting for orders. He shook his head. Conker moved back. Tye frowned, hesitated, and then did the same.

"So, Terlamaine," jeered the queen. "You are Hal's pet now. Is it because you are so obedient that he lets you leave off your collar and chain when you go out?"

"Do not let her rouse you, Tye," Hal said softly, as Tye hissed and raised her knife. "It's what she wants. It's the only power she has over you now. She can't harm any of us. That, at least, I could do."

Slowly Tye lowered the knife again.

"My leg hurts," Spoiler moaned. "Hal, for pity's sake . . ."

Hal dragged him to one of the carved golden chairs by the wall, and sat him down in it. Spoiler slumped forward with his hand over his eyes, but frozen on the ledge, staring through the open doorway, Leo clearly saw him peep at Mimi through his fingers. He knew that Spoiler was trying to work out if he could reach her, and the pendant, before he could be stopped.

"Guard him!" Hal said to Freda. The duck flew to the glass table beside the chair and turned to face Spoiler, her masked eyes glittering.

"This is all your doing, Hal," Spoiler said sullenly. "You had to meddle, didn't you? You had to mess things up for me, as usual. And they call you a hero. What a joke! You didn't even fight me for the Key. You stole it from me while I was asleep. You cowardly sneak! Call yourself a brother!"

He launched himself from his chair. Freda jabbed him hard on the arm with her beak. He fell back with a high-pitched scream.

Brother, thought Leo numbly. *Hal's Spoiler's brother. Hal's . . . Henry Langlander! Good, kind Uncle Henry. Not drowned. Not dead. Here!*

Suddenly it seemed so obvious. Suddenly so many things fell into place that it seemed astonishing that he hadn't realized it before.

Hal was looking at Spoiler with mingled pity and distaste.

"I took it from you because you'd lost all right to it, George," he said in a level voice. "You betrayed it. You couldn't use it to create wealth for yourself because you haven't got the imagination of a bowl of porridge. So in return for riches and an easy life you let *her* use it — for the worst of purposes."

Spoiler snarled at him. The Blue Queen snorted in contempt.

Hal looked back at Mimi. "Listen, Mimi, and understand," he said urgently. "The hair inside the Key is the tip of the brush that painted this world, and everything in it. The Key is Rondo's master. It can create, and it can destroy. If you give it to the Blue Queen, there will be another Dark Time — one that will never end."

Numb dread folded around Leo like a heavy cloak. Watching and listening from the balcony, unable to move or speak, he knew what Mimi would decide — what she *had* to decide.

Mimi had no choice. She couldn't betray a whole world for the sake of one life.

Just let it be quick, he thought dully.

The Blue Queen tossed her head. "The Dark Time!" she said scornfully. "That is what the plodding ones call it — the small ones, the folk with no vision who do not matter."

"Folk like Tye and me, and Jim and Polly, and every other normal, hardworking person in this world, you mean!" shouted Conker.

"Indeed," said the queen. "And all those who defied me and resisted me before will soon learn the error of their ways."

She fastened her burning eyes on Mimi once more.

"Enough of this delay!" she snapped. "Give the Key to me now, or your cousin will pay the price. And when he has gone, do not forget that I still have your little dog to play with. I have only to say his name and he, too, will do anything I ask."

Mutt, Leo thought with a shock. *I'd forgotten about Mutt. But surely, even for Mutt, Mimi couldn't . . .*

He watched in horror as Mimi slowly uncurled her fingers. *No, Mimi,* he begged her silently.

Mimi looked down into her cupped hand and gave a long sigh. Then she flattened out her hand.

The pendant gleamed on her palm. Leo could see it clearly, even from where he was. Briefly he remembered his first sight of it. Then, he had only thought it ugly. Now it seemed awesome. He saw that Conker, Tye, and Freda were gazing at it in fascinated horror. Clearly they recognized it. So did Spoiler, who was eyeing it with sulky greed. Hal's face showed no expression at all. He was looking not at the pendant, but at Mimi.

The Blue Queen nodded with satisfaction.

"That is better," she cooed. "I knew you would see reason, Mimi Langlander. You know what you want, and you will stop at nothing to get it. So. We are alike."

"No," Mimi said in a low voice.

"Yes," the Blue Queen insisted softly. "And because we are alike, you know I mean what I say. Come now. It is time to end this."

"Yes," Mimi said. "It's time to end it."

And without warning, she spun around and pitched the pendant straight into the middle of the fire.

The Blue Queen screamed piercingly. Spoiler bellowed and covered his eyes. Hal, Conker, and Tye shouted in horror.

Mimi, Leo thought numbly. *No!*

The queen sprang forward, seized a poker, and started trying to rake the pendant out of the fire. But it was too late. For a single instant the pendant flashed brightly among the blue flames, a small oval of silver and murky glass. Then there was a tiny cracking sound, and the pendant sank into the white hot coals, hissing, melting, burning . . .

"It is gone!" the Blue Queen shrieked, in a frenzy of rage and terror. "You ignorant fool! You have destroyed us all!"

She leaped at Mimi, clawing at Mimi's face. Mutt growled and snapped at her.

Hal sprang forward. He reached the queen in a single stride, pulled her away from Mimi and pushed her roughly back. She stumbled and fell screaming to the floor.

Mimi seemed to have taken no notice of the attack, or the rescue. She stood rigidly, staring at the fire as if she could not look away.

The fire roared. Sparks like blue stars sprayed the room. With a grating shriek, the black marble mantelpiece cracked in two, turned bone white, and shattered into a thousand pieces.

Mimi gave a slight start and turned away from it, her eyes glazed.

Don't you realize what you've done? Leo screamed at her in his mind. *Don't you remember what Spoiler said?*

The story goes that Rondo will end if the Key is harmed . . .

There was an ominous rumble. The room began to tremble. Crystal chinked. Wood creaked, groaned, and split. The silken wall coverings bulged inward.

"It's happening!" Spoiler screeched, leaping up. Freda half-raised her wings and flew at him, jabbing his injured leg viciously. He howled and fell to the ground, covering his head with his arms.

The floor quaked. Chairs, tables, and cabinets tipped and fell. Bottles and jars toppled and smashed, their contents spilling and mingling. The butterfly cage collapsed into a tangle of gold wire.

Panic-stricken butterflies filled the air. They swarmed through the balcony doorway, desperately seeking escape. Leo screwed up his eyes as they streamed past him, wings and legs heedlessly beating on his face.

He opened his eyes again to a scene of devastation. Everything in the queen's room was shaking. He wondered briefly why the balcony ledge wasn't quaking, too, and then gritted his teeth and put the thought out of his mind.

The balcony ledge would go soon enough. And he would go with it. He knew it. He told himself he accepted it. But it was the worst kind of torture to have to stand frozen, waiting, unable to move a finger to help himself or anyone else. Where he stood he was safe — for the moment. But he would far rather — a thousand times rather — have been in the quaking room, taking his chances with the others.

Especially, he wished he could be with Mimi. How must she feel, to have been the cause of all this? He no longer felt angry with her. Mimi had been driven half crazy by the decision she'd had to make. She'd felt cornered, and so as always she'd lashed out rashly, heedlessly, angrily, without thinking of the consequences.

It was so like her. Yet it was strange, too, because she must have remembered what destroying the Key might mean. And she loved this world. She felt more at home in it than she felt in her own. Leo had been sure she'd do anything to protect it.

As the thought crossed his mind the room shook again — even more violently.

Spoiler, facedown on the ground, screamed and drummed his feet on the rug like a child having a tantrum. Conker yelled as a cabinet beside him tipped, burying him under an avalanche of books.

Mimi staggered and fell to her knees. Hal was beside her, but though he glanced down at her, he made no attempt to help her to get up. He just turned away from her, leaving her kneeling on the quaking floor, Mutt hugged tightly to her chest, her eyes fixed and staring.

Watching, horrified, Leo saw Tye gliding sure-footed through the wreckage. Tye's head was held high. She had put away her dagger. She reached Hal's side and took his arm.

"So, Hal, this is the end," she said, raising her voice over the sound of breaking glass, crashing furniture, and the shrieks of the queen. "The Key is destroyed. Rondo will be undone."

"Well you don't have to be so calm about it!" roared Conker, emerging from a mountain of books and rubbing his head. "Where's Freda? Freda? Freda!"

"Here," said the duck, edging out from behind the overturned cabinet. She looked disdainfully at the mess on the trembling floor, and finally half-flew to settle on the moaning Spoiler's head.

"It's too soon to panic," Hal shouted. "We don't know what the destruction of the Key will do. We only know what has been said.

For all we know, the world might only adjust, and things might change. They might change utterly. We can only hope —"

At that moment, the rug turned red as blood. The silken wall hangings began oozing droplets of green slime. The white fur bedcover was suddenly alive with movement, as every silky strand became a writhing worm. The cover rose from the bed in a seething mass, swaying horribly, like some monstrous beast.

The Blue Queen shrieked again and again, her beautiful face distorted with mingled rage and terror. She crawled on the bloodred rug — crawled to the wall where the magic mirror hung. Clinging to the mirror's golden frame, she raised herself up, as if, with her world collapsing around her, she had to assure herself of her supreme beauty one last time.

Her image appeared in the glass. Then it changed — changed utterly.

Conker clapped his hand to his mouth. Freda quacked, and flapped her wings. The Blue Queen screamed — an earsplitting scream of anguish, outrage, and horror.

And what she had seen in the mirror screamed with her, its tiny eyes wide with shock, its ears flapping, its mouth gaping open beneath its pink snuffling snout.

Spoiler squirmed, and looked up. He gazed at the mirror and burst into hysterical, choking laughter. "Pig!" he screeched. "Pig face!"

All the blood drained from the queen's cheeks. Her eyes rolled back in her head. She crumpled, senseless, to the floor.

And Leo, suddenly released from the spell that bound him to the ledge, tipped slowly backward, and fell.

CHAPTER 33

Afterward, remembering how he'd felt when his feet slipped from the balcony ledge, remembering the scream of absolute terror that had burst from his throat, Leo didn't know whether to laugh or cry.

The long, deadly plunge he'd been fearfully imagining for so long just never happened. No sooner had the fall begun, than it was over. His back hit something smooth and soft, something that rippled beneath him like a waterbed he'd once tried at a friend's house.

I'm dead, he thought foolishly. *Dead or dreaming.* But the soft, cool breeze was blowing on his face, and he could hear voices very near, calling his name.

Cautiously he opened his eyes. The first thing he saw was the bottom of the balcony. It was so close that if he'd lifted his hand, he could have touched it. The second thing he saw was a row of faces staring down at him over the balcony ledge, not far above.

Leo blinked, but when he opened his eyes again the balcony and the faces were still there. Mimi. Hal. Conker. Tye. Bertha. Freda. They were calling to him, and their voices were all he could hear.

Dazedly he realized that the tumultuous quaking in the queen's bedroom had stopped.

He grinned weakly up at the row of shouting faces. Conker was waving and laughing. Mimi, pale and exhausted-looking, with Mutt in her arms, was half-crying with happiness. Hal was grinning like a boy. Bertha, still befuddled with sleep, was looking happily astounded. Even Tye was smiling. Freda, sitting serenely on the balcony ledge, was the only one to preserve a dignified silence.

The second thing Leo saw was that he was lying on a large rug. It looked the same — exactly the same — as the rug in his bedroom at home. But it was moving very slightly, and its white fringe was riffling gently in the breeze.

At that moment, many things became clear to Leo. He felt so weak with relief that he couldn't move. His arms and legs felt as if they'd turned to water. All he could do was breathe a long, long sigh.

Freda spread her wings and skimmed down from the ledge, landing flat-footed beside him. The rug tipped slightly, and in the split second before it righted itself, Leo caught a glimpse of seven shapes far below, bright white against the darkness of the moat.

"Down, please," Freda said to the rug.

The rug moved away from the castle wall, and glided down to land smoothly beside the moat. And so stunned was Leo that he wasn't even surprised to see seven confused-looking people climbing, drenched, out of the dark water where seven white swans had floated just moments before.

*   *   *

There was just enough room on the rug for everyone to ride back to Hal's house by the river. Even the hidey-hole found a place by the fringe.

"Turned out to be a pretty good night, all in all," it said to Leo, who was sitting beside it. "Mind you, I did get a few nasty bruises. Didn't mind the pig's trotters — that's all part of the job. But the other thing . . ." It quivered a little. "Sixth rule of successful hiding: *Never* jump out of a hidey-hole without warning it first."

"Sorry," Leo said.

"Just remember next time," the hidey-hole grunted, and Leo promised, hoping fervently that there would never *be* a next time.

His mind was buzzing with questions, but he had no chance to ask any of them on the short, crowded ride that followed. All conversation was directed at helping the seven strangers who had climbed out of the moat to understand what had happened to them.

Polly's family, Jim's parents, and the princess, Suki (who was, of course, extremely beautiful), only dimly remembered their lives as swans. Their last clear recollection was of the Blue Queen sweeping into their tiny village, laughing horribly, and raising her hand.

But they did know that their presence at the bridge, at the house by the river, and then on the castle moat, had not been the Blue Queen's doing, but their own.

"We just felt we needed to be there," Jim's father said simply, his arm tightening around his wife's shoulders.

They must have sensed the presence of the Key, Leo thought, meeting Mimi's eyes across the rug. *The Blue Queen used the magic of the Key to transform them in the Dark Time, so they were attracted to it. That's why they tried to distract the troll on the bridge by taking flight. Some instinct told them to try to protect us, because by doing that they'd protect the Key, too.*

"I still don't see how the spell over us was broken," said Polly's mother, Rose.

"Oh, that's easy," said Bertha airily. "The queen fainted when she saw me in the mirror. Her hold over you must have snapped right then, just like her hold over Leo did."

"But Leo was only bewitched," Suki objected. "And we were *swans*! If my stepmother had *died*, we might have changed back. But why would her just fainting have done it?"

"Well, it seems it did, Suki, and that's all that matters," her husband laughed.

"Indeed," Polly's father agreed heartily. "Bertha, how can we ever thank you?"

Bertha smiled and fluttered her eyelashes. "Oh, it was nothing," she said modestly. "I didn't really *do* anything. I'd dropped off for a moment, actually, and the noise woke me up, so I moved to the front of the mirror to see what was happening. I must admit I was a tiny bit startled to find the Blue Queen so close. But she screamed and fainted just at the sight of me!"

She sighed with satisfaction. "I suppose she'd heard of my reputation as a fighter," she added. "I can't think of any other reason for her to collapse like that."

She was so pleased and proud that no one felt like telling her the truth. Freda tried, but Conker held her beak closed and muttered to her till she agreed to keep quiet.

No one disagreed with Bertha's explanation of how the swans had been returned to their true forms, either, but Leo knew it wasn't right. With his own eyes he'd seen that the swans were still swimming on the moat long after the Blue Queen had fainted.

He caught Mimi's eye. She smiled, then hid her face by ducking her head and rubbing her cheek against Mutt's ears.

The rug settled to land in front of the willow trees that masked Hal's house. Leo, Mimi, Mutt, Bertha, Freda, Conker, Tye, and Hal climbed off. Jim and Polly's families remained onboard. They were longing to see their loved ones and didn't want to waste a minute.

The hidey-hole stayed on the rug, too. It said it would enjoy a change of scene, and the chance to meet a few forest-dwelling holes it hadn't seen for a while, and who were old friends. By the shifty way it spoke, Leo guessed that one of these friends was the burglary specialist. No doubt the hidey-hole was looking forward to boasting about its recent exploits to one who would really appreciate them.

The sun was rising as the rug skimmed over the river, then rose to soar over the forest canopy. The quest team watched till it was out of sight, then turned toward the house.

"I'd like to see Grandma's face when she hears that I saved her family," Bertha said with great satisfaction. "She'll get a shock, and it serves her right. 'A pig has no business going on a quest,' indeed!"

"Jim and Polly will be surprised to hear there was a quest at all," said Hal. "I sent a mouse to them last night, telling them not to worry because I'd make sure you three didn't go on to the castle, whatever happened."

"I heard you sending that message!" Leo exclaimed. "We thought you were writing to the Blue Queen. The mouse was so scared."

Hal laughed. "It was scared of the new troll," he said. "The bridge isn't as safe for messenger mice as it was."

"What's the world coming to, when a mouse thinks it can't out-run a troll!" exploded Conker. "Ah, the mice these days are a lily-livered lot."

They reached the house and trooped inside. While Mimi put down a bowl of water for Mutt, Conker set about building up the fire and putting the kettle on to heat.

"Is that why you ran?" Tye asked Leo, unsmiling. "Because of one cowardly mouse? Did you not trust us?"

"No," Mimi said bluntly, before Leo could think of a more tactful way of putting it. "You tried to lock us in, and —"

"Hal's plan was to get your dog back while you slept," Tye snapped. "You should have stayed where you were safe."

"We didn't think we *were* safe," said Leo. He repeated what he and Mimi had heard after they crept out of their room.

When he'd finished, Conker laughed uproariously. "Breakfast!" he said cheerfully, and disappeared into the kitchen.

But Tye frowned, and Hal shook his head ruefully.

"Tye and I were talking about my failure to tell you the ring was worthless," he said. "I should have told you straightaway, but I just couldn't face it. I thought if we got Mutt back first, it would be easier to break the news to you that you were stranded in this world forever."

He glanced at Mimi and Leo, his eyes dark with pity, then quickly looked away.

"Oh, come now, Hal!" Bertha giggled. "The coast might be a long way away, but it's hardly another world! Mimi and Leo can just *walk* back — the same way they came!"

"It's not quite as simple as that, Bertha," Leo said. He looked steadily at Hal. Bertha had risked her life for them. Leo didn't see why she should be kept in the dark about where they'd really come from, when everyone else knew the truth.

Hal hesitated, then nodded slightly.

So as Conker cooked pancakes by the fire, and Mutt fell into an exhausted sleep on the hearth rug, Leo and Mimi swore Bertha to secrecy, then told her their story. Bertha listened avidly, and wasn't nearly as annoyed about being deceived as Leo had feared.

She was actually quite delighted to find that the Langlander tales she'd been told as a piglet were true after all. She also said that she had always thought that there was *something* about Leo and Mimi that seemed otherworldly, though she hadn't quite been able to put her trotter on it.

She wasn't at all afraid of the idea that Rondo was simply a small box in some people's eyes. As she said, all worlds were probably small in comparison to what existed outside them. The important thing was whether the world you lived in was interesting, which she thought her own was. Very.

"You are a *most* unusual pig, Bertha," said Hal, regarding her with respect.

"I know," said Bertha, casting down her eyes modestly. "Macdonald always says the same. My brother says it, too. But, of course, *he* doesn't mean it as a compliment."

The only thing she seemed sad about was that her chances of becoming a film star were now fairly slim.

"Do pigs ever star in moovlies in Langland?" she asked wistfully.

"It *has* happened," Leo told her.

"Not often, I bet," Freda jeered. And Leo had to agree that it didn't happen very often. Pigs usually played minor roles.

"Oh, well," Bertha said, adjusting her hat, "I couldn't accept less than a starring part, so I'd better give up the idea. There's always my career as a model to fall back on. And questing, of course. I've developed quite a taste for that."

"There's nothing like a good quest," Conker agreed, setting a huge plate of pancakes on the table. "Have you thought about how many of us there were on this one?" He counted on his fingers. "Leo, Mimi, Bertha, Conker, Freda, Tye, and Hal. Seven! The perfect questing number."

"The hidey-hole made eight," Leo pointed out, but Conker just snorted and flapped his hands, as if hidey-holes didn't count.

Everyone gathered around the table and began eating pancakes with butter and maple syrup and drinking cup after cup of tea. For a time there was no talk at all. All of them were ravenous, especially Bertha, who explained, accepting a seventh helping, that she usually didn't eat much breakfast, but fighting evil queens always made her hungry.

Mimi ate her share, but kept glancing at the sleeping Mutt as if she couldn't believe that he was really there, and safe. Her face was radiant, but she didn't speak. It was as if her heart were too full for words.

"This quest could have ended in disaster, though, when you come to think about it," Conker said at last, wiping maple syrup from his beard. "The Key was taken right into the hands of the Blue Queen."

"We didn't *know*!" Mimi and Leo exclaimed in chorus.

"If you'd told them the ring was worthless, Hal —" Tye began.

"I know, I know!" Hal sighed. "Then they'd have told me that I must be wrong, because they'd come here *not* with the queen, but alone. And *then* I would have realized that they must have the real Key somewhere about them after all."

"Conker's fault," mumbled Freda with her beak full. "If he'd questioned them properly when they first arrived, instead of just assuming —"

"*My* fault!" exploded Conker, enraged. "What about you?"

"I was busy eating dots," said the duck with dignity.

"What happened was the Blue Queen's fault, and Spoiler's fault, and no one else's," Leo said flatly.

There was a short silence. Then . . .

"Leo's right!" Conker shouted, banging his fist on the table.

"The whole problem was caused by the queen and Spoiler wanting the Key. But now that the Key is destroyed . . ."

"It isn't, actually," Mimi said apologetically. She pulled an ugly silver pendant from her pocket, and put it on the table in front of her.

Hal gasped. Tye hissed. Conker goggled. Freda snapped her beak in shock.

But Leo smiled. And Bertha laughed aloud.

"You fooled the queen!" she chortled. "You fooled everyone! Except me, of course."

"Only because you were asleep," Freda muttered.

"But I saw the Key burn!" Tye gasped. "I *saw* it!"

"That wasn't the real Key," Mimi said, looking very pleased with herself. "It was a lemon drop that Conker had given me. I made it look exactly like the pendant by — by just thinking about it, and *imagining* it changed."

She shrugged at Conker's astounded expression. "That's how the Key works," she said. "You focus your mind on something and imagine —"

"I know how it works!" growled Conker. "That's what makes it so dangerous in the hands of bad eggs like the Blue Queen. But how did *you* work out how to use it, may I ask?"

"Well, I was desperate to escape from the Blue Queen and Spoiler," said Mimi, calmly mopping up the last of her maple syrup with a scrap of pancake. "I ran at the door, wishing, wishing it wasn't there, *imagining* it wasn't there. And suddenly — it wasn't. Then I remembered the ladder up the Flitters' tree, and being able to fly, and all the bears in Deep Wood —"

"What have *bears* got to do with it?" Freda demanded.

"I'm afraid of bears," Mimi said simply. "When I was little, I had a book of fairy tales with a story about bears in it. The pictures were very scary. Sometimes I still dream bears are chasing me. Those same bears."

Her cheeks had grown very pink, but she made herself go on.

"Jim said there were more bears in the forest than there had been before," she said. "We thought the Blue Queen had put them there. But why would she do that? She *wanted* us to get to the castle safely, to bring her the Key. And she didn't need the bears as spies — she had her blue butterflies for that. So I wondered if . . ."

"If you'd created the bears yourself!" Conker yelled, slamming the table triumphantly. "Just by imagining them!"

Mimi nodded. She was looking down, and her face was still very red.

"It was the same thing with the troll on the bridge," she said. "It looked exactly like a picture in the fairy-tale book as well. And just a little while before we got to the bridge, I'd been remembering that picture, and imagining the troll we were going to meet."

"So we have *you* to thank for that vicious beast," Tye muttered.

Mimi nodded. "And it ate the old troll," she mumbled. "It *ate* it!" Suddenly her eyes brimmed with tears.

"Never mind," Conker said, leaning over to pat her arm. "The old troll wasn't much of a loss."

"It certainly wasn't," snapped Freda. "Mean, smelly, gummy thing — always whining because it couldn't eat folk anymore, and had to live on dots and cake. What's wrong with dots and cake, I ask you?"

Mimi wiped her eyes with the back of her hand. "So, anyway," she said in a low voice, "I thought, that's why the Blue Queen wants the Key. She used it to change things in the Dark Time. But I can use it, too. If I can make bears appear, and a door *disappear*, I can do other things, as long as I concentrate hard enough."

"How *clever* of you, Mimi!" cried Bertha, absentmindedly helping herself to the last pancake.

"Excellent!" said Conker, nodding appreciatively. "Well, so it was *my* lemon drop that went into the fire! Lucky I gave it to you, eh?" He beamed around, as if expecting congratulations.

"I knew the Blue Queen would be able to tell the pendant was a fake, as soon as she had it in her hand," said Mimi. "So throwing it into the fire seemed the best thing to do. Spoiler had told us that if the Key was destroyed, Rondo would end so I created a few effects to convince him and the Blue Queen it was really happening."

"You convinced all of us," Tye said dryly.

"That was the idea," Mimi admitted without a trace of guilt. "I thought the more scared everyone looked, the more panicky the queen would get, and the easier it would be for us all to escape. I really enjoyed it. Everything I imagined just — happened, and

I got better and better at controlling it. Then Hal told Tye that things might just change, and so I tried that, too."

She grinned, remembering. "That was fun. The best bit was making that fur bedcover turn into worms."

"Sometimes I wonder about that girl," Leo heard Freda mutter to Conker.

"I wasn't very happy with the rug I put under Leo, though," Mimi said regretfully. "The pattern's much too modern-looking for a real flying carpet. But it was the only one I could think of at the time, and I had to work fast."

"It was when I saw the pattern that I realized what you'd been doing," Leo sighed. "What a relief *that* was." He was finding it hard to stop smiling.

There was just one shadow over his happiness. "I was hoping to get Spoiler out of Rondo," he said, looking down at his hands. "The thought of that kept me going quite a few times. But it didn't happen."

"What happened was almost as good," grinned Hal. "George fought the queen for the Key. I'd say the pact between them was well and truly dissolved last night. By now, George will be getting as far away from the castle as he can, and trying to find a hole to hide in."

Leo laughed. So did Mimi, who didn't seem a bit annoyed that Mutt hadn't been his sole concern. *Maybe,* Leo thought ruefully, *she'd suspected it all along.*

"Well, what I say is, all's well that ends well," said Bertha. "The Blue Queen and Spoiler think the Key has gone for good, so they'll stop plotting to get it back. But the Key hasn't *really* gone at all, so now that Mimi and Leo have got Mutt, they can go home whenever they like!"

"*They* can," Conker groaned. "*They* can use the Key and go from here. *We've* got to get across the bridge. And that troll —"

"Oh, the troll's a squirrel now," Mimi said casually. "I changed it as we flew past the bridge. I didn't know how to change its personality, so it's probably still pretty vicious, but at least it's small. I mean, it couldn't actually bite your leg off, or anything."

"Mimi," Hal began, frowning. "Don't you go —"

"I won't go around changing things just because I can, if that's what you're going to say," Mimi said hurriedly. "I *promise* I won't. But the troll was my fault, so I thought it was okay to change that."

"And we knew the seven swans weren't really swans at all, Hal," Leo put in. "Surely you can't blame Mimi for imagining them changing back to their real —"

"Of course not!" exclaimed Hal. "If only I'd known about them when I stole the Key, I would have done it myself — or tried to, at least. By the time Jim came to me for help, it was too late. The Key was out of my reach. I had to tell Jim I didn't have the power to change anything anymore."

He shook his head. "So now everyone thinks I'm a burned-out wizard," he said. "As if it isn't bad enough being called a hero when all I did was steal something from a weak, helpless fool, then go and hide it."

Leo knew exactly how he felt. He would have felt the same way.

"It mightn't seem very heroic," he said. "But you ended the Dark

Time, Hal, and you were the only one who could have done it. Who else knew enough to guess where the Blue Queen was getting her power? And who else could have taken the Key out of the Blue Queen's reach, and tried to arrange things so she could never lay hands on it again?"

"And all because of me," Conker said, puffing out his chest. "*I* was the one who fetched him, you know."

"*You* found a Gap into Langland, Conker?" exclaimed Bertha, very impressed.

"Oh, it was nothing," said Conker modestly.

"It was a complete accident," Freda snorted. "He fell into it, going after a particularly fast dot. It's just behind Posy's flower stall — in that blind alley between the bakery and the bank."

"I'd put the music box away after George disappeared," Hal explained. "I loathed the sight of it by then. I knew exactly where George had gone, of course. He'd been sneaking in and out of Rondo ever since our father first told us about it. For twenty years the box sat in a cupboard. But it was still wound up, just as George had left it, so —"

"So *I* was able to get through!" Conker broke in. "And I found myself squashed into this closet, see? Freda came after me, bless her heart, so then we were both stuck in the dark."

"Typical!" Freda snapped.

Conker grinned at her. "So we just banged on the door till Hal let us out. You should have seen his face when he saw us!"

"You should have seen *yours*," Hal retorted.

"You both yelled so loudly I thought I'd go deaf," Freda smirked.

"So we and Hal got talking," Conker went on. "After he'd — after *we'd* — got over the shock, that is. He explained about the music box. We told him how bad things were at home, and about the monster army, and all . . ."

"And I realized that my brother George was the man Conker called Spoiler," Hal said heavily. "It was a very nasty moment, I can tell you. I was certain that George was letting the Blue Queen use the Key — while keeping it safely in his own hands, of course — in return for power and a comfortable life. That would be so like him. So . . ."

"So you came here with Conker and Freda!" Bertha breathed. "Oh, Hal, what a risk! If you hadn't been able to get the Key, you wouldn't have been able to go back!"

"That's true," Hal said. "When I think about it now, it seems strange. I'd avoided risks all my life before that."

He shrugged. "Maybe I was tired of being careful, reliable, *predictable* Henry Langlander. Or maybe I was so angry with George, and so determined to stop him, that my natural caution just got swamped."

"Like Leo's, when he followed me," Mimi said thoughtfully. "You really are alike."

She clasped her hands and looked at Leo soulfully. "It's the eyes," she whispered. "The steady, responsible eyes."

"Shut up, Mimi!" Leo muttered.

Tye smiled. "The resemblance *is* remarkable," she said. "In more ways than one."

"The Blue Queen saw it, all right," Hal said grimly. "It made her loathe you, Leo, even more intensely than she usually loathes people who defy her. You must take good care in the future. The queen never forgets an enemy — especially one who has defeated her."

"Like *you* did, Hal, when you stole the Key from Spoiler," Bertha sighed in admiration.

Hal looked rueful. "We were lucky to find George alone in his room that day," he said. "If the queen had been with him, things might have been very different. As it was, I was able to get the Key without waking him. He was wearing it on a chain around his neck."

"Hal took me with him when he used the Key to wish himself back to Langland," Conker said proudly. "That was my second visit."

"And I told you it would be your last," Hal said, nodding. "I was determined that travel between the two worlds was going to stop, so that nothing like the Dark Time could ever happen again. I'd already talked to young Bethany about the music box, and written out the rules. All I had to do to complete the process was hide the Key. So instead of returning it to the place where it belonged —"

"Inside the silver ring on the lid of the music box," Leo put in quickly.

Hal raised his eyebrows. "Quite so," he said approvingly. "Well, instead of putting it there, I buried it, still threaded on the chain, under my old tool shed in the back garden."

"Yet somehow it got out of the earth," Tye said quietly.

"Like a curse!" Bertha breathed.

"Not a curse," Leo said, glancing at Mimi. "Mr. Higgs."

"*Very* loyal and *scrupulously* honest. And *so* good with camellias," Mimi chanted, as Hal looked confused.

"Mr. Higgs worked for Aunt Bethany," Leo explained. "The old shed was falling down, so Mr. Higgs cleared it away and built a new one. He probably found the Key then, and gave it to Aunt Bethany. She was always saying how honest he was."

"And Aunt Bethany put the Key in a box with all this other junky old jewelry she never wore," Mimi said, sounding rather awed. "She just *happened* to leave that jewelry box to my sisters and me in her will. I just *happened* to think the pendant was interesting, and chose to have it. Then I just *happened* to go and stay at Leo's place, where the music box was."

She looked at Hal. "It sounds to me as if the Key didn't like being hidden away. After all your trouble, it gradually worked its way back to the music box anyway."

Leo expected Hal to snort at this, but instead Hal nodded.

"Obviously it was a mistake to think that I could separate the Key and the music box forever," he said. "At the time I thought I could do it, though. I thought I *had* done it. I set things up to make it look as if I'd drowned. Then Conker brought me back to Rondo, and I've been here ever since."

"But why, Hal?" Leo asked, frowning. "I mean — why did you maroon yourself here? You didn't have to do it."

Mimi shouted with disbelieving laughter.

Hal smiled and shook his head. "Who would you rather be,

337

Leo?" he asked. "Dear old reliable Uncle Henry, who wears high starched collars and expects every day to be very much like the day before? Or Hal, who lives by the river, has friends like Tye, Conker, and Freda, and never knows what adventure each new day will bring?"

He laughed at the look on Leo's face. "You, however, are a different case entirely," he said firmly. He turned to Mimi. "And you, too," he added. "You're young, and you have your way to make — and people who love you dearly, though they probably don't understand you at all."

"What makes you say that?" asked Mimi, with a slight return of her old, prickly manner.

"You remind me of my aunt Alice, as a matter of fact." Hal said, grinning at her. "She was just a little thing, but she kept the family hopping! She was *very* fierce and determined — not at all what young ladies were supposed to be like in those days — and she played the harp like an angel. Ended up marrying a man who ran a traveling music show. It was a great scandal in the family at the time, but I understand Alice and Enzo were blissfully happy, so that's all that matters."

"Aunt Alice!" Mimi laughed in sudden, pure delight.

"Right," said Hal, suddenly very businesslike. "You must go — quite quickly. You've been here nearly three days already, and according to my father, three days is the Key's limit for return without time penalty."

"W — what?" Leo stammered. "What does that mean?"

"Well, presumably it means that you can stay here for three days without losing any time at all at home," Hal said vaguely. "As long as you've got the Key, of course. I've never needed to worry about it, myself. But Dad and Mother often came here for little three-day jaunts, apparently — whenever they felt they needed a change — and no one ever noticed they were gone."

Saying good-bye was harder, far harder, than Leo had imagined it could be. Especially saying good-bye to Bertha.

"I'm going to put off my move to the city for a little while," Bertha said, her bottom lip trembling. "I'm too soft-hearted for my own good, I know, but I can't bear to leave poor old Macdonald forever without so much as a good-bye."

"Of course you can't," said Leo.

"I should tell him what I've learned about foxes being good at keeping dots away," Bertha added. "Also, I'm feeling quite *drained* after fighting that wolf, and the troll, and the Blue Queen. I need a few weeks' rest."

"Of course you do," said Mimi.

Bertha sniffed, cleared her throat, and tossed the bobbing poppy out of her eye. "So," she said. "When you come back, if you don't leave it *too* long, you'll know just where to find me, won't you?"

"Yes, we will," Mimi and Leo said together. And Mimi straightened Bertha's hat and retied her ribbons, one last time.

"Best to leave from outside, I think," Hal said casually. "I'll take you."

So Mimi scooped up Mutt, who was still sleeping the sound sleep of a very relieved and grateful little dog, and she and Leo followed Hal out the front door and on into the shade of the willow trees.

"Just one thing," Hal said in a low voice. "I didn't want to say this in front of the others, but —"

"You don't want us to come back," Mimi muttered, all the light dying from her face. "You think it's too dangerous, because the Blue Queen —"

"Quite the contrary," Hal broke in, shaking his head. "You'll *have* to come back, I'm afraid."

As Mimi stared at him, overjoyed but obviously confused, he glanced at Leo to see if Leo, at least, understood.

"We'll have to show ourselves in Rondo quite often, and pretend we've never been away," Leo explained to Mimi. "We'll have to pretend we couldn't get home. Otherwise the queen will realize that the Key wasn't destroyed after all, and she'll never stop plotting and planning to get it back."

"Yes!" Mimi cried gleefully. "Oh, of *course!*"

"But that wasn't what I wanted to say," Hal went on. "I wanted to tell you —"

"That we mustn't depend on you to get us out of trouble every time we come here," Leo interrupted. "You're not good old reliable Uncle Henry anymore. Right?"

"Right," Hal said firmly. "But that's not —"

"You're afraid the Blue Queen will be so angry with us after what's happened that she'll be even more dangerous next time," Mimi suggested. "She'll want revenge, and —"

"Well, yes," Hal said. "Of course, but —"

"You're afraid that we'll play the music box for too long, or shut it before it runs down, so the blue butterflies will come out, and see us, and report back to the queen that we're out of Rondo," said Leo.

"And you're afraid we'll tell our parents all about this, so they'll insist on coming with us next time," added Mimi. "Then my brothers and sisters will come. And then word will spread and —"

"Will you let me finish?!" Hal roared.

Mimi and Leo looked at him, stunned. He thrust his hair off his forehead with long, impatient fingers.

"Right," he said. "Now. I'm afraid of all those things you've mentioned, yes, but I've finally decided it's pointless worrying about things I can't control. And that means you. I have to trust you to be sensible, and look after each other as true friends should."

True friends.

Leo and Mimi exchanged slightly startled looks, then grinned and nodded.

"No problem," Leo said.

"So what *did* you want to tell us, Hal?" Mimi asked.

Hal glanced back at his house. Bertha, Conker, Tye, and Freda were all peering out of one of the front windows.

He lowered his voice even farther. "I simply wanted to tell you something you may not have quite realized yet. It won't be difficult to deceive the queen into thinking you live in Rondo all the time. When you come back to see us you will find very little has changed. Because while the music box is wound up, whether it's playing aloud or not, life here goes on. But when the music runs down, life here simply — stops — until the box is wound up again."

Leo swallowed. He hadn't thought about it quite like that. "But that's — that's awful!" he whispered.

"Not at all," Hal said robustly. "Why do you think I'm here talking to you now, when I should have been dead long before you were born? It's not just because time goes more slowly here. It's also because time stops whenever the music box does, and we all have a rest."

He laughed at Leo's horrified expression. "There's nothing to worry about," he said. "We aren't *aware* that we're having these rests from time. To us, each rest is just the space between one blink and the next. That's all."

Mimi was nodding. But Leo shook his head. "All I can say is, I'm glad our world isn't like that," he said fervently.

"Oh?" Hal asked dryly. "How do you know it's not?"

And that gave Leo something to think about, all the way home.